Aaron Schmink's First Crazy Love

☹ 😐 ☺

Also by Arthur Plotnik

Better Than Great: A Plenitudinous Compendium of Wallopingly Fresh Superlatives

Spunk and Bite: A Writer's Guide to Bold, Contemporary Style

The Urban Tree Book: An Uncommon Field Guide for City and Town

The Elements of Authorship

The Man Behind the Quill: Jacob Shallus, Calligrapher of the United States Constitution

The Elements of Editing: A Modern Guide for Editors and Journalists

Aaron Schmink's First Crazy Love

: - {

A Novel by Arthur Plotnik

This novel is a work of fiction. All characters and events portrayed in it are either products of the author's imagination or are used fictitiously. Any resemblance to actual persons either living or dead is coincidental.

A version of the chapters "Fun at the Races" and "Big Winners" appeared as a story in *Balloons Literary Journal*, No. 7. A different telling of the chapters "Black Penny Loafers" and "I Make a Wreck of Things" was a *Glimmer Train* Honorable Mention in its Fiction Open and appears in *The Westchester Review*, Vol. 10.

ISBN13: 978-1092112154

For

Mary, Julia, Katya,
Sondra, Tara, and Anna

Contents:

What's ahead

1

Shul wasn't cool

IMAGINE a girl who can't help upchucking at the boy she loves. A girl who wants to just crawl away and die when it happens. Now imagine a boy with a talent for mimicking people to get a laugh—that was me a few months before turning thirteen. So when Keatsie Fairchild, the upchucking girl, entered my life, you'd think I'd have mockingly mimicked her, too.

But far from it. Being my softhearted mother's son, I couldn't help feeling sorry for anyone in real distress. That meant feeling sorry for Keatsie with her puking problem, and, very quickly, falling for her prettiness and smarts. The emotional mix soon turned to—well, love. My first big crush. So there I was, half hoping she would heave, spew, toss her cookies in *my* presence as proof of her affection.

My mother: The feel-sorry-for queen. She felt sorry for her aging parents, boozy boss, skinny daughter, the messed-up family next door, and also for herself—married to a good guy with a bad habit of staying out late to play cards.

Stuck with those Mom genes, how could I not feel sorry for *me*, starting with my name, Why oh why did I have to be named Aaron, instead of Al, Ash, or Ace? Nobody I knew was named Aaron! But that wasn't the worst of it. My last name was Schmink. Schmink! Not one person at school would ever call me "Aaron *Stink*," right? Except everyone.

Worst of all, I had to prepare for an unwanted bar mitzvah in December, which meant horrible Hebrew School—known to me simply as *shul*, a Yiddish word for synagogue, or the Jewish place of worship. Two afternoons a week toward the end of my twelfth year, I gave up my neighborhood street life and walked or took a bus from school to downtown White Plains and what I considered the most uncool dump in the universe: the Orthodox Hebrew Institute. Its square brick building was a block from Our Lady of Mt. Carmel church with its soaring bell tower and attached Catholic school. Mt. Carmel had a real gym where some kids I knew played genuine basketball. About twice a month after class, I suffered through the shul's Hebrew-school-hoop: An hour of unsupervised shuffling under makeshift rims in a dingy event hall.

My job was to learn enough Hebrew to read a section of the holy Jewish scripture so that in three months—December 3, to be exact—I could chant it properly and sweetly at a Saturday religious service. This, along with a speech in English, would be the bar mitzvah ritual in front of all the regular congregation and my family and their guests. A big scary deal, to be followed by another speech at a lunch reception.

The Hebrew School also included Jewish history and culture. It might have been okay if not piled on top of regular school and interfering with about a thousand more fun things I could think of. Or if I hadn't been required to attend eight Shabbat (Sabbath, "Day of Rest") prayer services during the year, sitting around watching mostly elderly guys pray and mumble stuff I couldn't understand. Or if the Institute itself hadn't seemed so ancient and musty to me, at least measured against my highest aspiration. What I wanted most, as you might have guessed, was to be cool or what we also called "sharp" or "slick."

A lot of exciting new stuff was in the air for my generation: coolness, greasers—collars up, taps on shoe heels—rebels, hoods, rock and roll, Elvis, and jazz, too. Some kids who "dug" jazz had other words for cool, like "solid," "mellow" "far out" and "real gone."

My new school drew from a rainbow of neighborhoods, with all the types of cool and sharp you could imagine. I thought black guys talked cool. (We politely called them Negroes then, but soon "black" was more acceptable, so I hope nobody minds if I use it just a few years early for the time.) Italians walked cool. Waspy guys were sports cool and dressed cool. Some Jews were smart cool.

I wanted to be all of that, all-around cool. But it wasn't going to happen at the shul. I'd wound up at the Orthodox institute mainly because it was closer and cheaper than the more modern Conservative or Reform Temples and my parents knew someone who was a regular there. We weren't Orthodox at home or regular temple goers or even considered religious. It was all about "carrying on the tradition" and getting bar mitzvahed so I could "be a man among *my people*." But here I was, trapped with some people I didn't feel were my *anything.*

For example:

--Mr. Rubin, the bony Jewish History and Torah instructor with fishy breath and a way of saying my name—A-*haa*-ron—so I got the full herring.

--My dozen or so classmates, some with embroidered skullcaps—*yarmulkes*—stuck on their pincushion heads with bobbypins. Bulldog-ish, redheaded Moshe Litvin was typical, acting grown up and righteous, Mr. Big Defender of the Faith. When I invented funny names for the Jewish holidays, like "Poor Him!" (pointing at Moshe) for *Purim*, Moshe twisted my arm.

--Bearded Rabbi Klein, head of the Institute, slumped behind his desk looking weighed down by the world and his meaty ears. One of his burdens was to deal with bad "deportment," but in my case he didn't have much leverage.

"You were joking in class, Aaron?"

"I guess so."

"You think studying Torah is a joke?

"I don't know."

"Did one single person laugh?"

"I didn't notice. But Moshe Litvin shoved me."

"I don't blame him. What I should do is call your parents, but with you they probably have enough aggravation. For now I'm taking off fifty points. You want prizes to take home? Keep being a smart aleck, you'll won't get even one."

The prizes, which you earned (or lost) with your behavior in class, were displayed in a wooden cabinet in the rabbi's office and consisted mainly of brass objects like candle-holders made in Israel or small plaster statues of elderly people in religious or village dress.

"Okay," I said, having zero interest in the rewards.

"Okay? Okay means what? That you'll disgrace your family by being a clown? By ruining the bar mitzvah they put so much hope into for you, that they sacrificed for?"

"I don't know."

"Maybe you're ashamed of being Jewish? Six million butchered for *nothing* as far as you're concerned?"

I hung my head. My cheeks burned. I felt plenty horrified from what I'd heard about the Holocaust, and right now even sorry for Rabbi Klein and his sad little statues. But would I go on making wisecracks in class and imitating Mr. Rubin? Probably. I couldn't help it, even if only one or two of my classmates laughed faithfully.

It was my way of coping with uncool captivity, like a monkey spitting from his cage at visitors. I might have told the rabbi that humor was a time-honored means of Jewish survival, if I'd known any such thing (or been more humorous). Nor did I know that some of the coolest, funniest kids around were doing bar mitzvah study in the Reform temple at the other end of town, just a couple of mansion-lined blocks from where Keatsie lived. If I'd known! But that neighborhood—that world—was Mars to me until my new friend Byron brought me into it and thus into the vicinity of his twin sister, Shelley Keats Fairchild.

2

Different you's

IT FELT like the world expected you to be one type of person or another; but you wanted to be *everything*—every hero you met in books and movies or on television. You ached to be every impressive thing you saw among your friends, family, classmates, and neighbors. You wanted to be a brainiac, tough guy, good kid, rebel, jock, artist, class clown, role model, leader, loner, understood, misunderstood.

For example, I liked to write letters and little stories and jokes. When people said I had a special talent for it I wanted to know every word in the dictionary so I could hold audiences spellbound. But I also wanted to be the silent type—*laconic*, there's a word!—the mystery man who takes care of trouble in his wordless way.

As it happened, I *had* to be at least three different people every day because I lived in three different worlds—even before Byron and Keatsie introduced me to a fourth. And I'm not counting shul, where I was both Smart Aaron (to learn the Hebrew) and Schmucky Aaron (to amuse myself).

Probably everyone lives in a few different worlds and each one seems different from everybody else's. Take your first world: Home. You're probably one person to your family and another person outside the house. At home I was pretty much the "good kid." It wasn't hard—bring in the decent report cards, feel sorry for my mother and older sister, make my bed, and go to the dumb bar mitzvah lessons. I could shoot my good-kid rating through the roof just with thank-you notes to aunts and uncles, at least in my mother's eyes.

Dear Aunt Sarah,

Please accept my enormous gratitude for the sensational and magnanimous gift of $5 on the occasion of my birthday. You are always so kind and thoughtful to remember me at this time each year, when sometimes I don't even remember me! I am tempted to "blow" this money on comic books, sodas, and other luxuries, but I think I will put it in my college education fund. That way, when I graduate . . .

Mom said I got my writing talent from her. She used her old, beat-up rhyming dictionary to enter jingle contests and actually won a vacuum cleaner in one of them. Sometimes I borrowed the dictionary to write poems like this:

You think you're so unique and sleek,
but you're a sneak and your feet reek
and when people smell you they cry "eek!"

Dad had his own notion of the "good kid." He used to train with boxers when he was young, so if I'd catch him between work and card games and put up my dukes, he'd stop and spar with me. He'd easily break through my guard to tap my nose and cheeks. But when I'd ask for actual training so I could hold my own in fights, he'd push my arms down.

"You got a brain," he'd say. "You don't need to fight."

"Why is that?"

"Because smart guys stay outta trouble."

"But what if somebody beats my brains out?"

"Just be a good kid, you'll be okay."

Armed with that advice, I had a record of about eight losses and one win in neighborhood fights, the single victory coming when I managed to twist Rocco Cabruzzi's pinkie until he gave up.

In truth, I was just barely a good kid, much less a great one. I didn't appreciate how hard life was for the family. Earnings from my father's work as a bakery-truck driver on the night shift and my mother's part-time secretarial work were never enough. I whined a lot. For example, I complained that I didn't have my own room, as my sister Joannie did—sort of. Her narrow "sun room" doubled as the entry hall to the apartment. My room was the so-called dining room, the fourth of our five small rooms in a row. I studied there and slept on a convertible sofa bed, snarling at anyone passing through to get to the kitchen.

Still, I did what was necessary to keep my rating. Being Good Kid meant that (a) I wasn't adding to anyone's misery, which I didn't want to do, and (b) I got trusted to do things on my own, like hang out with the neighborhood kids after regular school and even after supper on some nights. And given the neighborhood, these occasions demanded a second self, the Bad, But-Not-Too-Bad, Aaron.

We'd moved four years ago from the New York's Bronx borough to White Plains, a suburb with both rich sections and patches of struggling folks, including Italian and black sections. Our patch was a mix of small homes and a row of scruffy little apartment buildings, including the one we lived in with three families of Italian descent and a divorced Hungarian-American mother and her daughter. No blacks in this white section of town, not in those days.

Most of my neighborhood friends lived in the apartments, and so, as Bad Aaron, I would sit on the apartment stoops with Rocco, Googie, Chubby, and others, listening to terrible dirty jokes about traveling salesmen and farmer's daughters. The Bad Aaron learned to make farting noises with cupped hands under armpits. He tried to shoot bubble-gum spit through a gap in his teeth as Chubby did, even if Bad Aaron's too-small gaps caused backfiring. He rode his bike wildly with the pack, beyond the boundaries his mother had drawn. He took an occasional puff on one of Googie's Camel cigarettes. He strutted like a rooster in front of the neighborhood girls—Kay and Linda and Liz—as if, like Rocco, he was no stranger to necking and petting. And of course he talked Bad, like the others.

ME: "My old lady's a drag, man."

"How come?"

"She won't get me no loafers."

"So? Steal some money and buy 'em."

"I ain't no thief like you, man."

"Yeah, well at least I didn't kill Jesus. Kike."

"Shut up, Wop."

"Gonna make me?"

"God already made you: Ugly!"

Mostly it was all play. I wasn't about to make anybody shut up. That was the thing about being Bad Aaron—you had to know your limits. Moshe Litvin at the shul, or my father for that matter, would have slugged anyone knocking the Jews even in a joke. There were times I had a mind to do it, too. But throwing a first punch wasn't part of my Bad street self, not when returning an insult for an insult would do the trick. And since insults had to do more with words than punches I got pretty good at them, which would serve me well in my third self, Seventh-Grade Aaron in what was then "junior high school."

3

New world, same horrible name

EASTVIEW JUNIOR HIGH ran from seventh through ninth grades. My walk there was longer than to my elementary school and in the opposite direction. The old walk was along quiet, tree-lined residential streets. Now I walked through kind of an opposite world of parkway and street traffic and stores and big apartment buildings. The school itself seemed huge—a bunch of connected, dark-brick buildings climbing up a hill. A tall wire fence surrounded the paved playfield. Nearby shops sold candy and giant baloney sandwiches called "wedges," yellow mustard oozing from the seams of the Italian loaves.

Inside the enormous school hallways I bumped my way past students of every type, from all kinds of neighborhoods foreign to me. I'd never seen so many black kids in one place or heard them called such horrible names by white kids. Soon I would encounter even more Italians than in my neighborhood and kids with Spanish-sounding names, German, Jewish—even a "Lefevre" who I had to be told was French-Canadian. Plus a bunch of students with names I envied for their normality or pretty sound, like "Fairchild," as in Byron Fairchild, who would become my best friend.

Since my sister had gone to another junior high and was already in high school, I was probably Eastview's first and only Schmink. Oh, if only I could have left that name behind! It took about five seconds for the first "Hey, Aaron Stink!" But at least it helped me get to know Byron and through him his sister Keatsie.

Byron and I were in English, beginning Spanish, and math classes together, and we quickly discovered a common trait: class clowns could put us in giggle fits—as when pudgy Bruce Watkins would push his nose up into a snout and oink at us from the back row.

Byron's voice hadn't quite changed, and when he giggled or said one of his long words like *indescribable,* he'd go way up into the falsetto range. It was like a bird giving away its hiding place, and our math teacher, Mr. Trapazzo, would send us two gigglers into the hall for a time-out. But we didn't really get acquainted until the first meeting of the school Newspaper Club, where we volunteered to be reporters and heard the delicious term "byline"—your name in print at the top of an article you wrote.

It was a thrilling notion, that you could become a somebody every time the paper came out. But I had second thoughts. "The trouble with bylines," I said to Byron as we walked back to our lockers, "is that I hate my name."

Byron was thin and tall, towering over me, and when he looked down he had a way of turning his head like a curious bird. He was also kind of beaky. "Why is that?" he said. "Just because Schmink rhymes with stink?"

"Oh, it does?" I said. "Thanks for pointing that out."

"You're welcome. Anyway, join the club. I loathe my name, too."

"How come? Fairchild is pretty cool."

"Ehh. It's okay. But Byron is in*sufferable*."

"Yeah? Well Aaron is insufferable-*er*," I said, enjoying his smarty way of speaking, getting into it. "Byron's worse. Do you know a single Byron besides the doofus I was named after."

"Which doofus?"

"One of the dead and putrefying English poets, George Gordon Lord Byron."

"I'd take that name over mine," I said, though I didn't know what poets he was talking about. "'Lord' would be cool, too. 'Behold, I am The Lord Schmink!'"

"How about Percy Bysshe Schmink?" Byron said.

"Who?"

"Another putrefying poet. Percy Bysshe Shelley. My mother thinks these guys were the ultimate, ergo, we got named after them."

"Ergo?"

"Ergo means 'therefore.' From Latin."

"Okay. And who's 'we'"?

"I and my sister Keatsie."

"Keatsie?"

"Shelley Keatsie, after Percy Bysshe Shelley *and* John Keats."

" Does she hate her name, too?"

"I don't know," Byron said. "She's weird and inscrutable."

"Older or younger?"

"Younger by fourteen minutes. We're dizygotic twins."

"Di-what?"

"Fraternal twins. Different sperms, different eggs, exceedingly different people—you *do* know about sperms and eggs, right?"

"Oh yah, everything," I said, having read a juvenile facts-of-life book from the library not long ago. "So you guys don't look like each other?"

"Thank God, no."

"Then she must be great-looking."

"Very funny," Byron said. "Remind me to laugh."

"I will next week. Does she go school here?"

"Nah—she's in a private girls' academy. She hated Post Road Public. Couldn't *bear* the teasing."

"About what?"

"Long, boring story."

"What about you? You get teased there?"

"Why would I?

"I don't know. A longer, boringer story?"

"Ha. Actually, it's short one." He paused and stood stiffly. "You see, I am an alien from outer space."

"Oh," I said. "I figured."

By the time we got to our lockers, we had this jokey *rapport* going, comfortable with the kidding. He poked his beak into my locker, examined its ordinary contents (textbooks, mitt, sneakers) and made a face as if it stunk. I checked his out; on the upper shelf were several non-textbooks, including *Red Planet*, by Robert Heinlein.

"Any good?" I asked, pointing to it.

"It's *incredible*. It takes place on Mars. You ever read science fiction?"

"I'm not sure." I was just an occasional fiction reader, clueless as to the categories.

"I'll lend it to you when I'm finished," he said. "If you want. Or, maybe something from my massive collection at home. *Walls* of the stuff. You could take a look."

"Sure. Uh, where do you live?"

He gestured in a direction opposite from my own neighborhood and gave an address that meant nothing to me.

"Where—how do you get there? There a bus or something?"

"Dunno. I think so. My father drives me in on his way to work, and sometimes I go home with him or someone else picks me up. You want to come today?"

The invitation took me by surprise. But even if Hebrew school hadn't been looming for me that afternoon, I had no idea how I'd get back from his mysterious direction—way, way opposite my world. "I can't," I told him. "Maybe Friday? I can check with my parents and all."

"Cool. There's also ping pong, a basketball court, tennis court, badminton, and other assorted amusements."

"Where? By your house?"

"No, no—*at* my house."

4

From Keatsie's diary

(as seen by me much later)

I HATE my brother! Even if we were close when we were sweet little twinsies. Even if he's actually nice to me about once a year. But as soon as someone else is around, like when he brings a friend home, he has this sick need to be monstrous and put me down one way or another. Then he acts like it's no biggie, just "older" brother tormenting poor lil' messed-up twin sis.

Like today after school, he shows up with this new friend, Aaron Schmink—I can't believe that name—and he completely ignores me while he trots Aaron around the house and grounds. Aaron is kind of small and gawks at everything like he just popped out of a burrow. But he smiled when he saw me stupidly tagging after them, and he did seem nice in a shy way, so it mattered when Byron made me look like a pathetic jerk in front of him.

I'm not sure what Aaron knew about me being "Barf Girl"—or if he even knew the word "barf." But when he and Byron took off for the basketball court he looked at me that funny way, like one insulting word from him and I'd spew all over his Levis. And maybe I would, since I'm never sure when it might happen. The doctors keep saying its just nerves—just— but how come it doesn't happen, say, when I take a test? Okay, I do get too upset at things sometimes, and nervous around certain boys. Sometimes nauseated. Especially cute guys. It's crazy. But at least now, in my so-civilized, all-girls school, I don't retch every minute over some bozo. But it's not like I live in a nunnery. I see guys around. Like gorgeous Paul Lefevre, when he works on the grounds here with his uncle.

Anyway, I assumed that Byron being Byron had already opened his mouth, so of course I had to, heh, heh, even up the score while they were shooting baskets. I knew Byron would be coming to his room to show off his insane science fiction collection. Naturally I had to extricate about a dozen pairs of underpants from his dresser and tuck their elastic bands under the magazine bindings. Who wouldn't? It was quite decorative, like the bunting they hang from windows in a parade.

Okay, maybe he hadn't said anything to Aaron yet. But still, did my brother have to way overreact to an innocent prank? Storming into my room followed by Aaron and emptying out my top dresser drawer, where, unfortunately, I keep my own underthings? Here's how it went:

"Oh, you think you're funny?" Byron yelled at me. "Putting your pestiferous paws on my collection? Not to mention my unmentionables?" I almost laughed at "unmentionables" in spite of myself, but he was in a genuine snit fit.

"It was just a joke," I said.

"Well, ha-ha-ha!" he said. "Let's all have a good puke over it."

As soon as he said the word and I met Aaron's eyes, I felt it coming on; Aaron looked at me kind of sadly, maybe with pity—and my stomach did the plunger thing. The wave rose, the reflex, the heaves. The awful, acid taste and throat pain. I dashed into my bathroom, locked the door and ran the sink faucets to hide the sound. Not just of barfing, but crying, too. The foulness. The stink. I can't stand myself when it happens.

Mortified! By my own brother! I hated him, even if after a while he knocked on the door and said I should come out and get to know Aaron. "Come on, Keatsie-Weatsie." It was his crummy way of apologizing. But I wonder, did Aaron ask to come back and get to know me?

Through the door I croaked, "Pleased to meet you, Aaron. Sorry about . . ."

"No, it's okay," Aaron said. "It's nothing."

"I'm embarrassed."

"Don't be. At least your name isn't Schmink."

I heard Byron snicker at that.

"Maybe next visit," I said. "Are my things still all over the floor?"

"I don't know. I'm not actually looking," Aaron said.

I thought that was kind. Then Byron said, "I'm sending them out to be disinfected."

I shouted, "You're a total schmuck, go away! Aaron—nice meeting you."

"You, too," he said.

Ridiculous.

5

Describing Paradise

PHILLIPE LEFEVRE, the gardener, drove me home in his pickup truck. But just before we left the house, Byron's mother came crunching up the long gravel driveway in a white Cadillac. She stopped when she saw Byron and me in the truck and rolled down her window.

"Greetings, *Mater*," Byron called to her. "Meet my friend from school. Mater, Aaron. Aaron, Mater.

She was pretty cute for a Mater—pert, with graying dark hair in a short cut and the chestnut-brown, doe-like eyes the twins had obviously inherited. Also, their beak, but a smaller one than those of her offspring, more budgie than parrot. I waved and said hi, and she asked if I'd like to stay for dinner. I told her I had to get home, and she offered to do the driving instead of Philippe. We all protested. Byron and I wanted to ride in the funky pickup, and I didn't really want his mother to see my crummy street. Bad enough Byron had to.

"Well, come again," she said. She had a sleepy way of speaking, like a drawl. "Welll, come againnn." I loved it.

We had fun bumping along in the truck, which smelled of cut grass, manure, and Philippe's cigarettes. He spoke with a funny French accent, had big gnarly hands, and yanked at the wheel like he was outracing a mudslide. When we pulled up to my house Byron took in the row of ugly apartment buildings but didn't say anything. I thanked them both, and Byron said "See ya in school."

Rocco Cabruzzi from the apartment next door was sitting on the stoop and we exchanged little waves. He was my best neighborhood friend when we weren't tussling, and I felt like telling him all about Byron's house. I had to get inside, though, and it would probably have made him jealous and sad anyway.

But as I sat down to dinner I wouldn't shut up. "You can't believe this house!" I ranted, my mouth full of meatloaf and Ketchup and canned peas and carrots. "It's all white with two big pillars and its shaped like this gigantic T with *servant* rooms in the long part."

"They have servants?" my sister Joannie said. She was separating her peas and carrots with a fork, nibbling at the peas.

"There's a maid who also cooks, and a gardener—Philippe, the guy who drove me home? He's French-Canadian. But they don't live there. I mean, the maid has a servant's room she can use and Philippe has a little room next to the garage, but most of the servant rooms are empty, I think, and then there's the whole other part of the house with a big dining room and huge living room and parts they call wings with a library and a garden room and the kitchen but they don't eat there they get served in the dining room and then there's more rooms downstairs and *then* you go up this big staircase—"

"Slow down," my mother told me. "You'll choke." She stood behind Joannie with the pan of meatloaf, urging her to take more. Joannie waved it away with a face. "It sounds like a mansion," Mom said.

"It's like a castle! Upstairs there's Byron's room and his sister Keatsie's room and they each have their own big bathroom and down the halls is a guest room and the parents' bedroom—the *master* bedroom, Byron called it—and more bathrooms with glass showers and everything and—"

"Uh! To have *money*," Mom said.

"Mom—sit down already," Joannie said. She turned to me. "And what? There's more?"

"There's *another* floor that's a huge party room called the penthouse with windows all around and a great view and a bar and a ping-pong table and a piano and a deck and another bathroom and—"

"How many bathrooms they need?" Joannie said. "They have to pee all day?"

"No-o. But they don't have to go in their pants waiting for you to come out."

"Excuse me, you're the one who takes forever."

"No, you do. And Dad, when he sleeps in the tub." I remembered walking in on my father once: the water was up to his nostrils and he was snoring into it, making it bubble.

I looked at Mom, who was still hovering behind Joannie. "Hey," I asked, "isn't Dad coming home for dinner?" Joannie gave me a don't-bring-it-up look, but too late. Mom turned and slammed the pan on the stove.

"What do you think?" she said. "Do you see him here?"

I didn't have to ask further. Five and sometimes six mornings each week, from about three a.m. to noon, Dad drove a truck delivering bread and cake to factories and hospitals. When he got home he ate lunch, took a nap, and drove a few blocks up our hill to the Elks Lodge, one of a few former mansions along a broad street. There he'd gamble at cards for the afternoon. Afterward he was supposed to join us for dinner, but a lot of evenings he didn't. He couldn't quit the card game while he was on a hot streak, he would tell us.

I knew this would be one of those nights when Mom stomped around, seething until he came home to sleep before his next shift. She wouldn't talk to him for another day or two.

"Anyway," Joannie said, "is that it, or more bathrooms?"

"Wait, I didn't even tell you about the *outside.* It's as big as this whole block, except it's got all these lawns and trees and gardens with silver balls—"

"Silver balls?".

"Yeah, by the roses. Up on stands. Byron says . . . ."

"What's so funny?" Joannie said.

"Byron call's them 'Pop's enormous silver . . . .' You know."

"I get it," Joannie said. "What's his father do, anyway?"

"He's an optha something. He operates on eyes."

"Must be plenty of money in that," Mom said. She poked Joannie's back. "Stop slouching. Eat."

"And I *still* haven't mentioned the tennis courts and the basketball—"

"Enough already," Mom said. "Are you finished? You want Jello?"

"Yeah, okay. Anyway, Byron really wants to be friends, so I'll probably go over there a lot."

"We'll see. Don't forget you have Hebrew School. And who's going to drive you?"

"The servants!"

"The servants," she mumbled.

"I really like his twin sister, too," I said. "They're dizygotic twins. Not identical."

"Look at you, with the big words," said Joannie.

"You should hear Byron. He's super smart. Keatsie is, too—that's her name. Well, Shelley Keats Fairchild, actually. But she has this problem."

"What problem?" Mom said, slamming the refrigerator door.

"Well, she vomits when she gets upset. She threw up in the bathroom while I was there."

"The poor girl," Mom said. Joannie added, "It's a horrible thing. I know what she goes though."

"Yeah," I said. "I feel sorry for her. What if she vomited, you know, in a restaurant or something?"

Mom put a plate of quivering red Jello with milk in front of me. "Okay. Do we have to talk about vomit at the table? Eat up—I don't want to be in the kitchen all night."

Later, when we were watching "Truth or Consequences" on our almost new Philco TV, Mom got up to adjust the rabbit-ears antennae and then went into her bedroom without a word.

"She looks sad," I said to Joannie.

"What do you expect? Dad's a louse."

"He is not. He just has a gambling problem."

"Everyone has problems, that doesn't excuse them from being decent human beings. And by the way, I had the same problem as your friend's sister. Not always throwing up, but feeling like it when I got nervous."

"Really? Did you fix it?"

"It's better. I went to Dr. Zimmer. But I still can't eat if I'm worried about something."

"So don't worry."

"Yeah, Thanks. Oh, look," she said, nodding at the TV, "they're bringing in a dog they thought was lost. They're all crying."

My father came home at about 11p.m.—another night when he wouldn't get enough sleep. I heard some muffled angry words, and then, from my bed, saw my mother heading off with her bedding to sleep in the living room. I turned toward the wall and forced myself to think of something else. Keatsie. I pictured her as she'd looked following us around: tall and lanky, big eyes, freckles on her cheeks, long nose with a slightly beaky bump. and a great smile with beautiful teeth and dimples. Her hair was light brown, not as light as Byron's, and it spilled over her shoulders curling along the way. She'd worn a loose blue jersey with sleeves that came down to her knuckles, and snug jeans. As I drifted off I thought of her as "sexy," a word only recently inserted into my vocabulary, mostly by Rocco Cabruzzi's observations.

6

More imitations

MY NEXT TIME at Hebrew school, I fired off one of Byron's fancy words at Moshe Litvin. "Hey," I said, after he'd given me a shove, "keep your *pestiferous* paws to yourself!"

Before class, he'd shoved me for imitating Rabbi Klein. I had pulled my ears out wide and said in Klein's stern voice, "No prizes for Moshe until he loses some fat."

"You think you're smart?" Moshe said with another shove. "Big words? You don't even know what they mean."

But I'd looked this one up: "*Pestiferous,*" I informed him, "bringing disease. Evil."

"I'll bring you evil, all right, you *putz.*" He nosed up to me, but Mr. Rubin entered the classroom at that moment, driving us to our seats with a fierce look. For most of the next forty-five minutes we read lines of Hebrew text aloud, some of us with performances that made poor Mr. Rubin wince and drop his head to the desk. I had a decent knack for it, though, and when my reading got a "very good, *Aharon*," I turned around to the less-adept Moshe and thumbed my nose. Moshe shook his fist, but Frankie Solomon, a tiny kid who never looked well, had to stifle a laughing fit.

Frankie was my best audience in the class. He laughed at almost everything I did, which made me glad because I knew he had diabetes and, according to him, he might not even make it to his bar mitzvah. After the class broke up, with Moshe body-checking my shoulder as he left, Frankie begged me to do the Rabbi Klein imitation again. I did so, throwing in an extra mockery of Mr. Rubin. He sank to the floor, laughing and coughing so hard I was afraid he'd pass out.

As we left the building we got to talking about his insulin shots, and then, while on the subject of physical ills, I mentioned that I'd met a cute girl who threw up a lot.

"I knew a girl like that in Post Road," Frankie said.

"You went to Post Road? What was her name?"

"Uh, Kerry or something? No . . . "

"Keatsie?"

"Yeah, that's it!" he said. "Keatsie Fairchild. You know her?"

"Well, we just sort of met and said hi."

"Yeah, Keatsie. Except nobody called her that."

"What'd they call her?"

"Barf Girl." He giggled, then caught himself. "I mean, it was really rotten."

"*What* Girl? Arf Girl?"

"No, Barf. It was this new word for puking."

"Where'd they get that?"

"I don't know. Somebody heard it somewhere. It's from the sound you make, I guess. *Baaarf*!

"Huh. It sounds funny."

"Yeah. So everybody started using it and it stuck to Keatsie. I mean, I didn't call her that. Just the jerks did. There was this one eighth-grade hood she had a crush on—Sonny Rizzo?—and she was always running away from him, you know, running into the girl's room if she could."

"Really? What did he do?"

"The guys all teased him about it, so he started chasing her around like a zombie—*mwahhhh*—and making it even worse. Once she puked right in front of everybody."

"Wow. That's lousy. Did you know her brother Byron?"

"Yeah, a little. Smartest guy in the school but kind of stuck-up."

I told Frankie about befriending Byron at East-view. "I think he's okay, once you get to know him."

"Yeah, maybe," Frankie said, losing interest. Now attending Post Road's junior high school, he had a different group of classmates.

Waiting with him for his ride home, I gifted him with a Nat King Cole version of the bar mitzvah chant

I'd been practicing, singing it to Cole's hit tune, "Mona Lisa." Frankie hit the sidewalk.

7

"The Little Book of Drags"

☺ 😑 ☹

MY FIRST BYLINE for the *Eastview Dispatch* appeared over a short article on the Glee Club, with a schedule of the year's performances. My second story, co-written with Byron, was a report on Human Relations Day, when we had an assembly speaker talk about getting along with people of all races and creeds. My third—and most fun article so far—described a new craze in the school: *drags.*

A drag was a little insult or put-down you said to somebody. It was supposed to be funny or clever, and usually you got a come-back drag. It was like a duel, which other people at different times called "signifying," or "by-the-numbers," or "playin' the dozens." We called them drag fights. The drags going around Eastview weren't about respecting others' races or creeds. They were just about playing with words and getting a laugh. So naturally I was drawn to them.

For the article, I chose only the least offensive ones. These included some of the yo-mama drags I'd overheard, which insulted people by insulting their mothers—usually grounds for a fight, but fair play during the drag fad.

Yo mama loops (caddies) in combat boots.

Yo mama takes ugly pills.

Yo mama's a lifeguard at the birdbath.

Yo mama and daddy are in the iron and steel business. Yo mama irons while yo daddy steals.

Next were the appearance drags: *If ugliness was electricity, you'd be a powerhouse. You got friendly eyes—always looking at each other.*

Bad-breath drags: *Need a match? Your breath and a monkey's armpit.*

And so on. Like any hot new thing they would soon seem dumb and awful, but they had us stretching our wits. And somehow Mr. Salisbury, who supervised the Newspaper Club (when he wasn't overseeing the Stamp Club and Library Club or mysteriously disappearing for a day) let the article run in the *Dispatch.* The other teachers didn't say anything, at least not to me, but among a small bunch of classmates I was suddenly a writing star. I was cool!

They wanted more, more drags, more ammunition, which led to my first book—a two-inch-square volume of all the drags I could collect, about thirty little pages worth. I stapled it together in an edition of one copy with the title, *The Little Handybook of Drags*, kept on my person to read to the hungry masses, one at a time. Soon, by popular demand and with the explosion of new drags, I collected about forty more in a second edition.

One of my favorite sources, someone also in the Newspaper Club, was Betty Lee, a black eighth-grader nicknamed Happy because of her big fun-loving grin. Everyone liked her; she was smart and full of good cheer, but she gave me some seriously insulting drags from her rough neighborhood—a few of them too rough for the book and of course for any future article. Anyway Mr. Salisbury finally advised me to write about other things, so that was that.

Byron took great delight in the collection, generously sharing any drags he heard or could invent, such as *Yo mama is the Thing that Came from Outer Space*, and *Yo daddy feeds yo mama with his tentacles*, and *Yo mama is the Creature from the Black Lagoon.* He also suggested *Yo mama is the Fourth Horseman of the Apocalypse* (Death) and *Yo mama rides the Vomit Comet*, both of which I decided to reject: I didn't understand the first, and I feared Keatsie would blame me for the second.

"You wouldn't say the vomit one in front of Keatsie, would you?" I asked Byron.

"Of course I would," he chirped. But I didn't believe he'd be that mean—a second time. He took my rejections in stride, and in fact urged me to spend the coming Saturday at his house. I hesitated only because the Brooklyn Dodgers—my father's favorite team and thus mine—were on radio playing a big game in the pennant race that day. But when I thought of seeing Keatsie again as well as having fun with Byron, I decided that the Dodgers would have to wait.

8

I get looked over

MOM SHUFFLED wearily into the kitchen as I gulped down my Saturday morning breakfast: Cheerios with milk and banana; spongey Wonder Bread toasted on one side the way I liked it and blanketed with cream cheese and grape jam. Dad was at work. Joannie was still sleeping.

"Where are you running?" Mom asked.

"I told you—Byron's house. They invited me for the day."

"I'm sure they don't want you there all day."

"Then why would they invite me?"

She shrugged, looking unhappy. "Maybe tomorrow we could all do something together." She reached over and brushed some feathery hair off my forehead. "You look so handsome," she said.

"Too bad I'm not. But thanks anyway."

"You're my beautiful boy."

I looked at her. "Are you okay, Mom?"

"Eh. Don't worry about me. Have a good time today. Be nice and polite. And give me their number just in case."

"What are you doing today?"

"Me? What mothers do. Clean. Cook. Wash. Maybe some shopping."

"Have fun!" I sang, hoping to cheer her.

This time I was to meet my ride to Byron's in front of Macy's Department Store, in downtown White Plains. I got there by bus and waited outside the store until a light blue car pulled up with a black woman driving. Byron sat next to her in the front; Keatsie sprawled over the back seat. Byron got out and motioned his sister to change places with him. As she did so I nodded hello and she offered a pleasant little "hi" before I followed Byron into the back.

"Now who's this nice young man?" the woman said, turning around to me and raising her brows. Her graying temples framed a broad, friendly face with high cheekbones and smooth mahogany skin. Her right arm, resting across the seatback, looked solid and powerful.

"Leena, meet Aaron," Byron said. "Aaron, meet Leena."

"Hi," I said. "Thanks very much for picking me up."

"You're very welcome," she said. She looked at Byron. "You see now, this boy got some manners."

"*I* have *impeccable* manners," Byron said, going into his high falsetto.

Keatsie made a loud cackling sound. Byron reached over and tugged her hair. "You dare to mock me?"

"Ow!" she yelled. "You are so detestable."

"Why you twins always actin' up?" Leena said, pulling out into traffic. "You supposed to look out for each other."

"I did," Byron said. "I allowed *It* to come along."

"Let's just ignore him," Keatsie said to Leena, who shook her head and smiled.

It was an older car, noisy, and worn inside. But it got us to Byron's at mid-morning of a warm, sunny day. Leena left us to start preparing lunch for the family. Keatsie went with her, hanging on to her arm and laughing over something as they entered the house.

Byron and I retrieved a basketball from the garage. As we bounced it back and forth I asked him if Leena had been their maid a long time.

"As long as I can remember," he said. "She's like a parent who doesn't crab at you. Well, sometimes she does, but we love her to pieces. Keatsie hangs on her like a papoose."

"She's the maid *and* the cook?"

"Actually, we just call her the cook. She used to do some cleaning, but now someone else comes in, some kind of service." I must have had an odd expression, because Byron paused, then said, "She not a *slave.* She gets *paid* and everything."

"Yeah, I know. Once my mother hired a cleaning lady, then cleaned everything over again."

We shot some baskets, first playing one-on-one, at which the much-taller Byron murdered me. In "horses," I lost by only one thanks to a two-handed foul shot I had mastered in the Hebrew Institute's crummy gym. We chatted as we played, mostly about school, some movies we had seen, and a little about my family, including my poker-playing father. Byron warned me about his own dad, Walter Fairchild, who was due home at lunch along with Byron's mother and a friend of hers from the Westchester Woman's Club. "Pop can be a genuine pain," he said. "He'll probably try to embarrass you as he does everyone. Just play it cool."

"Cool, that's me, man," I said.

But I was already overheated and sweating when Leena came outside bringing a tray of sweetened ice teas with slices of lemon and sprigs of fresh mint. "Y'all clean up soon for lunch," she told us. "Ol' Baldy gon' be there, you know."

"That's my pater," Byron said, laughing. "Our secret name for him."

"And y'all better *keep* it secret," Leena said, heading back in. She seemed to walk with difficulty.

I washed my hands and face in Byron's bathroom, but my thin polo shirt was sweaty and stuck to my chest. You could see the outlines of my chubby boy-boobs, but all I could do about it was drown in shame as I was shown to my seat in the dining room between Byron and Keatsie.

I'd never eaten at a home with linen settings and heavy glassware and bunches of fancy plates laid out like in a restaurant; nor in a home with a huge chandelier over the dining room table and cushioned chairs with striped upholstery. I didn't know what to do with anything as I gaped at my oversized cloth napkin and a parade of silverware on both sides of the first dish, a wide, shallow plate of cold, light-green soup.

When I glanced up it seemed I was being studied in turn by each adult at the table: Mrs. Fairchild, smiling lazily at me; her friend, a Mrs. Bender, lean, tan, wearing white shorts and a loose blouse (a tennis outfit, I soon learned); and, next to her, Byron's father. He was settling his huge frame into his chair, looking at me over reading glasses as if I had just flown into his soup. He was way up there and as bald as a mountain top. Except for the glasses I thought he looked like a king, with bushy eyebrows, a commanding nose, full lips and big strong teeth. Two powerful, hairy arms emerged from his short-sleeve shirt; the fingers were long and graceful, with dark hair below the knuckles.

"Everyone," Byron announced. "Meet my new friend and famous author, Aaron Schmink. Aaron—you already know my mater—meet mater's friend Mrs. Bender, and my *paterfamilias*, Dr. Walter Fairchild."

I gave a sickly wave, thinking of the sweaty little Schmink they were beholding.

Dr. Fairchild looked at me. "So, Schmink—do you know what *paterfamilias* means?" His voice was big, with a trace of tease in it.

"Uh, 'father' something?" I ventured.

"Tell him, Byron."

"Head of the household," Byron said. "But actually, that's Leena."

Keatsie and Mrs. Fairchild laughed. The doctor did not seem amused. He took his seat, still looking at me. "You have amblyopia of the right eye," he said. "I can tell by the useless corrective lens."

Mrs. Fairchild sighed. "Walter—please." She turned to me. "Welcome, Aaron. We're pleased to have you here. . . . Shall we begin?" She picked up her soup spoon.

"It's called Lazy Eye," Dr. Fairchild persisted, starting on his soup. "It should have been corrected before you were five. Now it's too late."

I felt a flush of helplessness, but as I fumbled with my spoon a wonderful and surprising thing happened. Keatsie bumped her leg twice against mine and said to her father: "And is it also too late to get your hair back, Pop?"

Byron laughed and then, to my astonishment, Dr. Fairchild emitted a horsey chuckle. "My ungrateful, misguided offspring," he said in Mrs. Bender's direction.

More surprises were yet to come that afternoon.

9

Getting through lunch

I WATCHED how everyone else at the table did it, then filled my soup spoon by dipping it *away* from me gracefully instead of shoveling it in for a hearty slurp, as at home. The adult chatter hit a pause before the next course, and Mrs. Bender suddenly asked me what the "famous author" had written to be so famous.

"Me?" I said. "Well, uh, just some stuff for the school newspaper." I hoped to leave it at that, but Byron blurted out, "Aaron is author of the famous *Little Handybook of Drags*, volumes one and two."

"Really?" Mrs. Bender said. Now everyone's attention was on me. "And what are 'drags'?"

"Um," I said, trying to cut Byron off. "Just little jokes."

"What kind of jokes?" came the dreaded ques-tion from Dr. Fairchild. I froze. Was I supposed to reveal myself as the great insulter of parents?

"Come on, Schmink," he persisted, "the famous Aaron Schmemingway."

"Pop gives everyone a stupid nickname," Byron whispered to me as the others tittered uneasily. "Part of his charm."

Dr. Fairchild kept at me, but I was saved by the bell—a small brass one next to Mrs. Fairchild's water glass. She raised it and gave it a firm shake, ding, ding, ding. "Let's have these plates cleared and start on our salads," she said. Almost instantly the door to the kitchen swung open and Leena entered, wearing a crisp white apron and carrying a large tray. She greeted Mrs. Bender and collected the soup plates and spoons, stacking things up masterfully and carrying them back to the kitchen. In a minute or so, she returned with salads for three of us, then brought the remaining three. "More ice tea coming," she said. "Anything else?"

"No," Mrs. Fairchild said. "Thank you, Leena. The soup was superrrb."

Leena nodded and returned to the kitchen for a fresh pitcher of the tea, which she then poured for those who wanted it. The "salade Niçoise" in front of me was strange to my eyes: long string beans, potatoes, and hardboiled egg with tuna fish and flat slices of an oily, horrible-tasting fish, all on a pillow of fluffy lettuce. I could imagine my mother commenting, "Who ever heard?" as she did for anything different. I tried a small piece of the oily fish things and it was so strong and salty I almost spit it out. But I had to swallow it down and keep eating. I went for the string beans with fingers and a butter knife before Byron pushed my salad fork over. Luckily the adults were busy eating and talking about the tennis they intended to play later and how they would team up.

Byron leaned behind me so he could talk to Keatsie. "I bet they'll want me to play," he told her.

"So? You can say no."

"Even better, old Sis, why don't *you* get out there? I need a laugh."

"Then look in the mirror," she said, about to take a swallow of tea. Byron responded by pulling the skin down below each eye to create a zombie face, his tongue out to one side. Keatsie laughed at the wrong second, getting tea up her nose and making a ghastly sound as she slammed down her glass and started to hack and clear the channels.

Mrs. Fairchild sprang up in a panic. "Keatsie—are you . . . ?" Dr. Fairchild hurried around to Keatsie's side and yanked her chair back, away from the table.

"I'm *okay,* everyone!" Keatsie managed through her coughing. "*God.* I'm not . . . ." Her cheeks flushed, then went pale. She wouldn't look at anyone.

Dr. Fairchild lingered behind her. "Look, when you're feeling sick, you leave the table."

"I'm *okay*!"

"All riiight, all riiight" Mrs. Fairchild said after a moment. She sat down again. "Walter? Let us all just eat, please, so we might have an afternoon?"

10

Alone with Keatsie

TOWARD THE END of lunch, as the four adults sipped coffees, Byron suggested we go to the "penthouse" for a game of ping pong. He got us excused, and, with a quick stop in the kitchen to stack up on Oreo cookies—his "preferred confection"—he led me and Keatsie up to the third-floor party room.

Keatsie sat at the upright piano at one end of the room while Byron and I paddled a ping-pong ball back and forth—not that I got many of his shots either forth or back. Mainly I chased the ones he slammed past me as they rolled toward Keatsie. We found it funny anyway, especially when Keatsie started playing boogie-woogie and rock-and-roll piano as I ran after the balls. She was good. She played standing up and did a cool, crazy-legged, wiggling dance along with the beat. Byron had stopped to devour another Oreo when the expected call came from the stairway. Pop's voice.

"Hey, Little Lord Byron! Get your tennies on. Meet us on the court for doubles. Pronto!"

"I knew it," Byron said to us. He called back down, "But I have a guest!"

"Who, Schmemingway? Smelly-Feets can keep him company. Or they can come watch. It'll be you and Mrs. Bender versus your dear old parents. Hurry up."

"Heh, heh, perfect," Byron said to me. "I love destroying them. Want to come?"

"No he doesn't!" Keatsie said before I could answer. "It's my turn to beat him at ping-pong." Byron shrugged, and with the Oreo half-way into in his mouth, he headed downstairs.

Keatsie took a look at the ping- pong table, then decided she'd rather flop on one of the two rattan chairs near the piano. I sat by her on the other one.

"He's super-good at tennis," Keatsie told me. "He won a club tournament and everything. He also does gymnastics. Too bad he's such a jerk."

"Anything you guys can't do?" I said. "You can really play piano."

"Nah—I take classical, I mean, they make me take it. It's okay, but I don't practice a lot. I'm not much at sports, either."

"But you're smart, right? I mean at school?"

"I guess. So are you. I heard all about your little book."

"Oh-oh. It's not so . . . "

"No, I want to see it. I love drags."

"You *do*?"

She giggled. "Byron and I are always dragging each other. Here's one: You look like a million dollars—green and wrinkled."

"In my book! Where'd you hear it?"

"At school. It's old."

"Which school? The new one or Post Road?"

"I think Post Road."

"Hey" I said, "I know someone who knew you there."

She asked who, and I told her Frankie Solomon. She thought a moment. "Oh, yeah . . . that poor little guy. He passed out once."

"Really? Probably from his diabetes."

"Right, I remember now. He had to get these insulin shots. Did he say something about me?"

I hesitated. She squinted at me: "Aaron—come *on.* What did he say?"

"Well, he said you liked a guy named Sonny Rizzo."

Again, those pretty cheeks flushed deep pink, making my own face burn. I feared I'd said the wrong thing. "I mean, maybe it's not—"

"I *hated* Sonny Rizzo," she said. "He was the ickiest greaseball on earth. Why would anyone think I *liked* him?"

I stayed silent.

"What did Frankie *say*? You better tell me."

I took a breath. "He said you followed him around, and then he made fun of you."

"That is such *bull*! Rizzo *thought* I liked him because he was so conceited and thought *everyone* had a crush on him. I actually ran *away* from him whenever I could. What else did Frankie say?

"Nothing, really."

"I bet. Did he say I got sick in front of everybody?" She took my silence for a yes. "Well I did once, and you already know about *that* little problem thanks to my obnoxious brother. But it had nothing to do with Sonny Rizzo."

"Was he handsome?"

"I don't know. Why?"

"Just wondered. Was he?"

"Maybe. If you like big greaseballs who act all tough."

"He was big and tough?"

"Way big for his age. I think he got left back a year. And he was always showing off his disgusting muscles with his T-shirts rolled up. But so what? What do you care?"

I cared because I was small and four-eyed and didn't think I was handsome and certainly not muscular and no one had a crush on me as far as I knew and I'd probably be the last guy who could trigger Keatsie's problem by being really liked.

"I don't care," I said. "Just checking on what Frankie told me."

"Well, he's confused. Where do you know him from, anyway?"

"By the way," I said, sidestepping the question. "My sister says she gets nervous stomach. She gets nauseous when she's worried about something."

"You mean naus*eated*. Byron's always correcting me. Does she throw up?"

"I don't think so. Not any more."

"I wish all I got was nervous. How old is she?"

I told her a little about Joannie, four years my senior and in Mom's opinion fatally underweight. I got up and imitated how my mother sometimes stood over Joannie at dinner and poked her in the back. "*Uh*! Nothing but skin and bones," I said, poking Keatsie's lovely shoulder wings through her jersey. I got her tinkling laugh, which flowed through me like music. But the laugh ended abruptly.

"Did you *see*?" she said. "How Mom and Pop pounced when I choked on my tea? Like I'm some kind of freak."

"I don't think you are."

"Yeah, thanks. But maybe they're right. I mean, they're sending me to a *therapist*."

"Well, you didn't barf today," I said consolingly, wanting to take the stupid remark back at once.

"Oh, so you know that word."

"Uh, yeah, I've heard it."

"Well the thing is," she said, "at lunch? I really almost *did* barf."

We talked more, and after a while—with a few more imitations—I managed to get her laughing again. Her laughs began with a loud burst but sometimes stopped suddenly as if she'd just thought of something sad. She told me about her private girl's school and why Byron preferred to stay in public school (more cool people, fewer snobs). I thought we'd finally moved past Frankie Solomon and where I knew him from, but during a pause she brought it up again.

"I have a question first," I said. "What were those horrible little fish things at lunch? In the salad?"

"You mean the anchovies?"

"Is that their name? They tasted like dog-doo."

"Why do you keep changing the subject?"

"What subject?"

"You're being weird. How do you know Frankie?"

I sighed. "It's just boring. I know Frankie from Hebrew School, where I have to go twice a week to learn my bar mitzvah thing. You know, the Jewish ritual to become a *man*?" I raised my arms and flexed my paltry biceps as if to demonstrate manhood.

"I know what a bar mitzvah is," she said. "We've been to some, actually. And some girls at my school are having bat mitzvahs. So you're Jewish?"

"Sort of. My parents. Well, not religious. I hate Hebrew School."

"Why?"

It seemed too much to explain. "I don't know. It's so uncool."

"And you have to be cool?"

I snapped my fingers. "I got to be real cool, man."

She cocked her head, in a way similar to Byron's. "You're funny."

"Good funny or bad funny?"

"I haven't decided yet."

We didn't speak for a moment. She shifted in her chair, legs over one of the rattan arms. "There's some

Jewish blood in our family," she said. "My mother's grandmother? They were from Germany but they moved to England."

I was surprised to hear it; but was I pleased? Did I care? I wasn't sure how to react except with a wisecrack. "So part-Jewish? Now I see why you get nervous."

"Why, are all Jews nervous? Are you?"

"You mean right now?" For a second I thought I should admit I was. But I couldn't. I couldn't reveal how much I liked her and wanted her to like me. "I was just kidding," I said.

"But are you a nervous type?"

"Oh. I don't . . . . Maybe a little. I'll be nervous at my bar mitzvah—you know, in front of a whole audience."

"I'd be, too. But our church has nothing like that."

"You go to church? What church?"

"Unitarian. Well, Mom goes and sometimes I go with her. It's not really religious—just about understanding life, humanity, doing good, acceptance of everyone, things like that."

"Does Byron go?"

"You kidding? He's a big atheist. Hasn't he tried to make you one?"

"Uh, no."

Well, he will."

11

Giant slimy green octopus

KEATSIE THOUGHT we should go watch the tennis match before it was over, so I followed her downstairs and through the gardens and lawns to the court. I was curious to see how Byron played, but I'd have gladly stayed alone with Keatsie all day if she'd wanted to. But I guessed she didn't.

The teams had changed, and now it was Byron and his father against Mrs. Fairchild and Mrs. Bender—who was clearly the best player. Between games Keatsie asked for the score and Byron said they were tied at four games apiece, which meant little to me, the tennis know-nothing. "But you should have seen the first set," Byron hollered. "I was *phenomenal*."

He looked phenomenal enough to me as they played three more games, even though his team lost when Mrs. Bender smacked some fast serves past them. His parents were good, too, but Byron could scoot after most shots no matter where and whip them back, even if they landed out of bounds some time.

As we returned to the house, Keatsie trailing us, Byron offered to teach me the game if I was interested. I just nodded and let it go. It had taken me long enough to build a little confidence in basketball and street baseball. Based on my showing at ping-pong, tennis was sure to be a disaster.

At the house, Keatsie went into the kitchen to hang out with Leena, and I waited in Byron's room while he took a shower—something I needed before sitting at a table again. But of course I couldn't—not in someone else's house, not without a change of clothes.

Byron had a large desk in his room with a swiveling chair. I sat in it and spun around for a sweeping view of his bookshelves. He had plenty of regular books and some comics, but his science-fiction–and-fantasy-magazine collection took up most of the space, every title on earth, it seemed. I got up and started reading the spines: *Weird Tales, Amazing Stories, Astounding Stories, Fantasy and Science Fiction, Galaxy, Fantastic Story, Fantastic Adventures, Thrilling Wonder Stories, Other Worlds, Future, Startling Stories, Unknown Fantastic Fiction, Dynamic Science Fiction, Marvel, Famous Fantastic Mysteries, Imagination . . . .*

"Do you *read* all these magazines?" I asked, after Byron had emerged in undershorts from the shower and was getting dressed.

"Easily," he said. "But of course, *we* read thousands of pages a second."

"Who's we? Oh, wait—I forgot you were an alien."

"That's. Because. We. Have. Perfected. Our. Human. Disguise," he said in a nasal alien voice.

I looked him up and down. "Not really."

"Sorry. I. Do. Not. Understand. Earthling. Humor."

"And do you believe in God, Mr. Alien?"

"What?"

"Keatsie says you're an atheist."

"Well I am since there's no God," he said, returning to his earthling voice.

"How do you know that?"

"How do you know there *is* one?"

I thought a moment, since I hadn't cogitated much on the subject. "Because how else could everything have started from nothing?"

"Possibly a spontaneous electro-chemical event in an infinite atomic soup. No need for mythical father figures and divine hocus-pocus."

"But where did the soup come from? Campbells? And how can you prove there's *no* God?"

"I can't, and I can't prove there's not some giant slimy green octopus out there running the universe. They're both the absurd kind of ideas we invent because we don't have the scientific answers. Yet."

My head was already spinning. "So all religions are absurd?"

"Absolutely."

"The Unitarian thing too? Keatsie says she and your mom go to their church."

Byron looked peeved. "It's not really a God church, and I don't care what Keatsie does, since she'd demented. She shouldn't have kept you from the tennis game. You missed the best part."

The tone took me by surprise. I felt a rush of shame, deserved or not. "Keatsie wanted to . . . I mean she just wanted to talk a while, and then we came down."

"I thought you were here to visit me."

"I am. I just didn't know how to . . . ."

"You could ignore her. Before she pukes all over you."

I faked a little laugh and immediately felt mean and stupid. "That's kind of rotten," I told him. "She says great things about you."

"That," he said, lightening up, "is because I *am* great."

We got past that huffy moment and soon we were sorting through a pile of board games and making up more drags. About half an hour later Leena appeared at the door. She was breathing heavily from climbing the stairs. "Your mama's callin' you," she told me. "Y'all can use the phone out in the hall."

I sat at the small phone table in the hallway, near the door to Keatsie's room. Mom came on, in an unusually cheery mood: Miracle of miracles, Dad was home early from his card game and wanted to take us all to Yonkers Raceway tonight. We'd gone once before and I'd loved it, watching the horses pull their drivers around the racetrack on two-wheel carts called "sulkies" while the crowd screamed for the nags they'd bet on. You could also get salty junky food there and pump unlimited Ketchup and mustard on it.

Mom said they would pick me up if I got them directions. I hesitated, not quite sure I wanted the Fairchild's to meet my parents yet or see our old car. But at least it would get me out of begging a ride home and sitting through another awkward meal here. "I'm all sweaty," I told my mother.

"I'll bring a clean shirt and sweater," she said. "So you're coming? It'll be fun."

"Okay, I'll ask how to get here. Hold on."

As I laid the phone down, Keatsie's door opened and she popped her head out. "I can give you directions," she offered.

"Oh, hi. You overheard? Uh . . . ."

She put her hands on her hips. "What?"

I knew Byron might be coming out any minute. "No, it's okay, I'll get them from your genius brother."

"Okay, suit yourself," she said, closing her door hard, right on my heart.

I was waiting in front of the house with Byron when Dad pulled up in our old Plymouth. He was wearing his "lucky" black fedora and looked like a gangster, which I ordinarily thought was cool. I was hoping no one else would come out—Mrs. Fairchild was off somewhere with Mrs. Bender—but Dr. Fairchild appeared on the front porch and strolled over, examining the car like a state trooper.

I introduced everyone, Byron-style. "Mom, Dad, Joannie—Byron and his dad."

"Walter Fairchild," said the doctor, extending a big hand through the window and nodding to my mother and Joannie.

"Izzy Schmink,"my father said, giving the hand a hearty shake. "Helluva place you got here."

"I'm Vivian," my mother announced, leaning over Dad. "And my daughter Joan. Thank you for your hospitality. I hope Aaron behaved himself."

"Aaron the famous author?" Dr. Fairchild said. "We're lucky to have him stop by. So you're off to the races?"

"The trotters," Dad said. "A sucker's game, but it's a good night out."

"Never been. Polo matches, closest thing."

"So come on, hop in the back," said Dad. "I'll teach you how to lose your money."

I exchanged a look with Byron. I was dying. What if Dr. Fairchild had said 'yes'? Squeezed in the back seat with us? But he smiled, tapped on the door, and stepped back. "I'll pass, but thanks anyway. Nice meeting you all. Have fun."

As we pulled away, Joannie looked up from her screen magazine. "Why didn't you just invite everyone?" she asked Dad. "The whole family, the maids, the gardener?"

"Next time I will. How d'ya like that place, huh? Looks like a President's house."

"Didn't I tell you?" I said to Joannie.

"I thought you were exaggerating."

12

More from Keatsie's diary (as seen by me much later)

WHY DIDN'T I just go out and say good-bye to Aaron? Kind of rude. And I shouldn't have slammed my door on him. What's wrong with me? I guess I was miffed at how he snubbed my help in favor of Byron's. But why shouldn't he? Byron's the one who invited him here. Byron's the one who really needs a good friend. I don't care myself.

But I did have fun with Aaron, and I think he wants to be my friend, too. Maybe even more, the way he tried to be so pleasing. Or, he just feels sorry for me, probably because his sister has a problem like mine. Of course he hasn't seen what Sonny Rizzo and half of Post Road and my family and others have—the real picture when I barf. The mess, the stink, me looking like I just got pulled out of the grave, wheezing, with slime dripping down my rotting clothes.

I don't know how I held it in at lunch today. Maybe I just couldn't bear the idea of Pop yelling at me in front of guests and everyone backing away from the mess and covering their mouths and saying it doesn't matter, it doesn't matter, when it really does.

Anyway, I should be nice to Aaron, even if he's not exactly my type, whatever that is. And I should probably try to understand Byron when he hogs attention and shuts me out. Byron always acts like it's a big privilege to know him because he's so good at everything, but that just makes people think he's a snob. He never seems to have a real friend. Of course he'll say he doesn't need any buddies, any girlfriend, any God, or anything but his own wonderful self. But didn't Leena tell me in secret that she's seen him crying after this or that hurt his feelings? It made her cry, she said.

I hope Aaron stays friends with him, and with me, too. First thing I have to do is straighten him out about Sonny Rizzo. Okay, I had a crush on Sonny for one second. I think I was just terrified of him, even if my therapist says the problem is partly my fear of becoming a woman and sexual attraction and all that stuff. Boys. Boobs. Periods. Moods. God, sometimes I just want to go play with my old dolls.

13

Fun at the races

WE ARRIVED at Yonkers Raceway before the first race and found seats way up in the grandstand. Joannie held our places there, her nose in a movie magazine, while we wandered off. Mom headed for the betting windows to play her "hunches"—lucky numbers, or names reminding her of a relative or friend, or anything that clicked for her, like "Mama's Boy." The bets were marked on tickets, and after the race you'd trade in the winning tickets for cash at the pay windows and throw the losers on the floor.

Dad went down by the track to get a closer look the horses and drivers as they paraded before each race. Usually I'd stand with him along the track railing as he explained his "system" for picking the winners. With a printed racing program in hand, he'd make all kinds of notes on the horses' and riders' records, how they'd done with different competition on various tracks. Then, at the last minute before the races, he'd run to the betting windows and make wagers so complicated I couldn't figure out which horse to cheer for. But when the races started he'd tell me which ones were his and I'd join in the screaming—or moaning when they lost.

Between races, when I wasn't with him, I'd roam the betting areas and check out all the characters—men puffing on big cigars and women in fancy dresses smoking cigarettes. They stood gazing up at "tote" boards showing which horses were the "favorites"—getting the most bets—and which "longshots"—fewest bets—would pay a fortune if they miraculously beat the favorites. Other characters shuffled through the litter of discarded tickets on the cement floors. They'd bend way over like ostriches, looking for a winning ticket that may have been dropped accidentally. Sometimes I joined them in this treasure hunt that never yielded anything, not to this ostrich anyway.

With money from Dad, I'd also go get food to bring back to our seats for everyone: Franks, burgers, french fries, pickles, corned beef sandwiches, popcorn, candy. Joannie wouldn't eat anything except little bites of hamburger. "It's all disgusting," she'd say, as Mom eyed her.

After half the night's races Dad had won a little money on his favorites and lost on other horses ("It was fixed!"). Mom hadn't won anything. Then something crazy happened.

As if I knew what I was looking at, I liked to peer over Dad's shoulder as he sat and studied the program, scribbling on it with a stubby pencil. While I looked my eye caught the name of a stable that owned a horse in the upcoming race. My heart jumped: *Shelly Farms.*

"Dad," I said, "you have to bet this one, number six!" He looked at the entry. The name of the horse was Stroke of Dawn, which meant nothing to me. But Shelly! Not the same spelling, but close enough.

"She's a bum," Dad said, looking at the horse's record. "No better than fifth in two years. Lousy times. Disqualified in three races for breaking stride. No wonder she's—" He looked at the tote board showing the latest and near impossible odds of winning—"thirty-to-one. Whaddy'a see in this dog?"

I pointed to the name in the program. "Shelly Stables?" he read. "What's that mean?"

"It's his new *girl*friend," Joannie piped without looking up from her magazine. "Byron's twin sister."

"She's not my girlfriend," I said. "I just like her name. Come on, Dad."

Mom, listening in, lowered her own program. "*I'll* bet two dollars on it. It's a good hunch."

"You're both nuts," Dad said. "Shining Pride's gonna win by ten lengths. But you wanna throw money away, I'll make the bets for you."

I went with him to the window. He bet on his own pick, plus number six for the rest of us. Then—"Aw, what the heck"—he added another bet on number six for himself.

14

Big winners

☺ ☺ ☺

WELL, YOU KNOW what happened, or I wouldn't be telling the story. But the *way* it happened. Halfway through the race, Stroke of Dawn from Shelly Stables was in seventh place, pinned in by another sulky, with the favorite Shining Pride way out in front. Then something magical got into number six, the "bum" we'd bet on. Her driver maneuvered the sulky into a clear path and she took off—her legs flying in the graceful pattern called a "trot," front-right leg moving with back-left, then front-left with back-right. She moved up to sixth . . . fifth . . . fourth . . . *third*, coming down the stretch toward the finish line.

We were going crazy. But in the last seconds, though she held her position, she seemed to lose the energy to keep gaining on the two lead horses. It looked like she would finish third—except that trotting races can be especially weird. Horses that try to run too hard at the end often lose control of their trotting stride. They "break" into their natural gallop—and according to trotting rules, that means automatic disqualification. And guess who broke? Both Shining Pride and the second horse, a big grey one named Dutch Treat.

We were winners!

Not only was I the night's hero, pocketing my unbelievable sixty-dollar share from the wad of bills distributed by Dad. Now, also, I knew that Shelley Keats Fairchild was my destiny.

15

Rocco's advice

OUR HIGH SPIRITS carried over to the next morning. Lots of jabber, no silent treatments. Dad was up and about, eating with us at our Sunday breakfast, my favorite: smoked salmon and bagels, cream cheese, tomatoes, dill pickles, and olives. Even Joannie dug in, smooshing olives into chunks of cream cheese on an onion bagel.

"You shouldn't lick your fingers," I told her as she did so. "It's bad manners."

"Oh, suddenly you're high society?" she said. "You with your elbows on the table?"

I put one arm in my lap, remembering that the Fairchild's ate that way.

After breakfast, Dad sat up in bed smoking his Chesterfields and checking racing results in the Sunday *New York News*. He had his night's winnings piled up on the dresser, and when I stopped by he asked me what I was going to do with my own share.

"Bet it all again," I said. "On horses from Shelly Farms."

"Yeah, that's just what a dope would do. Put it in your college fund."

"No, thanks. I'd rather buy some cool loafers for a very poor kid."

"What poor kid?"

"Me."

"Wise guy," he said, turning back to the race results.

Mom cleaned up in the kitchen and stayed there drinking coffee and paging through *The New York Daily Mirror*. Both Joannie and I did homework until early afternoon, when I joined Dad at the television to watch the fifth game of the World Series. Mom came in, too, since our beloved Brooklyn Dodgers were playing the New York Yankees, with the series tied at two games each. Joannie watched an inning here and there, going off to listen to pop tunes on her new 45rpm player.

We got excited as the Dodgers went ahead 4 to 1, but before long it was 4 to 2, then, oh-oh, 4 to 3, and we groaned and clutched each other until the Dodgers put it away 5 to 3. It was one of those days I felt lucky to have my family around me, happy that we were having fun together.

But it was a different story next door, where Rocco Cabruzzi lived. The walls were thin between our two apartments, and when Rocco's parents had one of their frequent fights and screamed at each other, we could hear almost every word. And they weren't pretty. Sometimes the fury spilled over to Rocco, and we heard his sobs mixing with his parents' threats and curses. In the worst of the fights we heard sounds of physical violence followed by shriekings and wailings that Mom said broke her heart.

Joannie, as usual, knew all the "dirt": Rocco's father—Rocco Sr.—had a girlfriend in town; the mother—Adele—had her own drama with our landlord's son Mario. He lived upstairs from her apartment and was said to be crazily in love with her. One night he'd stood at her door with a butcher knife, threatening to kill himself if she didn't let him in. Luckily, Rocco Sr. had been somewhere else or we'd have heard gunshots along with Mario's hysterical cries. Those cries ended only when Adele opened the door and somehow calmed him down.

About an hour after our dinner, a new round of muffled growls and swearing came from Rocco's apartment. Joannie pressed her ear to the dining room wall to hear better. "It's about money," she whispered to me. "Adele says she doesn't have a nickel for Rocco's needs, and no wonder he gets left back in school." The voices got louder. "Now the father's saying they're both spoiled rotten. He's had a lousy week, he says. He's owes a lot of money." She held up a finger for silence. "Now Adele's screaming about his girlfriend. She says Rocco gives her their money. Ooh, now she's calling her some filthy words."

"What words?"

"Never mind."

After a while we heard someone slam out of the house. We ran to Joannie's window and saw Rocco, Sr., speed off in his shiny black Buick. Later the door slammed again and we watched as an angry Adele strode up the block in high heels and a black dress. She was headed for our bus stop.

"Poor Rocco," Joannie said. "Look how they leave him all alone."

"I know. Maybe I could go keep him company. But Mom doesn't like me going over there."

"So go out the back door. She's watching the Jack Benny show, she won't even know."

I slipped out to the back-stairway landing that connected our two apartments. Rocco let me into his kitchen and slapped my extended hand. "Hey, man." But he looked away when I saw his red eyes.

"I heard the fighting," I said. "It's okay, man, everyone has fights."

"I hate them both," Rocco said, wiping away the last tears. "I wish they'd die."

"Don't say that, man. It might come true."

"It don't make no difference. If my old man hits us again I'm gonna kill him."

"He hit you?"

"Come on, let's go in and do something."

We headed toward Rocco's room, which like Joannie's overlooked the street. The apartment had the same layout as ours but was littered with garments, bedclothes, ornaments, crucifixes, newspapers, and full ashtrays. I thought of the word *festooned*—hung with decorations—which I had heard Byron use after Keatsie had draped his underpants from the bookshelves.

Rocco picked up a broad-brimmed hat lying near the front door and put it on. "I'm a gangster like my old man," he said from the side of his mouth before throwing the hat down again. I already knew that Rocco Sr. was a "bookie" who took cash bets from people on lucky numbers, horse racing, and other sports. He collected the money for his bosses, who allowed him to keep a share of profits. Thinking of him reminded me of my own winnings.

"I won a bunch of money at the race track," I boasted.

"No lie? You went to the track?"

"Yeah, my old man took us, and I bet on a horse because of a girl I know, and it won."

"That's shahp, man. Hey, maybe you can loan me something if you got any extra."

"What for?"

"You know, clothes and stuff. Bus fare."

"I don't know. I think I have to save it."

"Yeah, never mind."

"Maybe I could—"

"Nah, never mind," Rocco said, shrugging it off. "Lissen, I got this new game in a box, but I don't know how to play it or nothin'."

I felt wave of pity for him, thinking of all the great things to do at the Fairchild's house and how little Rocco knew about anything compared to Byron and even me. Then I felt bad for thinking it. But Rocco did have a way with "chippies," as he called the neighborhood girls who seemed to adore him. He was just my age, but already a little lady-killer, slim and full of confidence in the flirting department. His face with its dark-eyes showed the best of his mother's Latina and father's Italian features. He combed his black hair wet and swept it into a wave, a few strands falling loose to meet his heavy brows. A chipped front tooth gave him an impish smile.

"Wanna watch TV?" he asked as we passed their set, newer and bigger than ours. "I got cigarettes, too."

"Nah, I can't stay too long. You know what, though? I could use some advice. About girls. *A* girl."

Rocco brightened. "You come to the right place, man."

We flopped down on the big velvet sofa across from the TV, moving aside two empty soda bottles wedged between the cushions.

"Well," I began, "her name is Keatsie. She's beautiful and all, really sharp, but . . . "

I paused, unsure of how to present the problem. "I mean, I think she likes me, but she goes for big, tough guys, and they, uh, make her kind of sick?"

"Huh?"

"Okay. Here's the thing. How do you get a girl to really like you? Like for a boyfriend?"

"That's easy, man. Be like Rocco."

"Come on. How do you even start?"

"You ask her on a date, man. Like to the movies. You dress sharp and you buy her stuff and sweet-talk her."

"What kind of sweet talk?"

Rocco grabbed a throw pillow near him and placed it between us, on top of the sofa back. He put his face against it.

"Baby, you're so fine," he murmured. "So pretty. I love your eyes. . . . I love your hair. . . ." He stroked the pillow's imaginary hair. "I love the way you smell. Mmm. . . you know I'm wild about you, don't you? . . . "

"Wild?"

"Wild, crazy, nuts. It don't matter." He brushed his mouth against the pillow. "Mmm . . .your cheek's so warm, baby, and your lips are driving me ga-ga. . . . . Can I just kiss them a little? Please . . . ." He stopped. "What are you laughin' about, man?"

"*Ga-ga*? You'd really say that?"

"I told you, it don't matter what you say. You just gotta keep talkin.'"

"I couldn't do it."

"Why not?"

"I don't know. I'd get it all wrong. And I don't think Keatsie would like it."

"They all like it, man. Does what's-her-name got a *fahn* body?"

"Real fahn."

"Then, you know, man," he said, moving his hand lovingly up and down a sofa cushion. "Show her you like it.

16

Dodgers win!

MONDAY was overcast, just the right gloominess for my lessons at the Hebrew Institute after school. And to make matters worse, the Dodgers had lost to the Yankees that afternoon, with one final game to go.

Moshe Litvin sat in his usual place, giving me murderous looks, but Frankie Solomon's chair was empty. That worried me. After class, during my individual bar mitzvah practice, I asked the teacher Mr. Rubin if he knew where Frankie was.

"He's not here, that's what I know."

"Maybe he's sick."

"So then it's good he's not here. Let's continue, please, and pay attention for a change. Practice this passage here."

He pointed to some lines of Hebrew text. It was an effort for me to switch gears.

"Schmink?" he said. "Wake up. Do I have all night?"

"Okay." I stumbled through the lines, trying to make a song out of them. "*Cházôn ovad'yäh Koh-ämar Adonäy Adonäy leédôm sh'mûäh shäma'nû mëët y'hväh w'tziyr BaGôyim shuLäch qûmû v'näqûmäh äleyhä laMil'chämäh . . .*"

"Stop," Rubin said. "This isn't the Hit Parade. *Chant*, like last week when you were doing so nicely."

I tried again. My voice had changed earlier in the year, so at least I could handle the lower notes of the chant. Still, time was getting short and I was going backward. My stomach fluttered as I thought about performing before a crowd, and I was already a nerve case thinking about Keatsie all day and how to get her out on a date.

On Tuesday, in a game that started during our afternoon classes, the Dodgers beat the Yankees 2-0 and won the World Series. The Eastview principal had halted all instruction and put the radio broadcast on the PA system. Later, everyone seemed to be celebrating the fun of a dramatic week, honking horns, yelling on the streets, even people in Yankee hats.

I was looking forward to celebrating with Dad, but he had gone to the Elk's Club for the afternoon and didn't come home till supper was cold. "Some game, huh Kid?" he said to me in passing, bopping me on the shoulder. Then he closed himself into the bathroom and ran a bath. Dodger victory or not, Mom was not happy.

When everyone had settled elsewhere, I sat on my bed trying to get up the courage to call Keatsie. Soon it was too late at night.

In school on Wednesday, Byron and I hurried from math class to Frida's grocery a block away to buy our lunch: baloney wedges slathered with yellow mustard. We sat on the curb outside, downing the doughy mess with swigs of Coke and sharing a package of Oreos. I'd been dying to tell him about all the money I'd won at the races betting on the Shelly Farms horse. But knowing he didn't like me focusing on Keatsie, I just told him we'd all won some money. As we headed back to school and our Beginning Spanish class, we had a laugh-fit twisting our tiny new vocabulary into Yo-mama drags.

"*Yo mama es un burro.*" (Yo mama's a jackass.)

"*Yo mama come las cabezas de los perros.*"(Yo mama eats dogs' heads.)

"*Yo mama no tenga la cabeza.*" (Yo mama has no head.)

After classes, we met up again in the library, where Mr. Salisbury ran the Newspaper Club meetings. Five of us sat around a long wooden desk, and Mr. Salisbury coached us on how to begin a news story—by telling the who, what, when, where, how, and maybe the why of something in the first paragraph, the "lead."

"The World Series is a good example," he said. Sitting next to him, I smelled what seemed like alcohol on his breath. "Let's say the Dodgers are the 'who.' What did they do? They beat the Yankees. When? Yesterday, Tuesday. Where?"

"Stinky Stadium," I said.

"Yankee Stadium," Mr. Salisbury continued, unamused. And how?"

"They cheated," said Alfred Gano, a Yankee fan.

Mr. Salisbury paused, continued. "The 'how' is by a score of two to zero. Is there a 'why'?"

Betty Lee, with her famous smile, said, "Because the Yankees had whupped 'em all four times before in the World Series and the Dodger weren't about to take it anymore. They had heart."

I noticed Byron looking at her as if she'd just solved all the world's problems. It was the first time I'd seen him look at anyone like that.

"Good!" Mr. Salisbury said. "So what have we got? Let's put it all together in a sentence or two, everyone. Include Betty's 'why' or your own interpretation. I'll be back in a minute."

"Off for another swig," Alfred said after he'd gone.

17

The call

I'D BEEN HOPING that Byron would invite me to his house during the weekend and that I could sneak in enough time (and courage) with Keatsie to ask for a date. But at Newspaper Club I couldn't pry him away from Betty Lee. And then Thursday I had Hebrew School, and Friday he never said anything about getting together. Instead he seemed edgy about something, but I didn't think it had anything to do with me. I hoped not. So if I wanted to ask Keatsie out for this weekend, my one choice was to call her.

I paced around the apartment like someone on Death Row. By late afternoon, all I'd done was sit at our rickety telephone table in the hallway and dial the Fairchild's number—several times, but with the phone hung up. I'd never called a girl before, much less actually asked one out on a date. I'd flirted some with neighborhood girls in Rocco's company, but the closest I'd come on my own was to invite a former neighbor named Linda to ride bikes together. We did so three or four times without saying much before she moved away.

At dinner I acted-out like a jerk, complaining about lima beans and fishy-smelling fish. "You're in some mood tonight," Mom said, and I snapped, "Can't you make food I *like*?" Finally Dad—who was home early Friday night for a change—slammed his palm down. "You should be ashamed of yourself. Be thankful you got food on the table!"

Afterward I isolated myself in my room, brooding over what I might say to Keatsie once I called. Finally I made my way to the phone, but now the television was blaring from the living room and I wouldn't be able to concentrate. I gave up for the night. A bad night, with all my favorite night fears—polio, bar mitzvah speech, infinite cosmic nothingness—bubbling up between dreams.

Mid-Saturday morning, however, as the sun crept into the house, everything seemed less frightening. With Dad still at work and Mom and Joannie busy, I marched myself to the phone, picked up the receiver, and dialed the Fairchilds.

Dr. Fairchild answered. I hung up.

I tried again in an hour. This time it was Leena's voice: "Good morning. Fairchild residence. . . . Hello?"

In a panic, I did the only thing that seemed safe. I asked for Byron.

"He's not available," Leena said. "Who's calling please?"

"It's Aaron. Aaron Schmink, his friend?"

"Well, hey there. How you doin'?"

"Great, thanks."

"That's real good. But Byron's out playing tennis with his folks and his kinfolks, the ones from England. Uncle Otto, auntie Alice, cousin Boyd, they're all here."

"Oh. I didn't even know about them. When did they come?"

"Came last night. Gonna be around this whole long weekend, makin' a whole lot of work for me. It's Byron's birthday, too, I got to bake a cake or go find one. Anyway, I can tell him you called."

"No, that's okay. Tell him happy birthday. But is . . . uh . . ."

"What."

I took a breath. "Is Keatsie with them?"

"No, she's up in her room or somewhere."

"Can I—could she—I mean, could I speak with her?"

"You want to speak to Keatsie?"

"I guess so. But please don't, you know . . . ."

"Say anything?" Leena laughed. "Tell you what. I can't go chasin' after her right now, but give me your number."

"She'll call me?"

"Maybe. Hard to say with that girl."

I gave her the number and said goodbye. The receiver was wet with my perspiration when I put it down and I hadn't even talked to Keatsie. I paced around a while waiting for a call. Took a stab at some homework. Nibbled at a cheese sandwich my mother had left me for lunch—she and Joannie were off on errands.

At about 2:30, the phone jangled. I picked it up, heart galloping, and said hello. It was Keatsie.

"Hey, Aaron. You called me?"

I slid to the floor, back against the wall. "Yeah. Hi. I mean, I wanted to, uh . . ." I froze, unable to think of anything but to chide myself. *What's the matter with you? Calm down.*

"You wanted to what?"

"Uh, how are you?"

"Me? I'm fine," she said. "Well, bored out of my gourd actually."

"Really? How come?"

"Didn't Byron tell you? Our cousin Boring Boyd is here with his boring parents."

"Oh, right. Leena said they were. How come you're not with them?"

"They're all at Dad's club right now. The *Club*. Some big party or something, and while they were here they mostly played tennis—it's a big competitive deal with them. Even on Byron's birthday I have to listen to Boyd talk about his wonderful Harrow prep school and his cricket and rugby and their stupid practical jokes, which are decidedly unfunny."

"Yeah, I hate unfunny jokes. Like mine. Does Byron like him?"

"Not really. He tries to be nice, but Boyd's so competitive he makes it impossible. You should see him when he loses—all red-faced and *livid.*"

"Huh," I said, guessing what "livid" meant and storing the word. So why aren't you at the party?"

"I hate those things—they're dress-up, and super snooty. Besides, Dad isn't especially eager for me to go."

"Why not?"

"Why do you think? He's afraid I'll barf."

"Oh."

"Heave all over the gardens."

"It might be good for the plants," I said, worrying that I shouldn't joke.

"Yeah, Miss Fertilizer," she said with a laugh.

I laughed, too. Then silence. My sweat flowed again.

"Anyway," Keatsie said, "why'd you call me?"

"Uh, just kind of to say hello." *Idiot. That's not why you called. Tell her!* "I didn't, you know, get to see you guys this weekend."

"Aww. Did you miss us?"

"I guess."

"Both of us?"

"Well, yeah."

"That's sweet. I'd have liked to have seen you, too."

"Really?" I squeaked, marveling at what she said and her fancy grammar.

"Sure. I think you're fun. At least when Byron unchains you for a minute."

"I know. He didn't like me sharing the visit."

"Tell me about it. I know he needs friends, but still."

"Hey," I said, finally taking the leap, "what if we snuck out by ourselves some time? Went somewhere fun?" *I did it, I said it!*

"Out? You mean like a *date*? You and I? I haven't really gone on dates."

"Neither have I." I held my breath.

"Hmmm. Weird," she said. "Where would we go?"

"Wherever you like. Movies or something. I won a load of money at the horses. In fact, I'll tell you a secret if you promise not to tell anyone else."

"What's that?"

"I bet on a horse because of your name. It was from Shelly Farms? No one ever expected it to win, but we all bet on it and it paid out a bunch of money. Thanks to you."

She paused a moment. "A crummy horse had my name?"

"No, no—it was fabulous! . . . . Like you." *Oh god, what did I just say? How did that come out?*

"Wow. Thanks. Except, I'm not sure I'm so fabulous. I can't even control my guts."

"That's doesn't bother me."

"Don't be so sure. Anyway I guess I could go to a movie with you. I think. If we just meet there and nobody knows. Sounds like fun."

"Really? Yay! When could we go?"

"I don't know. It would really be hard on school days, and I have piano Saturdays and pretty much have to be with the family on Sundays."

"There's no school this Monday," I said. It's "Columbus Day."

"Yeah, but they'll still all be here. Maybe we could figure out something next week, okay?

I didn't have a choice, as much as I wanted to be sitting next to her right now in a snug movie seat. "Okay," I said. "Great."

And just the hope of a date *was* great, considering my fears. I hung up, got to my feet, and danced The Stroll, whooping all the way to the kitchen.

18

The perils of Columbus Day

ON MY STREET if you hung out most of the day with the neighborhood guys, someone was going to challenge you to do something stupid. But hanging out seemed the only choice this Columbus-Day Monday. I'd finished my homework, even practiced my bar mitzvah reading, and nothing else was going on.

Dad was snoring away after a long night on the delivery truck. Mom was typing envelopes, which she often did at home for extra money. My sister was off somewhere with her best friend Barbara Katz. She was all excited about a call Sunday from our Aunt Ada—one of Dad's sisters—inviting her down to Biloxi, Mississippi, over the Christmas vacation. Aunt Ada was the family rebel; she'd divorced a bossy, violent husband and left Brooklyn with their daughter Maureen to start a new life in the South, working at an Army base. Maureen was now about Joannie's age and would "show her the town."

I'd have been jealous, but now, buzzing with the excitement of a date with Keatsie, I was happy to spend the rest of this warm October day doing nothing. That was the specialty of the street guys—doing nothing, until someone talked us into some activity, usually a dumb one. We started out on the front stairs of my building—me, Rocco, Googie, and Chubby, plus Dickie—a sour-pussed redhead with a chip on his shoulder—and a tall goofy guy named Brent. We chewed our Fleers bubble gum and spit the juice on the steps, then migrated to Chubby's building after our landlord Mr. Apolitano came out of his basement apartment hollering at us.

Some of the neighborhood girls strolled by. Chubby did his loud, two-fingered whistle. Rocco sang out some sweet talk. The girls waved and moved on. Googie lit a cigarette and told an old joke that only Brent laughed at. I tossed a "yo mama" joke Googie's way: "Yo mama's sells cigarette butts to the hobos." Again only Brent laughed. We threw a pink rubber ball around for a while, sat down again. Googie made fun of my blocky Buster Brown shoes for about the fiftieth time this year, twisting its advertising jingle.

I'm Buster Brown, I live in a shoe.

My dog Schmink, he lives there, too!

The talk turned to movies. Brent said that *Rebel Without a Cause* with James Dean was coming to the RKO Keith's. "Dean's real cool," Chubby declared, which led to Googie's report that Dean, just twenty-four, had died in a car accident two weeks ago. "Everyone knows that," Dickie said, but it was news to me. I guessed they'd been talking about it at school, but my mind had been on the

World Series and this was the first time I paid any attention. Googie said he'd heard the new movie was a lot like Dean's life, including someone dying in a car accident. I wondered if it would be a good movie for me and Keatsie.

"Hey, any ya's guys wanna wreck a mansion?" Rocco suggested out of the blue.

"What mansion?" Dickie asked.

"Up the hill. Nobody ain't in it."

I knew the one he was talking about—just two properties away from the Elks Lodge where Dad played cards. A big white building on a huge overgrown lot. It looked something like Byron's house, but with boarded-up windows.

"Why'd I wanna do all that work?" Dickie said.

"For fun," Rocco said.

"Shoot, my old man gets paid to do that crap."

And yo mama wrecks bird houses for a living, I thought of saying. But Dickie had a mean build and quick temper.

The idea died. And then Chubby, jetting gum juice through his teeth, named the one activity that would reliably send chills down our spines. "Let's go down the ledge. Spit on cars or something." He got up and started off. "Come on," he said, turning to wait for us. "What, you guys, chicken?"

The ledge. At the bottom of our hill, past the last apartment building, our street crossed over a two-lane parkway and continued a few blocks to a dead end. The overpass had stone walls up to our chests on each side, but a sidewalk ran only along one wall. That wall was "the ledge," where neighborhood kids congregated.

They stood on the sidewalk and leaned against the stone, looking down at traffic over the foot-and-a-half-wide top. They carved initials on the ledge. They threw trash over it. Older kids flipped cigarette butts into traffic after a final dramatic puff.

If you were tall enough to hoist your rear up to the surface or if someone hoisted you, you sat on the sidewalk side of the ledge, dangling your legs.

And if you had no fear of heights, you might swing your legs over to the outside edge, just a slip away from plunging to the concrete parkway or colliding with a speeding windshield.

And if you were nuts or showing off or afraid of being called chicken, you stood up on the ledge.

And if you were forced to prove something or you made a stupid bet or were driven to it by a bunch of mental bullies, you walked across the ledge from one end to the other. This was what every neighborhood kid promised his parents he would never do. This was the challenge that came up now and then from some fool who had done it himself. And why Ozzie Assim would never move his limbs again, if he was even still alive.

Parents used the legend of Ozzie to scare us all, and it did the job perfectly on me. We'd moved here after Ozzie's family had gone, but Rocco and Googie had seen him around, a slow teenager who didn't want to disappoint anyone, not even the punks who got him to drink beer with them then challenged him to walk the ledge. Wobbling across, he'd almost made it before falling off the last stretch, landing just where the road met the grass bank. A little sooner, he'd have hit all cement and probably been dead and run over.

Today was just the kind of idle, hanging-around time that could lead to dopey challenges. I felt it coming when everyone got themselves up on the wall and Chubby and Dickie swung their legs to the outside. Then Rocco, sitting next to me, did the same. Cars whizzed underneath, making a swooshing sound under the bridged street.

"Hey, Stink," Dickie called to me. "Why don't you get your Buster Browns up on the ledge?"

"Me? Why'd I wanna do all that work?" I said, mocking his earlier remark.

"Oh, you're a little wise guy, ain'tcha. And a chick-en."

"I just like being able to walk. Why don't you get your smelly shoes up there?"

"Yeah, chicken. Cheep, cheep. What about you, Cabruzzi? I dare you to stand up."

"Why don't you?" Rocco said.

"Shoooot," Dickie said, sliding back from the edge and getting to his feet. He did a slight shuffle. "Come on, Cabruzzi."

"Don't," I said to Rocco. "You don't have to do what he says."

But Rocco slowly maneuvered his feet under him and rose—shakily, it seemed to me. "I ain't no chicken," he said.

The two stood a while, egging others to do the same. Chubby had started to rise when a black Buick pulled around the corner and screeched to a stop at the sidewalk. Before Rocco could climb down, Rocco Senior leapt out of the driver's side, ran around the car and grabbed Rocco junior by the belt, hauling him off the ledge.

"Whadda you *doin'* whadda you *doin'*? You moron! You imbecile!" He whacked his son in the back of the head. "You wanna die? *I'll* kill you. Get in the car! Get in there!" He looked back at the rest of us. "I'll throw ya's *all* off the bridge next time!"

I saw Rocco in tears in the passenger seat before the car took off.

19

Back at the Fairchilds'

THE FOLLOWING FRIDAY, after math class, Byron invited me to come to his house the next day and stay overnight. Dr. Fairchild would be away at a medical conference in New Orleans, and Mrs. Fairchild had said she was fine with the idea—had even encouraged Keatsie to invite a friend of her own for the weekend.

"It is *imperative* that you appear," Byron told me.

I thrilled at the chance to spend more time at the Fairchild mansion and have the fun of an overnight, maybe even sneaking some moments with Keatsie. Except that I still had to get permission from home. When I asked Mom for it at dinnertime, she wasn't too happy with the idea. But then she wasn't too happy to start with. That day at work, her boss had come back drunk from lunch, imagining he was an Army officer and shouting orders at the "troops." She tried giving him papers he had to sign and he threw them on the floor, yelling, "Nazi forgeries!" Later he sat sobbing with his head on his desk, so of course she felt sorry for him. On top of that, Dad hadn't come home yet from the Elks Club and Mom was starting her slow burn. Finally, Joannie complained of stomach sickness and said she didn't feel like eating.

"So what am I cooking for?" Mom said. "This one doesn't eat, that one loves his card game more than his family, and you want to race off the first chance you get."

"Well, *I* want to eat," I said. "And it's not racing off. Everybody goes to sleepovers."

"You've been to plenty of sleepovers."

"At cousin Alan's? That's the only one I ever do. I don't even like staying there."

"So why can't you spend a nice weekend here?"

"Because I've been *invited*. By a nice *friend*."

"Your fancy rich friend. We're not fancy enough for you here?"

"That has nothing to do with it. I just want to have fun with my friends. That's *normal*. God, you never want me over at Rocco's, you don't want me at Byron's—"

"Okay, so I'm a lousy mother." She slammed a wooden spoon into the sink.

"I didn't say that. You're a great mother, I know you care about me. But please—I really want to go."

She sighed and put a hand on her hip. "Who's going to watch you there?"

I explained the situation, just how I would take buses, call when I arrived, and get a ride home.

She gave it a long moment. "Go," she said. "I don't want you moping around all weekend. You want Ketchup with the chops or not?"

I felt slightly ridiculous carrying a suitcase up Byron's street from where the second bus let me off. The case was the smallest we had in the house, but still too big for the change of clothes, pajamas, and bathroom items I'd packed with great care. Workers tending the neighbors' huge lawns paused and gave me funny looks—they felt funny, anyway.

I arrived at lunchtime and made the call to Mom. Today, instead of sitting in the Fairchilds' formal dining room we were all to grab something in the kitchen and eat it there at a big white table or wherever we liked. Leena had made ham and cheese sandwiches with devilled eggs and a salad containing—phew!—no anchovies.

"That ham okay with you?" Leena asked me as she put the sandwiches on the table for us.

"Sure. I love ham."

"Cause some Jewish folks don't eat it."

"I know. But I'm not religious. I eat bacon and everything."

"Nothin' wrong being religious."

"I beg to disagree," Byron interposed, his mouth already full. "There's *everything* wrong with it."

"There you go again," Leena said, bringing the salad and eggs. "You headed straight to that other place you keep talkin' like that."

"There is no other place if there's no first place."

She shook her head and looked at me. "You an intellectual, too?"

"Me? No, just a smartypants."

Leena chuckled. "What y'all want to drink?"

"Milk, Coca-Cola, and many Oreos," Byron answered.

Just as we were finishing up Keatsie entered the kitchen accompanied by a petite girl with glossy black hair, wearing a turtleneck sweater and a skirt over dark tights.

"Hi, Aaron," Keatsie greeted me. "This is my friend Miki from school. She's supercool and a great dancer."

"Not either, really," Miki said.

"And this is Aaron, the famous author."

I looked around. "Nobody famous here."

"Soon to be *infamous*, Byron said. "Anyway, I'm afraid we ate all the sandwiches. There's some stale bread left, though."

"Don't listen to that fool," Leena said. "Sit down, I'll bring 'em out."

"I never listen to that fool," Keatsie said.

Miki extended a hand to me and said "Nice to meet you." I shook it. "You, too." She had a delicate hand and smooth skin except for an outbreak of acne on both cheeks. The eyes were dark—pretty Asian eyes beneath large glasses. As we all paused for an awkward moment, I snuck a glance at Keatsie and quickly looked away when she met my eyes. I think I blushed, as if some passionate secret hung between us instead of just a date in the offing.

"Come on," Byron said to me, rising from the table and gathering a fistful of Oreos. "Let us reconnoiter in my sanctum sanctorum."

I figured he meant his room, and that's where he led me, leaving the girls behind. Outside it was warm but foggy and drizzly, so we played some board games and pored through another of his collections, science-fiction and horror comic books. I loved the dripping gore and drooling monstrosities leaping off the pages—which I had to turn very carefully per Byron's instructions. Some of the words spoken in the voice balloons were explained at the bottom of the pages. *BEM* stood for Bug-Eyed Monster, and *Squa tront!* or *Span fon!*—meant "Oh my God!" in Martian or maybe Venusian. Byron, of course, had built a whole alien vocabulary from the stories. He liked to shout something like, "*Svoort za znukuxa, Gwanqu!*"—"You must die, Earthling!"

While we talked I asked him how well he knew Keatsie's friend Miki.

"She's been over a few times," he said. "She's nice, but they giggle a lot together."

I asked if she was Oriental, a word we used then for most Asians. Byron told me her father was Japanese, but born here. "He's a musician, but I think they gave him a rough time during the war."

"Oh. Well, she's cute."

He nodded. "She's the right height for you, too."

"Thanks," I said, wondering what he'd think of me out with taller Keatsie. "Who do *you* think is cute?" I asked.

"Who cares?"

"Wait. I bet it's someone in Newspaper Club."

"What makes you say that?" He looked down at his hands.

" 'Cause I saw you making eyes at Betty Lee?"

"Really?"

"Definitely really. Couldn't take your eyes off her, actually."

He threw his hands in the air. "I confess! I think she's *incredible*."

"Yeah, she is, man. I dig her smile. She's sharp and brainy and funny and everything."

"Hey, better stay away from my girl, or *svoort za znukuxa*."

"Okay, I'll let you have her. But you should ask her out." I sounded like Rocco to myself.

"Out?"

"On a date, man."

"Hmm. You think she would?"

"Why not?"

"I'm white, for one thing."

"But you're not prejudiced or anything."

"Of course not."

"So?"

Byron thought for a moment. "Maybe her family wouldn't allow it. I don't know."

"What about your family?"

Byron rubbed his chin. "I think Mater would be okay with it. Pop, you never know. I've heard him make some stupid jokes about Leena."

"Well, you should try asking her."

"Yes, maybe. Must think. Must run equation through superior brain circuits."

20

An overnight

THE DRIZZLE stopped and Byron and I set up the badminton net for a few games before dinner. He let the girls join us for one of them—Miki, a skilled player, and I against Byron and Keatsie, who played like she was dancing rock and roll or swatting at killer bees, laughing all the way—my kind of opponent. Miki politely praised my wild swings as "good try!"

I looked for some sign of special interest from Keatsie, but didn't see it—and not at dinner, either, which we ate briskly so Leena could go home for her Saturday night. Mrs. Fairchild's friend Mrs. Bender had come over in the afternoon and was dining with us. She had somehow learned that I'd been practicing for my bar mitzvah and asked where it would be held. It wasn't a topic I wanted to trot out, but I told her where.

"At the Hebrew Institute?" she said. "Why, are you very religious? Orthodox?"

"Me? No!" I said, maybe too emphatically.

"I see. So maybe you should look into my temple, the JCC. It's Reform."

"Well, my parents . . . "

"Oh, okay. I didn't mean to interfere. I just think our ceremonies are more, uh . . . modern."

"They're cooler," Keatsie chipped in. "And Aaron digs cool."

"Yeah," I said. "But when it comes to bar mitzvahs, I think mine's gonna be pretty square."

Mrs. Bender laughed. "Anyway, think about it for the future."

"She's on the Booaaard there," Mrs. Fairchild said, tapping her friends arm. "You might keep it in miinnd."

When it got dark outside and the weather cleared, Byron led me to a set of outdoor chaise lounges near the rose garden where we could lie back and gaze up at the emerging stars.

"There's Ursa Major, the bear," Byron said, pointing somewhere among the millions of visible pinpricks in the night ceiling. He moved his hand. "And Ursa Minor."

I looked at the clouds of stars. "I don't see any bear."

He tried pointing out the dots that made up the pattern, but there was no way I could follow his hand.

"I'll take your word for it," I said.

"Astronomy is so cool. We've barely begun to know what's out there. There are billions of stars—*billions* of suns and their planets and galaxies and nebulae and all kinds of strange phenomena."

"Plus aliens."

"Extraterrestrials, absolutely. It's absurd to think of Earth as the only suitable planet for life."

"But no God up there, no Heaven, right?"

"Absolutely not."

"You know," I said, "the Jewish God is very wrathful. Don't get him mad."

Byron laughed. "Tell Him not to get *me* mad."

We watched the stars silently for a while. Suddenly a dot of light streaked across the sky. I'd heard about such things but had never gazed up long enough to catch one. "Wow—did you see that shooting star?" I said.

"Not a star," Byron said. "A meteor burning in the atmosphere. You see a lot of them over time."

"Pretty neat. Aren't you supposed to make a wish or something when you see one?"

"Another fairy tale."

"Well just in case, you should wish that Betty Lee falls all over you."

"Hmm."

"What?" I said.

"Nothing. Whom would you wish to fall upon you?"

"You mean who do I like?"

"Whom."

"*Whom* I like?" I fought back a surprising urge to confess about Keatsie. "I like 'em all, man. I play the field." I heard Rocco coming out of my mouth again.

"What field? You mean at school?"

"Mostly some neighborhood girls." It was a safe lie.

Later, as we left the rose garden, the sound of wild piano-playing and giddy laughter came from the penthouse party room, where lights glowed and some of the French doors had been thrown open to the terrace. I took that territory to be forbidden as long as I was Byron's guest, but I was having fun anyway and it looked like Keatsie was doing fine without me

It was a long evening, and finally we settled down in Byron's room. A comfy roll-out bed had been set up, and I slid in under a fresh-smelling top sheet—a luxury that had never made it into our bottom-sheet-only household. We talked some more and got on the subject of future careers, which I'd thought of only in modest terms.

"Maybe a math teacher," I said, "or some kind of writing, like a reporter. What about you? Space traveler?

"I wouldn't mind. Pop wants me to be a doctor, like a surgeon, which might be my first choice even though he wants it. Maybe a neurosurgeon so I can drill into people's brains."

"Echhh."

"A psychiatrist would also be cool—or psychoanalyst, the high priest of psychiatry. A shrinker of heads."

"You mean the doctor who talks to crazy people? My mother's always threatening to send my sister to a psychiatrist for not eating but says she can't spend a fortune just for a talk."

"But it's a lot more than talk. I've been reading Sigmund Freud's *Interpretation of Dreams*—you know about him?"

"I think maybe. I'm not sure."

Byron offered some background on the pioneering Viennese shrink, a bit more than I could absorb as sleep beckoned. The last words I remember before drifting off were "sexual symbolism," but I missed any juicy parts after that and couldn't remember any symbolic dreams in the morning.

21

The man in the truck

BYRON HAD TOLD ME that he liked to sleep late, and sure enough when I opened my eyes at about eight-thirty Sunday he was dead to the world and still that way about an hour later. Even after I'd gotten out of bed and washed up, he lay asleep on his back, his eyes covered by a pillow and nose sticking out like a shark's fin. He snorted and snarfed as he breathed, maybe dreaming Freudian dreams.

I decided to get dressed. While doing so I heard laughter from the direction of Keatsie's room, followed by what sounded like the two girls galloping down stairs and out the front door. From one side of Byron's room I could see the front driveway, and there they were: Keatsie and Miki headed toward Philippe's pickup truck, which awaited them with its motor running. Miki had her overnight bag with her.

They greeted the driver, whom I couldn't quite see because that side was away from me, but I assumed it was Philippe there to take Miki home. The girls climbed in and the truck took off, spinning its wheels on the gravel. The house was quiet now save for Byron's nose music. Finally he stirred, sat up, and asked what time it was. I told him it was after ten-thirty. "Mmmf," he said, and flopped back down, pulling a pillow over his whole face.

"You're gonna suffocate," I said, "unless aliens breathe through their butts."

"Only on the exhale. I'm getting up in a minute anyway."

It was more like fifteen minutes as I looked through more of his books and out the windows of the corner room. I could see the side parking area and the basketball court as well as the front driveway. Finally Byron got out of bed and staggered to the bathroom. "Gotta shower."

He'd been running the water just a minute or so when I noticed Philippe's truck returning up the driveway and coming around to the parking area. Again viewing just the passenger's side, I saw Keatsie say something to the driver, pause a moment, then suddenly bolt out of the truck. She sank to her hands and knees on the parking surface with a convulsive *guhh*—

I couldn't make myself look away, as much as I needed to before I might get sick myself. I won't go into detail, but this was no "dry heave." It was prolonged. It was a lot. It was gross to see, puddled on the dark asphalt. I felt a welling in my own gut and started to turn away when the driver jumped out of the truck and hurried to Keatsie's side, leaning over her and putting a hand on her shoulder. She batted it away as she stood up and wailed something before running into the house, leaving him standing there. I heard her run up the stairs and, as I opened Byron's door a crack, saw her dash into her room, turning the lock behind her.

Outside I saw the driver unravel a garden hose from a faucet attached to the house. Quickly, he had a stream of water blasting the yellowish puddle and dispersing it into the dirt base of surrounding bushes.

But who was the driver? It wasn't Philippe. It was a big teenage kid who looked slightly familiar.

"What's going on?" said Byron, appearing behind me in a white terry bathrobe, a kind I'd only seen in movies.

I pointed outside. "Who is that?"

He looked. "Oh, that's Paul Lefevre. Philippe's nephew."

"What's he doing here?"

"Must be working. He helps Philippe sometimes, or he comes on Philippe's days off to do extra stuff. Pretty nifty guy—strong as an ox and has a French-Canadian accent like his uncle."

"Have I seen him before?"

"Not when you were here. Oh—you may be thinking of his younger brother, the one who goes to Eastview. You know, Henry Lefevre? Ninth grader? He looks like Paul, but not such a hairy ape."

"Oh. Maybe. How old is Paul?"

"I think he just got his license. Sixteen?"

"He looks twenty."

They watched him run the hose until mud started to ooze from the bushes.

"What's he doing, anyway?" Byron asked.

Could I tell him what I'd seen? I was afraid he would just make fun of his sister again, or expect me to do so, or even ask why I'd been watching her. All silly thoughts, I knew, but she looked so terrible I just felt I shouldn't rat on her. Bad enough I had to wonder what was going on between her and handsome hairy Paul.

Paul exchanged the hose for a big rake, Byron got dressed, and we went downstairs and raided the refrigerator. Leena was off, and Mrs. Fairchild was reading a newspaper in the library. She'd be going to her Unitarian Church later. Byron and I shot some baskets and horsed around a while before my mother called to tell me that they wanted to pick me up soon. Since it was unlikely I'd see Keatsie again before evening, when Dr. Fairchild would be back, it seemed a good time to leave. Besides, my father was taking us to a restaurant managed by one of his Elks Club "brothers," a place I loved for its shrimp cocktails served with crushed ice in silvery goblets on a white tablecloth.

This time Mrs. Fairchild greeted my parents and sister when they pulled up, exchanging some cheerful words with them. But I focused my attention on the broad-shouldered guy across the lawn, raking leaves.

22

Before the big event

EVERYONE AT SCHOOL and in the neighborhood was buzzing about the new James Dean movie, opening this coming Saturday at the big RKO Keith's theater downtown. The young, brooding, sweet-faced Dean had already been a big star and teen idol. He'd played a misunderstood son seeking a strong father figure in *East of Eden*, which ran earlier in the year. In that movie he came off as loveable and easily hurt, but also tough and manly when he had to be.

Before he died in the car crash, Hollywood had been grinding out one romantic story after another about him, so by the time *Rebel Without a Cause* came to town with ads showing Dean in jeans and cool red jacket, a cigarette dangling from his lips, it was the must-see movie and Dean was the must-see rebel representing all us moody, misunderstood youth.

Now I had the perfect movie for the special girl who said she'd go out with me. I just needed to pick up the phone and make the date. But every time I thought of how miserable Keatsie must have felt on Sunday, or how easily someone else might answer the phone, I got cold feet.

Then, Tuesday night, a wonderful, astounding, unbelievable thing happened: Keatsie called me

Joannie yelled from the hallway "Aaron—it's your girlfriend!"

"Quiet!" I hissed, coming out of my room. "What if she heard?"

"I had my hand over the phone."

I took it from her and waved her away.

"Hello?" I said, as if I didn't know who was calling.

"Hi, it's Keatsie!" sang the beloved voice. "Hope it's okay that I called."

"Sure! Hi! I was going to call you."

"You were? What about?"

"To ask if you wanted to go see *Rebel Without a Cause* with me."

"That's *exactly* what I want to see!"

"Really?" I said.

"Really. Everyone's going."

"But I mean, do you want to see it with me?"

"Well, yeah," she said. "I was going to invite you along with me and Miki. We're going Saturday."

"Oh." I felt a little plop inside. I didn't know what to say.

"What's the matter?" she asked..

"I don't know. I was thinking of, you know, a date?"

"You and your dates," she said laughing. "But you can call it that if you want."

"But it's not the same with three people."

"Why, what's different?"

I pondered the question. Rocco would have had a fast answer.

"Don't you like Miki?" she asked.

"Oh sure, she's nice and all. I just thought of us sitting together, you know. You and me—I?"

"So? We still can. You on one side, Miki on the other. But if you don't want to go . . . ."

"No, no—I do! I'll even pay."

"You don't have to."

"I want to. I still have all those winnings."

"Maybe, then, Thanks."

She set up the place we'd meet and the time—before the theater's second afternoon showing. "After my piano lesson," she said.

"What about Byron?" I asked. "Are you going to say anything?"

"Not me. Are you?"

"I don't think he'd like it."

"He's a pain," she said. "So we'll just keep it to ourselves, right?"

I agreed. Now it seemed more like that "date" I'd proposed, where we would "sneak" off together. And even if Miki would be there, I could still work in some sweet talk, Rocco-style, and—who knows, maybe in the darkness of the theater?—score my first kiss.

23

Black penny loafers

NOW, three days before my date, it was time to act on Rocco's second piece of advice: *dress sharp.*

I had to have those black penny loafers that every sharp dresser on earth was wearing, sometimes with pennies stuck in the shoe tongues, sometimes with metal taps nailed to the heels. Flat feet or not, I wanted those shoes to wear with jeans and white socks like the "troubled teens" in movies and probably James Dean himself.

The loafers had been calling to me a long time from the Thom McAn shoe-store window on Main Street. I passed by there every week as I walked from Hebrew school to the bus that took me home, and now I had the ten dollars to buy what I wanted with plenty to spare. What I didn't have was permission from Mom. But it was my money and my feet, right? If she didn't understand how important they were to me, she didn't have to know. Not before my date, anyway.

Instead of going to Newspaper Club, which met every Wednesday afternoon, I skipped it and went directly from school up the long hill that led to the start of Main Street. A few more blocks and I passed Macy's and the RKO theater, where life-sized posters of James Dean cried for me to hurry and get those shoes, never mind my lingering worries. And I did worry still, not only about Mom's reaction but about my absence from Newspaper Club. I'd have to make up something to tell Byron, since he knew I'd been at school.

But once I walked inside Thom McAn's, the shoe salesman who greeted me made everything seem right. He was a well groomed man with a thin grey moustache and dress shoes so polished they reflected the ceiling lights.

"How can I help you, son?"

"I'd like a pair of black penny loafers, please."

"Excellent. I assume you're making a purchase on your own?"

"Yes."

"A trusted young man, eh? Well let's check your size."

I removed my worn Buster Browns, which he pushed aside like they were dead rats. He placed each of my feet on his metal measuring device, then fetched the shoes from the stock room. The leather smelled delicious coming out of the box. So black. So smart. The heels and tan soles without a mark on them. He removed bundles of tissue paper from the shoes and worked my feet into them with a shoe horn. I held my legs straight out to admire the instant transformation, from square to sharp. Too mellow! The coolest! The most!

"Beautiful, huh?" he said. "Our most popular shoe. Go ahead, see how they feel."

"They feel okay."

He smiled. "You should walk a little on the carpet, make sure they fit."

I stood up and paced the two carpeted aisles. The smooth leather skated over the rugs, but the shoes hurt in three places: the heel, the arch, and, one of them, around the toes.

"A little tight," I confessed. "But they'll break in, right?"

"Usually," he said. "Let me see 'em."

I took them off and he worked his knuckles into the mouth of each shoe, then bent the soles back a bit. "They're the right size," he said. "Try 'em again."

Another customer, an older man, entered the store.

"Go ahead, I'll be right back," the salesman said.

I walked the aisles again, telling myself they hurt a little less. And so what if they hurt? I wasn't going to wear them every day. Yet I could hear my mother warning me, "They'll ruin your feet."

The salesman returned. "So?"

"You think they're okay for flat feet? I had special shoes."

"Yes, I saw. But all our shoes are scientifically designed to support the metatarsal bones and arches. The kids love wearing this model. You're lucky I have your size." He glanced at the other customer. "So, do you want them?"

"Yes."

At the cash register I had him put the new shoes in their box, which I carried home in a bag and smuggled into the house like it contained a stolen baby. Joannie was in her front room, nose in homework. She looked up just as I hurried through. "What's in the bag?"

"Just gym stuff from school," I called back to her.

I'd become such a liar. A liar and a sneak: I hid the forbidden goods behind my sports stuff in the hallway closet, which also held a small box of rarely used tools and an accordion that nobody played anymore.

24

The day of the rebels

I THOUGHT SATURDAY would never arrive. First came school, then Hebrew school, and on Friday a weird conversation with Byron. He asked me if I was going to see *Rebel Without a Cause*, and, liar that I'd now become, I shrugged and said I wasn't sure I really wanted to. Then I asked him if he was going to go. And he answered much the same way, adding one of his typical Byronisms: "I expect it to be minimally amusing." But neither of us said anything about what else we might be doing on the weekend.

This year I'd already gone to a few downtown movies with neighborhood guys, including Rocco, and it was fine with Mom, as long as she knew the kids and where I'd be and when I'd get home. We usually went to a cheap theater we called the Ranch House to see action serials like "Superman" and "The Lone Ranger" and a bunch of cartoons. So when I lyingly asked my mother

Friday night if I could go to a movie with Byron and some friends the next day, she surprised me by saying sure, as long as I promised this and that and that and this. She was in a good mood, mainly because Dad was home and he was taking her out tomorrow for their anniversary.

"What are you going to see?" she asked.

"Just some new feature at Keith's. About teens."

"Which *you* will very soon be, my bar mitzvah boy. Keith's is expensive, you know."

"So? I'm loaded."

She laughed. "Well you don't have to spend every penny. Save it for college."

Saturday did finally get here, a pretty fall day. After grabbing an early lunch I scrubbed myself, fussed with my feathery hair, and dressed my sharpest best: V-necked sweater over a collared shirt, bluejeans turned up at the cuff, and white athletic socks.

Dad would be taking Mom out later in the day, but he wasn't home from work yet. I waited until she was busy in the kitchen to say goodbye, then hurried to change from my Buster Browns to the penny loafers I'd hidden. I was halfway out the front door, waving goodbye to Joannie, when she said, "You're going to *Rebel Without a Cause*, aren't you."

"So?"

"You're not really old enough. You're underage."

"They never check. And everyone's going."

"I know, I'll be there with my friends tomorrow. But I'm not twelve."

"Thirteen, almost," I corrected. "Anyway, hope you like it. I have to go."

"What are those shoes? Are they new?"

"I gotta go! G'bye!"

I slipped out and hurried up the street toward the bus, feeling Joannie's eyes on me. I wasn't sure I could trust her not to say anything, but it was too late to worry. The only sure thing was how much the shoes hurt. Too late to worry about that, too.

I arrived early at the theater, joining a long line for admission to the afternoon show. It was past two o'clock when I paid for three tickets. The movie would be starting in a half hour and I didn't see a sign of Keatsie and Miki. I paced around under the marquee, feeling panicky. I gazed at publicity photos of a suffering James Dean, trying to scrunch up my features to look like his. As I did so, someone flicked one of my ears from behind. There they were, my two movie companions, giggling. Quickly I took off my glasses and brushed a few hairs over my forehead.

"Sorry we're a little late," Keatsie said. "Late for our date, heh, heh."

"Hi. It's okay. I have the tickets already."

"Let me pay you," Miki said as I gave the scrip to her. I noticed that she wore a black leather jacket and snug jeans, looking cute and cool at the same time. Keatsie, beautiful as ever to me, wore a scarf over her usual floppy sweater.

I refused the money gallantly, and we moved aside to allow the people from the first show to pour out of the theater and into the street. Everyone seemed to be jabbering wildly about the movie, some laughing, some blotting tears. I recognized and nodded to a few kids from my school, and the girls did the same with three or four schoolmates they knew. And then, at the tail end of the crowd came someone the three of us knew all too well. But only I recognized the girl with him, and I couldn't believe it.

25

Thrills of the silver screen

BYRON SPOTTED US just as we spotted him with his movie date, Betty Lee.

I did a double take and so did he, as if neither of us could decide whether to act surprised or normal. Keatsie looked just as confused, while Betty and Miki seemed merely curious.

Byron halted, because Betty was already smiling at me and saying, "Hey, look who's here. Hi, Aaron!" Byron now felt he had to introduce Betty to the girls, while slipping me an annoyed look.

"You guys are going to *love* this movie," Betty said.

"Was it more than 'minimally amusing'?" I asked Byron.

Ignoring the question, he looked from me to Keatsie and back again. "Did you run into each other here, or come together?" he asked. I didn't know how to answer. Should I lie to my friend, too? But Keatsie gave my arm a little tug and said, "We should really go in now if we want good seats."

"Yeah, we should," I said, moving a half step toward the entrance.

"Well, nice meeting you," Betty said to the girls. "Enjoy it, all of you."

"Okay, thanks," I said. "See you guys around."

Byron scowled at his sister before we all parted. As he and Betty moved through the crowd, though, I looked back and saw that we weren't the only ones interested in them. People froze and gaped as if watching a pair of escaped criminals. Some of the older folks made faces and muttered comments into their hands. A few punks made louder remarks, ugly ones, which caused Byron to glare at them until Betty, looking straight ahead, pulled him forward and out into the street. "Yeah, take her back to Africa!" a voice yelled.

"God, I hate those lousy, stupid dopes," I told the girls, who were equally upset. "And I think Byron's mad at me, too."

"Not just you," Keatsie said. "But that's his problem. Did you know about him and Betty Lee?"

I told her what I'd known.

"Those horrible prejudiced jerks! And she seemed super nice. I can't believe my shy brother asking her out. I wonder what Pop would say though."

We let the question go as we found and settled into three seats on one side of the big theater. I hurried off to get refreshments. The coming attractions and short features were just starting when I returned, taking my seat on the aisle and handing out boxed buttered popcorn and Almond Joy candy bars. *You dress sharp and you buy her stuff,* Rocco had advised. Keatsie sat next to me, as promised, and Miki on her other side.

"I shouldn't eat this stuff," Keatsie said. "But I hardly ate any lunch and I'm starving."

We dug into the goodies while cartoons and the Pathé newsreel ran and the packed house chattered away. From the balcony above and behind us came hoots and catcalls and clouds of cigarette smoke. But with the start of the movie's dramatic music and title frames, the audience hushed. I put on my glasses and drank in the opening scene.

Seventeen-year-old Jim Stark (James Dean) appears in a police station, picked up for intoxication. Also there: A high school girl named Judy (Natalie Wood), for curfew violation, and a messed-up fifteen-year old loner named Plato (Sal Mineo), booked for shooting a litter of puppies with his mother's gun. Both, like Jim, have serious family issues.

Jim is new to town and still the troubled kid he was before moving to this Los Angeles suburb with his parents. They've moved a lot. We meet his strong-willed mom and weak-willed, apron-wearing dad when they come to pick him up at the station. As they try to deal with him, their opposite ways cause Jim to cry out, his face tortured, his body curled up in pain, "YOU'RE TEARING ME APART!"

At his new high school, Jim runs into Judy again, but she brushes him off as "a real yo-yo" before going off with her boyfriend Buzz (Corey Allen), leader of a gang of school "delinquents."

"You liking it?" I asked Keatsie.

"Yes. And I'm *loving* poor Jim. It's so sad about Dean."

Miki leaned over her. "Aaron—thank you for taking us. It's super good!"

"Yeah, thanks," Keatsie said.

I nodded—Mr. Big Spender—and we turned back to the screen.

A school outing at an observatory and planetarium. Buzz and his gang taunt Jim into a knife fight. Jim defeats Buzz, holding him down and throwing the knives away. But now Jim is challenged to a "chickie-run," where the two rivals will race stolen cars to the edge of a cliff. The first to jump out is the chicken, the other the winner. A crowd of kids gathers to watch the night race. Plato, who hangs on to Jim as a father figure, is among them. Buzz tells Jim privately that he actually likes him. Jim asks why they're doing this crazy race. "You gotta do SOMETHING, now don't you?" Buzz replies.

Buzz take off, but as they near the cliff Buzz's sleeve catches the door handle and he plunges to his death. Jim jumps out of his car at the last second.

The gang runs off, leaving Judy alone. Jim drives her home. She warms to him. Back at his house, Jim agonizes over the death; he wants to go to the police, but mom says no, overruling dad as usual. Jim cries and wails as he grabs his father roughly, urging him to be a man.

"I actually wish my father was more like that," Keatsie whispered to me.

"You mean wearing an apron?"

"No," she laughed. "Just nicer."

Jim takes off for the police station, hoping to confess to a sympathetic sergeant who'd talked to him earlier. But the sergeant isn't there, so Jim runs off again, chased by Buzz's gang. He gathers Judy and they hide in an abandoned mansion that Plato has discovered. Soon they're joined by Plato, also running from the gang and now armed with his mother's gun.

The three troubled characters share their stories of being misunderstood, rejected, and confused. They pretend they're a family. Jim and Judy soothe the panicked, needy Plato and get closer to each other. Romantic music. Judy tells Jim she's been looking so long for love and now she loves someone— Jim— and it's "so easy." Jim says "for me, too."

Rocco's third piece of advice: *Sweet-talk 'em.* If I was ever going to act, right now was the moment with all that love in the air.

"I think you're prettier than Judy," I whispered to Keatsie.

"What?"

I repeated it, this time stroking her hand, which was on the arm rest between us.

"What are you doing?"

Miki looked over. Then quickly looked away.

"Just touching your hand," I said. I felt a cold sweat under my shirt and sweater.

"What for?

"'You know. Cause I like you. 'Cause we're on a date. Sort of."

"Okay, but I didn't say anything about touching."

"Sorry," I pouted, taking my hand away. "Never mind."

"Oh, don't be mad. Come on, we're missing the movie." She gave my arm a little friendly squeeze, let go, and turned back to the screen.

Things go from bad to worse in a hurry. The gang shows up at the mansion. Plato puts up a fight, then shoots one of the boys. He runs off to the observatory. Jim and Judy join him there. The police arrive. Jim gets Plato to empty out the gun's bullets, but a frightened Plato charges the police waving the empty weapon. Jim screams, "I GOT THE BULLETS! LOOK!" But too late. Plato is shot dead.

Agony all around. Jim's dad makes his way there to comfort his grieving son. He promises to be a stronger father from now on. Jim makes peace with his parents, introduces Judy—"My friend." Closing shot: At dawn, a stranger walks toward the observatory unaware of all the drama.

The three of us sat still for a moment. I wasn't quite ready to step out of Jim's world. Like probably half the audience, I had identified with Jim and even Plato to some weird degree. Keatsie and Miki seemed lost in their own reactions, maybe identifying with Judy. As our section emptied, I stood and took Keatsie's arm.

"Now what are you doing?"

"Helping you up."

"All right. I feel kind of . . . queasy."

"What's queasy?

"Sort of nauseated? I shouldn't have eaten all that junk."

"You think you might, you know—"

"No! Let's go. I just need some air."

Were the popcorn and chocolate causing the problem, or could it possibly, possibly, have anything to do with her liking me? Whichever, I took advantage of her "condition" by locking her arm in mine until the three of us exited the theater. It almost felt as if I had a girlfriend out on a date. Then she slipped her arm away.

26

She barfs for another

WE MOVED AWAY from the theater crowds and headed down Main Street, tall Keatsie between us two shorties. It was still light outside, still pleasant. I removed my glasses again.

"You okay?" I asked Keatsie. She seemed pale.

"I'm not sure. Maybe." She paused and looked my feet. "But *you're* walking funny."

I hadn't realized it showed. "What do you mean?

"I don't know—like an old man?"

Miki giggled. I laughed, too. "New shoes. Kind of tight."

"But very cool," Miki said. "Just like the delinquents."

"That's the idea!" I said. "Gettin' me a switchblade, too."

She laughed again. She was a good audience, like Frankie Solomon.

We walked on, more or less toward the next bus stop, but Keatsie stopped in front of an alley to take a breath. "So where we going?" she asked. "I need to get back by dinner."

"Well," I said, "I was thinking of sodas or ice creams at Schrafft's. My treat."

"Ugh," Keatsie groaned. "The last thing I need right now."

"But *I'd* love a soda," Miki said.

An inspiration hit me. I looked from one to the other. I turned up my collar and made the best Jim Stark-James Dean face I could, squinting and grimacing. I doubled up in pain. "*You're tearing me apart!*" I bawled.

Bingo. They both squealed with laughter. "That is so *perfect*," Miki said. And Keatsie, catching her breath, to Miki: "I love his imitations."

"*I got the bullets. Look!*" I cried out, mimicking Dean's frantic movements in front of the police.

"Oh, God, stop!" Keatsie gasped, holding her chest. "Wait, just one more—the 'tearing-me-apart' thing."

Now on a roll, I redid the Jim-Stark-James-Dean look of agony. But a big voice cut off my performance.

"Hey—Barf Girl!"

Keatsie froze. I turned around to see a husky bruiser with a curly black mane. Two boys swaggered along with him, one almost as big, the other lanky and vicious-looking.

"Oh God, not you!" Keatsie said.

"Did you miss me?"

"Just go away, Sonny," she told him. "Leave us alone."

So this was Sonny Rizzo. With bushy black eyebrows and thick black eyelashes over blue eyes, with ruddy cheeks and good teeth and a manly voice. Crap!

"Whatsamatter, Shelly girl," he said, "Still tossin' your cookies?"

Rizzo's friends snickered, just like Buzz's cronies in the movie. It was all getting creepily like the film—and I was no Jim Stark, even though I found myself posing something like Jim did before his knife fight.

"Why we doin' this?" I said in the Jim Stark voice.

Rizzo looked at me as if I'd crawled out of a sewer, then at Keatsie. "Who's the little homo who thinks he's James Dean?"

"None of your business," Keatsie said. "Just go away."

"Oh, you own the streets now, Barf Girl?"

Keatsie looked about to cry. I had to say something. "You shouldn't call her that, man."

Rizzo made a who's-this-insect face. "Oh really, *man*? How about Hurl-Girl? Or the Vomit Comet?" More snickering. "Why, you gonna do something?"

"Let's just go," Miki said, pulling Keatsie away. The vicious-looking one took a step to block our way on the sidewalk, locking us into the alley. The other big kid joined him. Rizzo moved to within a few inches of Keatsie.

"Aww," he said, "you mad at me? Did you change schools just for me? Come on, let's make up." He took her by the shoulders, and I could see it coming. Keatsie put one hand to her stomach, another to her mouth, and gagged once, gagged again . . . .

Rizzo jumped away. "Hey, look, I still got the touch!"

Keatsie bent over and lost her popcorn and her Peter Paul's Almond Joy and whatever else had been occupying her stomach. Rizzo's cronies jumped back with exaggerated groans of disgust. Even for me, the sight and smell were hard to take without gagging.

Miki screamed at the three: "Look what you've *done*, you morons!"

Keatsie seemed limp enough to collapse. I took her arm to hold her up, telling her, "It's okay, it's okay. Don't worry . . . ." Miki took the other. "It's over," she said. But it wasn't. There was another convulsion and its result.

"And by the way," Rizzo said, not yet satisfied. "I saw your creep brother at the movie with his coon girlfriend. It made *me* want to puke."

"Why don't you shut your mouth, man!" said a voice. Whose was it? Whoops—it was mine! Even a chicken has his limits when mad enough, but I still couldn't believe my own fighting words. I had a good idea what would happen next, and it happened. Rizzo's ham of a hand slapped me so hard across the face I fell down, almost in some of Keatsie's, er, product.

Keatsie screamed. Miki tried to drag me away as I stood up. But the slap had me seeing red, a good rage, and I came up swinging wildly at about Rizzo's chest level. I might have landed a harmless blow or two before Rizzo knocked my arms away and hit my forehead with the heel of a hand that felt like a missile. I went down hard, and a kick from Vicious Guy kept me down until a crowd of onlookers started to close in and Rizzo and his friends sauntered off.

We declined some offers of help and got ourselves to a pay phone. Miki called an older sister to come pick up the two of them; Keatsie had no intention of getting on a bus, even after cleaning off the worst bits with tissues. While they waited for the ride, Keatsie apologized to me for making a mess of things. I waved it off, a bit sullenly.

"And you were so brave," she said.

"Our hero," Miki added. "Are you all right?"

"No, I got my butt kicked, and I feel like a . . . ."

"But you—"

"I didn't do anything. I just wish I could fight."

"Come on, one guy against those three hoods?" Miki said. "And Rizzo is huge."

"I *hate* him so much," Keatsie said. "I completely *despise* him."

Yeah, right, I thought, shrugging at her. I felt powerless and somehow betrayed. I wanted to get away, go home. I turned down Miki's offer for a ride and mumbled goodbye before walking off toward my bus stop. When I got there I looked down and noticed that Keatsie had left me a souvenir on one of my shiny new black loafers. I wouldn't be the most popular person on the bus.

27

More from Keatsie's diary (as seen by me much later)

☹ ☹ 😐

I THOUGHT TODAY was going to be fantastic, a new James Dean movie and everything, but what a disaster!! Lot of good it did me to go to the shrink this morning instead of my piano lesson. Maybe Byron is right when he calls Dr. Nusbaum Dr. Nut-Bin. All Nusbaum does is sit and listen until I've said something stupid and emotional and then he tells me I've got father issues and brother issues and self-image issues to deal with, and that this is a stage that highly sensitive people often go through and that therapy will help me through it eventually (as long as my parents keep paying him whatever fortune it costs).

But today the same old thing still happened, thanks to that horrible ignorant loathsome idiot Rizzo. Plus, I messed up Miki's and Aaron's days. Poor Aaron—he was trying so hard to make it a nice "date." And he fought for me, like David taking on Goliath. So as a reward he got beaten and kicked and he'll probably be sore for weeks. I think I hurt his feelings, too, the way I acted when he tried to get romantic. But I couldn't help it. I like him a lot, but not in a boyfriend way. It's pretty obvious he likes me that way—I mean like a girlfriend, so I shouldn't encourage him if I don't feel the same way, right? I just wish that Byron and I could both be close friends with him, but even that's hard because Byron is so weird about sharing anyone. He's the one who should be seeing Dr. Nut-Bin.

Anyway, this may have been the worst barfing I've ever done in public, and I couldn't even clean up until I got home. Thank God I made it up to my room before anyone saw me. I felt so ashamed and disgusting, especially getting into Miki's sister Yoshi's car. I know how I stank, but Yoshi never said a word about it. I love those two.

But now I have to ask myself, honestly, like Dr. Nusbaum says I should, what set off the reaction? Sure, eating buttered popcorn and chocolate on an empty stomach didn't help. Plus all those tense scenes in the movie gave me stomach butterflies. And to tell the truth, Aaron made me a little nervous saying how pretty I was and everything. But I know it takes more than all that stuff to set me off. Okay, the truth now, Shelly Keats: Was it Rizzo or wasn't it? Think.

I know I don't have a crush on him any more. That ended long ago. In fact, I'm sure that when he first showed up I didn't feel the gagging thing. Just angry and scared. But then when he grabbed my shoulders and kept making fun of me I felt, I don't know, this sadness in my gut, like a weight. I tried to breathe, I tried to swallow, and—bleeeaah.

Once that started and he just kept going and insulted Byron and Betty and knocked Aaron down, I wanted to collapse and cry like a baby. Dr. Nusbaum says barfing may be my way of crying, of letting off emotion, because I almost never cry the usual way, with sobs and tears. I wish I did, though; it would be a lot less messy.

Of course, that crying theory doesn't explain what happened with Paul Lefevre in Philpe's truck, after we drove Miki home. He didn't do anything that would make me cry. He was all sweetness and polite manners. Sometimes he did seem to be flirting, but more like pretend-flirting with a little kid. He's four years older than I am after all, and looks ten years older. But with that accent and those big shoulders and gorgeous hair, he does kind of make my heart cry

28

Bad kid Aaron

☹ ☹ ☹

MY FIRST DUMB MISTAKE when I got home: heaving the soiled loafer against a wall in my room and flopping down to whimper into my pillow. That drew Joannie out of the kitchen, where she was heating up some supper. Mom and Dad were still out on their anniversary date.

"What's wrong, Aaron?"

"Nothing."

"Don't tell me 'nothing.'"

"Then everything."

She sat next to me on the bed and put a hand on my shoulder. "Was the movie that bad?"

"My new shoes hurt, my date stank, and I got in a fight."

"A fight! Are you okay?"

I sat up and turned to her.

"Oh, God—look at your face. You have two red welts. What happened?"

My side is sore, too, where a guy kicked me. Three big guys from Keatsie's old school. They know how to fight. I *don't*."

"You shouldn't have to know."

"Bull! I want to learn, and Dad won't teach me!"

My second mistake was leaving the smelly shoe where I'd thrown it. When Mom and Dad got home at about nine o'clock, neither looking very happy, Mom sniffed it out like a hunting dog or probably saw it lying out on the floor and then gave it a quick sniff. She held it at arm's length as she came into the living room where I was watching TV in my socks.

"What is this?"

"A shoe."

"It's a loafer, isn't it? Where did this come from? Did you go out and buy them when you were told not too?"

"Mom, I'm trying to watch—"

"*Did* you?"

"Yes! Yes I did, because everyone in the world has them except me and I was tired of having to ask for every little thing when I could buy them myself!"

She dropped the shoe to the floor. "Do you know how much we've done for your feet? Do you want to throw away every dime we've spent?"

"I won't, if I just wear them sometimes. I hate my other shoes!"

"Poor you! And what did you get on this one that it stinks! Did you step in something and bring it into the house?"

"No. It's not that. I'll clean it off. Can I please watch this show?"

She was already pretty worked up. Now she stormed to the TV, turned it off and flipped on the living room light so she could see the rotten son. "Oy, like the shoes are not enough with you. Look at your face. What happened?"

"*This* is what happened because Dad won't teach me to fight!"

I think Mom was ready to throw the shoe at me when Joannie came in from her room. "Mom, he got beat up in front of his date."

"Date? What date? He was supposed to be going with his friend Byron."

"I didn't know about that. But he had a really bad day."

"Oh, you think he's the only one? You think I'm having such a great day? On my *anniversary*?"

It turned out that Mom and Dad's big anniversary date at the romantic Patricia Murphy's Candlelight Restaurant in Yonkers didn't go as planned. They hadn't made reservations, thinking they'd be arriving early. But the old Plymouth stalled on the way, and Dad had to call for road service from Jimmy Cushman, the gas station mechanic who'd sold him the car. Jimmy got it going (dirty carburetor), but by the time they reached the restaurant they had to wait in line over an hour for a table, a bad table in a dark corner near the restrooms. The restaurant had run out of its best dishes. And on the way home the car kept stalling between starts and they had an argument about Dad's loyalty to Jimmy's used cars. Joannie gave me all this background Sunday morning, making it clear why Dad had shut himself in for a hot bath soon after they'd gotten home Saturday night.

Knowing what had happened, I should have waited for a better time to confront my father than after our Sunday breakfast with a lot of angry looks around the table. But he was the one who started on me about disobeying my mother and lying and getting into trouble. So when he sat down in the living room to have a smoke and read the papers, I stood in front of him and pointed to the marks on my face.

"You see these?" I said. "And this?" I pulled up my T-shirt and showed him the purple bruise on my ribs. "These are you're fault."

He put the paper down and crushed his cigarette. "Whaddya talkin' about?"

"How many times did I ask you? Dad, teach me to fight? Dad, teach me to fight? If you'd ever taught me maybe I could have done something yesterday. Defended myself instead of looking like a sissy in front of everybody!"

"Hey, it ain't being a sissy to stay out of fights. It's being smart."

"Will you stop *saying* that? *You* fought. Were you stupid?"

"The place where I grew up you didn't have a choice. You fought with a gang or you got beat up every day."

"What about the boxing? Why'd you do that?"

"You know why. My best friend Billy Rancoff needed a training partner, for when he fought lightweight? I was all he could afford."

"Well *I* need a training partner."

"For what?"

"To win my fights! So I can be a man!"

He started to pull another cigarette from the pack, but tossed the pack aside instead. "For chrissake, Kid. Fightin's got nothin' to do with being a man. Are we gettin' you bar mitzvahed or not? That's when you'll be a man, not when you slug some dope and think you're a tough guy."

"I hate the bar mitzvah thing! I *want* to be a tough guy."

"Yeah? Let me tell you where Billy Rancoff is today. In a nursing home, because his brains got bashed in the ring. He drools instead of talks. He can't walk. And he ain't the only one I know like that. I seen guys lose all their teeth, go deaf, get blinded, end up wearin' a diaper. And I don't want that for my son, understand? You got a thousand other choices."

"Maybe I'm your son," I said, holding back tears, letting the worst impulse rise to my lips. "But you're not a real father!"

With that I turned and headed to my room.

"No?" he shouted after me. "I don't work six nights a week so you can eat and have clothes—"

"Stupid clothes!"

"—and go to movies and do whatever you want? Grow up, ya crybaby!"

Crybaby. He must have heard me sobbing as I dragged myself down the hall.

29

Down the slippery slope

I WAS ALREADY in a crummy mood, and things went downhill from there. Monday at school Byron nodded hello but obviously didn't want to get into a conversation or deal with my questions: How did you like the movie? How did it go with Betty? How is Keatsie doing? I got shrugs and one-word, non-answers. I didn't feel like asking him what the problem was; I already knew. It wasn't until I saw Betty in the hall that I got a big smile and some sympathy for the now-purple bruise on my forehead.

"I heard all about what happened," she said. "Those lame-brains. You did right fighting 'em."

"Yeah, you mean trying to. I hope you and Byron had a good time at least."

She put a finger to her lips. "Shh. Mum's the word, Aaron. Too many people know already, and I've heard some real nasty comments."

"Like what?"

"Never mind what. A lot worse than *The Little Handy Book of Drags*, I'll tell you that."

The Newspaper Club meeting was canceled Wednesday, with Mr. Salisbury again "under the weather." I didn't feel like writing my assignment anyway, the one for the next, delayed issue of the *Dispatch*. Who cared about "The History of Thanksgiving"? It wouldn't even be funny.

Thursday evening at Hebrew school Mr. Rubin ended class early so he could attend to some personal business. He gave us the choice of going home or shooting baskets in the Hebrew Institute's so-called gym. Five of us, including Frankie, Moshe, a girl named Madeline, and a tall kinky-haired kid went over to the events hall, where we removed our shoes and heaved two basketballs at the shaky portable backboards and their rims. The court was about half official size, and if you missed the backboard the ball went up on a small stage and rolled into its curtain—which happened when Moshe tried a wild hook shot and missed by a mile.

"Nice shot, Moshe babe!" I called, as he climbed on to the stage. "Hey, maybe you could sing to us while you're up there."

"I don't know any songs," he said, retrieving the ball. "Not your songs."

"What about 'Song of Solomon?'" I cracked, picking the only biblical "song" I knew of. "With a rock beat, man."

Frankie laughed, Madeline giggled and tossed me the second ball. As I lined up a shot, Moshe yelled,

"Hey, Schmink! Think fast!" I turned to him and got a cannon ball fired smack into my chest. "How's that shot, you schnook? You better learn some respect."

It hurt like crazy and it was humiliating. I had to strike back. "Go roll yourself up in the Torah!" I shouted as he came off the stage, grinning. "Yo mama catches gefilte fish. Yo mama gets drunk in the bar mitzvah bar. Yo mama takes a bath in Manischewitz wine."

He was no longer grinning when he came up to me, thrusting his chest against mine and pushing me backward. "You're dragging my mother now? And the Torah? Huh? You want a real punch where somebody gave you a tap? He cocked a fat fist in line with my forehead. "Schmuck. If I thought you knew, I'd really give it to you." The fist trembled in place, as if he was trying his best to hold it back. The other three kids stood frozen, gawking at us.

"If I knew what?" I asked timidly, hoping to keep that fist at bay.

"My mother is sick," he said. "She's might die. That's what." He pushed me away and dropped the fist. "I'm tired of you and your mama jokes." He moved off to get his shoes.

My skin buzzed as if electrocuted. Blood rushed to my cheeks while my neck and forehead felt clammy and cold. I was publicly shamed, stupid beyond measure. The other three wouldn't look at me. I had to fight a sensation like paralysis in my legs before chasing after Moshe.

"Wait—Moshe! I'm sorry. I didn't know."

He kept walking.

"I'm really sorry," I persisted. "I never would have . . . ."

"Who knows what you would do?" he said, sitting down to put on his shoes. "You're a pathetic *nebbish*, a real *lets*!"

"What's that mean?"

"You want a Yiddish lesson? You're a *putz*. A *yold.* With a *shkots* like you we don't need the *goyim* to insult us.

The kinky-haired kid brayed at the words. I was pretty impressed with them myself even if stung by Moshe's anger. "Come on," I asked him, "tell me what they mean."

"Just get away from me—before I give you the *zets* you've been asking for."

I stood still as he walked away and left the gym. When I turned around, the others were gathering their things, not looking at me—probably because I was just an inch tall, or feeling that way. Frankie and Madeline mumbled goodbyes as they passed, but the kinky-haired kid paused by me.

"So Aaron, you don't know what he said?"

I shook my head.

"You should learn Yiddish. He called you a nobody, a dork, a jerk, a sap, and . . . a bad Jew."

"Oh. That's all?"

"Uh . . . oh yeah, one more—a *lets*. Smart-aleck."

30

I make a wreck of things

NEBBISH. That was me. A nobody, a sadsack. I felt mad at everyone and most of all at myself. Worse than if Moshe had given me that *zets* in the mouth instead of showing me up. And all those great insults he knew—they made yo-mama jokes look pretty sad. As if I would ever say the stupid things again.

By the time I got up Saturday morning, I could hear the neighborhood guys playing street games outside. They didn't yet know about me being a nebbish—or maybe they already thought so. I heard a rubber ball making contact with the cut-off broom we used for stickball, then banging into fenders and hoods of parked cars. Shouts of *you're out* and *safe* and *bull* made it into my room, tempting me to get out there. But I was stuck inside until after lunch. Mom had commanded me to practice my bar mitzvah readings all morning as punishment for "throwing money away" on loafers—"those foot-killing loafers"—without permission.

I made a fuss, but did some grumpy work on my chant—I needed the practice—and then a little math homework before gulping down a sandwich and heading for the door.

"Put a jacket on," Mom yelled after me. "And be home before dinner, you hear me?"

"Yeah, yeah."

The nebbish, the smart-aleck, was free to go.

The stickball teams included some of my regular associates, but also a few older kids I'd seen around. They were playing a more serious game than we usually did and not everyone was getting chosen for the teams. Unathletic Rocco sat on the curb watching, and Dickie, not wanting to be lumped with him, sat a couple of yards away. I joined Rocco.

"You play at all?" I asked him.

"Nope. Don't even wanna, with these guys."

"I don't feel like it, either," I lied, figuring I wouldn't be picked anyway. "What's happenin', man? Where you been all week?"

"Nowhere. I was around. Where you been?"

"Bad week, man. My date didn't go so great, and—"

"You dated that girl? Did you do what I told you?"

"Yeah, I tried. She didn't like it or maybe just me. Then I got punched and kicked by three tough guys for sticking up for her. Then I got in trouble for buying cool loafers, then I got reamed out for dragging somebody's mama who was dying but I didn't know."

"Man."

"What about you?"

"Lousy. My old man and my old lady . . . you know. And I cut school a whole lot."

"How come?"

"'Cause I hate bein' the dummy who got left back."

I shook my head in sympathy. "You're not a dummy." We were quiet a moment.

"Hey, you wanna do something?" Rocco said.

"Like what?"

"I'll show you that mansion we can get in—you know, up the hill?"

"I don't know, man. What for?"

"You chicken?"

"Of what? I don't care. I'll go if you want."

Dickie looked at us when we got up. "Where you losers going?"

"We're giving you a chance to get picked," I said.

Dickie made a nasty gesture. "I'll kick both your butts any time."

Rocco had small taps on the heels of his loafers. They clicked and scraped on the sidewalk as we climbed the hill. I eyed the sneakers I was allowed to wear, an old high-top pair with extra arch support, white, not fashionably black. At the top of the hill along North Broadway, I pointed to the Elks Club lodge. "That's where my old man lives."

"At least you know where he lives at," Rocco said.

We crossed the wide boulevard and walked toward the other two mansions along it. Both were unoccupied, but the first was fenced in and maintained. The second, set back on a huge and now overgrown plot, had wood planks nailed over the doors and windows. A crumbling stone wall around it was posted with no-trespassing signs.

Rocco slipped through one of the wall's gaps and waved me along to a small basement window. It's metal screen had a long tear in it. Rocco pried open a space to climb through.

"You ain't gonna believe this place."

I shouldn't go in there, I thought. A hundred questions had to be answered: Who owned it? What if someone was inside? But I said nothing as Rocco squirmed past the mesh. I followed, scraping my arm on the ledge. We stepped through the mud and debris of dank basement rooms, then climbed a small stairwell to what had been a pantry and kitchen. Sunlight leaked in around the window boards and revealed ruptured pipes, decay, and heaps of beer bottles. But a tall cupboard still had all its glass panes, until Rocco heaved a bottle into them.

I jumped. "What are you doing?"

"Why you think we're here, man?"

"I don't know. Why?"

"I told you before—to wreck the place."

"Yeah, you said. But I mean, what for?"

"Cause I didn't finish last time," Rocco said, as if that made perfect sense to me. He picked up two bottles and handed me one. "Wait'll you see."

We climbed an old servant's staircase, then another, and came out on the balcony of the mansion's great ballroom. Rooms off the balcony were entered by French doors, which ran along three sides of the room. Most of their glass panes were in place. Strong sunbeams poured in from half-boarded windows, allowing us to see this level and much of what lay below, including large mirrors at each end of the room. Only a fancy wood railing, rickety in parts, kept us from falling maybe twenty feet to the ballroom floor.

The ceiling and much of the walls were water-damaged, stained and cracked. From the balcony level, we were only a bottle's throw from two grand chandeliers dripping with hundreds of crystal drops.

"It's like a castle," I said.

"Yeah," Rocco said. "Watch this." Holding the railing, he hurled a bottle into the edge of the nearest chandelier.

The throw yielded only a tinkling of crystal and broken glass, followed by the clunk of the bottle. He threw his second bottle and missed entirely. I felt a mix of admiration and sympathy for Rocco, not much of a thrower, not sports-minded at all.

"Here you go," I said. I put a bottle to my chest like a pitcher beginning his windup. "Big Aaron checks the bases. Ninth inning. Two outs. Two strikes. He winds up. Fast ball—strike three!" I whipped the bottle into the second chandelier and racked up a shower of broken fragments. My forward motion carried me to the balcony railing, which moved scarily.

Rocco grabbed another section of railing and worked it loose. I joined him, and with another few tugs we tore the section out, falling backward. "God," I said, dizzied by the plunge I'd risked. I stood to peer over the edge.

Armed with our club-like rails, we went to work on the house. Lights, panes, mirrors, china fixtures—everything cried out for punishment. We dodged the spew of glass, laughed, cursed, whooped, cheered the crack of surfaces. Soon the wreckage brought out cries against all villains, all who tormented us, all who would oppose our will—

"Die bookie old man!"

"Die Buster Brown shoes!"

"Die Dickie!"

"Die Rizzo!

"Die school!

"Die shul!

Our frenzy turned toward a row of built-in bookcases. The shelves split under the force of our blows.

"Die, old lady's boyfriend!"

"Die, Elks Club!"

Outside again, we collapsed in the tall grass, exhausted, laughing at the sight of each other covered with dirt and dust.

"Look at my clothes," I said. "My mother'll have a fit."

"Tell her you got lost in the woods."

"You kidding? What woods? Look—I have all these little cuts on my hands. We should scram before we get caught."

Rocco jetted some spit through his chipped tooth. "Why? We didn't do nothin.'"

We made our way through the estate's back property and emerged on a quiet street that ran behind the three mansions. I wanted to head home by way of the Elks Club, and we climbed its steep driveway to the parking lot. There I saw what I'd feared I might: Dad's car. He'd left it unlocked while he was playing cards, probably thinking he'd quit after a few hands like he always promised Mom.

I climbed into the back seat and Rocco followed. The scent of Dad fresh from a bath and shave at home blended with the sweat and yeast aromas I loved best—the scent of the bakery truck driver, the sometimes man of the house.

I put my feet up on the seatback and looked at my filthy sneakers with their many little eyes, feeling thrilled and frightened to be such a stranger to myself. Nebbish, maybe. But now truly a Bad Aaron, too.

31

Badder and badder

☹ 😐 ☺

LATELY I had managed to stay out of trouble in Mr. Trapazzo's math class, where Byron and I competed for the best quiz scores and shot our hands up to answer the hardest questions. But on Monday this week I had trouble paying attention and got myself and Byron called out for whispering in the back of the classroom during a lesson. And I'd started it: I'd leaned over to the next aisle, where Byron sat, and asked about his weekend: Did he do anything special? Did he see Betty? Was Keatsie okay? But again, he gave short replies—"Nothing much," "No, I couldn't." and "Not okay in the head."

Mr. Trapazzo stopped short, turning from the blackboard and pointing a piece of chalk our direction. "Okay," he said. "I'm through competing with all the whispering back there. I think it's time to break up Murderer's Row.

"Do you know about Murderer's Row?" he said to the class. "The 1927 Yankees had six great batters in a row. They murdered the ball, murdered their opponents, and murdered the leagues. The only hope for other teams was to break up that row. So—who was doing the whispering?"

Byron and I looked at each other and slowly raised our hands, heads bowed.

"How about that? The same two guys who murder the quizzes, now trying to murder my lessons." The other students laughed. "Okay—Mr. Fairchild, why don't you switch your desk to that empty one by the window?"

I waved my hand in the air. "Mr. Trapazzo, I'm the one who started it. He was just . . . It was my fault."

"Okay, Mr. Schmink, then *you* go move over there."

"Sorry," I said to Byron in the hallway after class.

"Eh. I'm still his star pupil. Thanks for taking the blame, anyway."

"Yeah, my stupid fault. Hey, you want to go to Frida's at lunch?"

"Nah. Too cold. And I have a sandwich. "

"Yeah, okay, me too. See you in the cafeteria?"

"Okay."

When lunch time came I found Byron unpacking the egg-salad sandwich Leena had made for him, along with pickles, a thermos of milk, and, of course, Oreo cookies. I sat across from him and unwrapped the American cheese sandwich I'd have gladly thrown away for a baloney wedge.

"Are you mad at me or something?" I asked through a mouthful of the mushy bread. "About the Murderer's Row?"

"Nah, not about that. I *am* kind of peeved you didn't tell me about you and Keatsie."

"I meant to. But . . . .you know, there wasn't much to tell, and you were kind of weird about it."

"*I* was weird?"

I took a breath to start explaining, but couldn't figure out how to express it without making things worse. "It's all weird," I said. "It doesn't really matter anyway. I don't think she likes me." I waited for him to say, *No, she told me the exact opposite!* But he didn't. Instead—

"She told me what happened after the movie. Sorry about that, but bad things go along with Keatsie. She got me in a nice mess, too."

"No lie? What mess?"

"She had to open her mouth to Leena. You know, about me and Betty Lee? She thought Leena would see it all as cool and interracial and everything."

"She didn't?"

"You kidding? She's even more old fashioned than I'd thought. She says people should stick to their own kind. That I would only hurt Betty and get her in trouble. She *even* threatened to tell my old man if I kept it up."

"*Leena* said that?"

"Yep."

"Wow. So what are you gonna do?"

He shrugged. "Don't know, I should talk to Betty, but she's been kind of . . . . Anyway, Keatsie can go barf on herself for all I care."

There wasn't much I wanted to say to that. Or to anything else. I thought of bragging about my house-wrecking exploit, but wasn't sure how he'd take it; his house wasn't so different from the one I'd helped trash. So I brought up the James Dean movie and we talked about it briefly (he thought Natalie Wood was way too hot for the Dean character). By the time the lunch period ended, things felt awkward again and we didn't mention anything about getting together.

That left me still in my hangdog mood from the previous week. And today was Monday, a shul day. Halloween Eve, too, although I really didn't care about knocking on the same old doors in my same old homemade pirate costume. Besides, last year a few kids from the next block pulled some bad pranks—broke windows, painted on doors—and Mom didn't want me anywhere near those guys..

After my last class at Eastview I headed for the Hebrew Institute; but when I thought of facing Moshe and the other kids who'd seen him put me down, I made a decision I knew might lead to the worst possible consequences. I couldn't help it: I decided to skip Hebrew school and the bar mitzvah lesson.

I headed up Main Street and wandered the downtown streets. Kids in costumes were already galloping from store to store, cheeks full of candy. Usually on my walk from Eastview to the shul I went by way of the White Plains Public Library, a low red brick building on the crest of a hill. I'd stopped in now and then to borrow a book or look at magazines; I even had a library card. But this evening the library would be my cover-up, my refuge during the time I was supposed to be in shul.

I'd only recently discovered the adult area, having spent most of my time in the children's section. Even as I shivered at the consequences of skipping bar mitzvah practice, I felt a thrill of rebellion being here in the reading room, sitting at one of the long oak desks and acting as if I were a regular. I started doing some homework, got restless, wandered around the room looking at the shelves of popular reading and reference works. The sight of a several science fiction novels reminded me of Byron, and then of a book he'd recommended to me that day we'd talked by our lockers. I went to the reference desk and asked the librarian if the library had *Red Planet* by Robert Heinlein.

She accompanied me to the card catalog, which I more or less knew how to use, found the title, and showed me where to locate it in the stacks. And there it was: One of two copies. I checked it out, brought it to my seat and opened it. From then on until I had to leave, I existed in a different world.

The thin air of Mars was chill but not really cold. It was not yet winter in southern latitudes and the daytime temperature was usually above freezing.

I was in the world of Jim Marlowe, schoolboy resident of a Martian colony, and his pet Willis—a furry, careening, basketball-sized juvenile Martian with collapsible eye stalks and bumps; Willis, who could imitate any sound and who overhears and repeats to Jim a most sinister plot against the colonists.

I was in the world, too, of adult Martians, vastly evolved beyond humans and barely tolerant of them.

I was in the world of a kid rebelling against those who would mess with his life.

For the next two days *The Red Planet* pushed most everything else out of mind. I finished the book in bed Wednesday night, after forcing myself through Spanish and math assignments. Earlier, as I'd rushed through supper, Mom had asked me how Hebrew school and my bar mitzvah lessons were going. "Okay," I'd said, my stomach tightening.

"Is something wrong?"

"No, why?"

"You've either had your nose in that book or been moping around and acting strange. It's not still about those shoes, I hope."

"No," I said. "Nothing's wrong."

It was the last time I could tell this lie. Because very soon, wrong exploded all over the place.

32

Consequences

THURSDAY. At first, things seemed to be looking up. Byron seemed a little friendlier, and when I saw him and Betty Lee talking in the hall I got a cheery wave from both of them. I shined in math and English classes and got a laugh in Spanish class for exaggerating my double-*r*'s: *el perro esta corriendo* (the dog is running)—*perrrrrro . . . corrrrrriendo*.

But when the hour came to go to Hebrew school, I still couldn't face showing up there. Again I went to the White Plains Library and killed time working on my Thanksgiving article for the *Eastview Dispatch.* I promised myself I would go back to shul on Monday, after the long weekend—tomorrow was Armistice Day and Eastview would be closed.

It was already dark when I got to my apartment building. Rocco was outside, parking his bike by the front stoop. We exchanged "How's it goin'" greetings, and

Rocco asked what I was doing tomorrow. "They got new stuff playin' at the movies."

"Which movies?"

"The Bughouse. Wanna go?"

"To wreck the place?"

"Nah," he laughed.

"Okay" I said, "maybe, if I can. I gotta go in now. See ya."

But I wouldn't see him, not that night or the next day. As soon as I entered the apartment, Joannie said, "Wait." She stopped a McGuire Sisters record in the middle of "Sincerely" and waved a finger at me.

"You," she said, "are in big trouble."

She followed me through the apartment to the kitchen, where my mother stood fuming. She stirred a pot on the stove like it contained something deadly. And of all nights to be home on time, my father had chosen this one. He sat at the table giving me the executioner's eye.

"Where were you?" Mom demanded. I was already dizzy with panic and her tone of voice jellied my knees.

"When?" I said weakly.

"What when? Where were you *tonight*, after school?"

"I . . . you know."

"No, we *don't* know, because you weren't at shul!"

"Who said so?"

"Who? Rabbi Klein, that's who. With all he has to worry about, he had to call us tonight because he was concerned about *you.* Why? Because you didn't show up at *all* this week and he thought something might be wrong. And besides, he said you've had attitude problems all year but he didn't want to trouble us. So you better tell us right now, *what's going on*? " Her voice trembled, on the edge of crying. I couldn't remember her being so upset at me. I stood there mute.

Dad slapped the table. "Answer your mother!"

I took a breath. "I was in the library downtown, both nights. Something bad happened in shul last week and I was embarrassed to go back, okay? But I was going to go Monday, I *promise*."

Mom stirred the deadly-thing pot again, threw the spoon back in it. "You know what, Aaron? Your promises stink. When I think of everything we do for you, how we sacrifice so you can *go* to shul, *have* a nice bar mitzvah, and then you decide to throw everything away, everything we've slaved and paid for, because some little thing bothered you? What was so terrible that you can *do* this to us? *Lie* to us?"

"I'm *sorry*. I can't explain it. It was just embarrassing."

Dad broke in. "What are you, a little baby, you can't take it?"

It was a bad time for my tears to start welling and my voice to go into baby mode, but I couldn't help it. "I could take a lot if you ever taught me to fight!" I cried at him. "And I never *asked* to go to Hebrew school. I never *asked* to be bar mitzvahed. I *hate* shul!"

Mom and Dad looked at each other as if to say *should we throw him in the garbage now or later?*

I'd forgotten that Joannie was standing behind me "Mom," she said, "I think he just had a couple of lousy weeks. His girlfriend doesn't like him. He got beat up. He can't wear his new shoes—"

"Oy, those shoes! Another thing he lied about."

"I didn't lie," I whined. "I just didn't tell you because I spent *my money.*"

"Well it ain't your money no more," Dad piped in. "That dough was for being a good kid, not a lyin' dummy."

"I won that dough."

"Shaddup. I oughtta smack you one. You go back to shul, hear me? You do your bar mitzvah like a man, and we'll talk about money."

"*If* it's not too late to go back," Mom said. "I'll have to apologize to the rabbi. And you'd better change whatever attitude you put on there. I don't care what happened, or anything about girlfriends—which you're too young for anyway. You'll just forget about all that stuff and go back, you understand?"

I shrugged, which got my father out of his chair and waving a finger at my face. "Tell us you understand, dammit!"

"O*kay*. I understand," I said glumly.

"And I don't wanna hear about the fight stuff no more. It don't have nothin' to do with nothin'."

You mean "with anything," I felt like saying to him, Byron-style. But I just nodded to get it over with.

"Go. Wash your hands," Mom said. "And don't think you're leaving the house this weekend. You have *three weeks* before your bar mitzvah, you realize that? You'll practice your reading and your speech."

"For *three days*?"

"Go!" she said, turning back to the deadly-thing pot.

33

Byron to the rescue

WE HAD A SUMMERY spell for the holiday weekend, and I could hear neighborhood life exploding outside. It made my house-arrest even harder. A sad-faced Rocco came to the door twice on Friday, and twice I had to send him away even sadder-faced. With days to fill and my light homework done in the first couple of hours, I had no choice but to work on my *Haftarah* reading and speeches.

For Haftarah practice I had one copy of the reading in Hebrew script and another with the words spelled out in the regular English roman alphabet. I worked mostly with the Hebrew, because there might not be a roman cheat-sheet during the ceremony. I found that I had the words pretty well memorized by now, and with Mr. Rubin's coaching on the chant for another two or three weeks I'd probably be okay. It wasn't that hard and most of the audience wouldn't even know if you screwed up.

The English speeches were another matter. The shul had supplied me with models of talks for both the synagogue and the later family lunch, and I didn't like any of them. At the synagogue, wearing a silk skullcap and the religious prayer shawl called a *tallit*, you were supposed to thank everyone, including the teacher and rabbi, then say some serious stuff about how much the reading and ceremony of manhood meant to you and what wonderful things you were planning to do for the world. You kept it short and looked lovingly at your parents and made them cry. But I wanted to be smart with words and funny, too. I started tinkering with one of the model speeches to try to make it cooler.

I decided to write something much different for the lunch reception, where some favorite aunts and uncles and cousins and invited friends would make up the audience. Here I wanted to be really cool and funny, as nervous as I'd be; maybe do one-liner jokes like Henny Youngman, the famous comedian who kept interrupting himself with his violin. Something like, *Today I am a man. So what was I yesterday, a bagel?*

I set to work on it, and somehow between the creative effort and a little Saturday television I got through the first two days of my confinement. On Saturday evening, with Dad home, everyone seemed in a better mood. Mom said she heard me chanting the text and what a beautiful bar mitzvah boy I was going to be. She didn't say "cool," of course, but, ugh, "beautiful." She had talked to Rabbi Klein, and I'd be allowed to resume my torture on Monday evening *if I changed my attitude.*

Saturday night after supper the phone rang in the hallway and I picked it up. I couldn't believe it: Byron was on the other end, asking if we could do something tomorrow.

I explained my situation to him.

"You skipped Hebrew school?" he said. "Excellent!"

"I'm not so sure. I gotta go back to that dump and have my bar mitzvah or I'll get killed—by my whole family *and* the rabbi."

"Hmm. You should switch to JCC temple. Mrs. Bender thinks the rabbi there is the coolest."

"Yeah, I wish, but I don't know how I could switch now."

"I could ask her."

"Well, anyway," I said, weary of the subject, "guess what? While I was in the library I borrowed *Red Planet* and I finished it this week. It's so great, man!"

Byron was delighted. We gushed for a while about what parts we liked best. He rattled off all the other Heinlein and similar books he could lend me if I wanted. "You know," he said, "I could just bring one of them over to your house tomorrow."

"Here?"

"Yeah, if it's okay."

"Neat! I'll check."

"I might bring something else of extraordinary interest."

"Really? What is it?"

"To be revealed."

34

Forbidden secrets

😐 😐 😐

MOM wasn't very hot on the idea of a visitor, my fancy friend at that. But after seeing me work so seriously for two days she decided to give me a break—well, more like she caved in after I'd begged, pleaded, bargained, and whined.

Byron arrived by taxi, about an hour after we'd finished our big Sunday breakfast. Mom now wanted to make good impression on the "guest," so I'd helped her tidy up beforehand and convert my messy bed into a sofa. With all the dishes put away, she still insisted on offering Byron the whole Sunday breakfast, lox, pickles, and all. He politely declined in favor of mayonnaise on white bread and a glass of milk.

"I never heard of such a thing," Mom said amiably as she smeared the Wonder Bread with thick mayo.

"It's alien food," I explained.

"Alien. Whatever that means."

"It's okay," Byron said. "Your son is confused."

She chuckled. "I'll say."

When Dad emerged from the bedroom, where he'd read his Sunday papers and had a smoke, he shook Byron's hand and took in his height. "You're gonna be some tall guy," he said. "Stay away from cigarettes. See how they shrunk me down?"

"I think that's a myth," Byron said. "It's all genetic."

"That's right," I said. "That's why I'm Schmink-the-Shrimp."

"Wise guy, this one," Dad said to Byron. "The truth is, it don't matter if you're two feet tall."

As Dad and Mom drifted back to their Sunday routines, Byron and I settled in my so-called room, where I sat at my desk/dresser and he plopped on the sofa bed, eyeing his surroundings like an inspector.

"Interesting arrangement," he said. "You have no privacy."

"I know. But I've trained my parents to hurry through without looking."

"I like your parents. They're amusing."

"They're okay. Well, pretty good, actually. Most of the time."

Byron nodded and opened up the gym bag he'd brought along. "Here's the next Heinlein you can read," he said, pulling out a copy of *Between Planets.* He put his hand back in the bag. "And *this* . . . " He looked around again, like he was hiding a stolen necklace.

"Don't worry, no one's coming through," I told him. I could hear the TV going, and Joannie was off somewhere with friends.

"Okay, *this* will be of profound interest to you, for reasons I find challenging to comprehend. Nevertheless . . . . "

From the bag, he withdrew a fat notebook with red leather cover and shiny clasp. He held it out to me. "I present. . . Keatsie's diary."

"*What*?" I bolted to the sofa and grabbed the book, turning it over and over like a strange animal. "How'd you *get* it?"

"Easy. Walked into Keatsie's room and pulled it out of a drawer. Remember when I dumped her underwear from the dresser? I spied the diary at the back of the next drawer down."

"But where is she? Won't she see it's missing?"

"Oh, Mater took her to Mrs. Bender's beach house for the weekend. In Connecticut. It's nice—I go sailing there sometimes in the summer."

"Pater didn't go?"

"Nope. Pop doesn't like Mr. Bender. So—shall we have a reading?"

"Did you read it already?"

"Some."

"You think it's okay to read? I mean, it's private and all. What if she finds out?"

"Would serve her right for blabbing to Leena about me and Betty. I think Pop suspects something now. Plus, Keatsie must pay for saying that I '*cry because I have no friends.*'" Byron wiped imaginary tears from his eyes as he mocked the words. "Utterly untrue!"

"When did she say that?"

"Right here—look." He opened up the diary, thumbed through it, and thrust the page at me. I had no choice but to read it. Well, okay—I did have a choice: to be moral and make my friend feel like a skunk, or to be the skunk and, with luck, keep both Byron and Keatsie as friends.

"You think she'll figure out we have it?" I asked.

"Nah. I'll put it back before they get home."

He was waving the diary in front of me. I steadied it and read the paragraph he pointed to:

> Anyway, I should be nice to Aaron, even if he's not exactly my type, whatever that is. And I should probably try to understand Byron when he hogs attention and shuts me out. Byron always acts like it's a big privilege to know him because he's so good at everything, but that just makes people think he's a snob. He never seems to have a real friend. Of course he'll say he doesn't need any buddies, any girlfriend, any God, or anything but his own wonderful self. But didn't Leena tell me in secret that she's seen him crying after this or that hurt his feelings? It made her cry, she said.

Each revelation hit me like a head-butt. *I'm definitely not her type? I'm Byron's only real friend? Byron cries?* No—he denied that last one. So maybe other things weren't quite true? I read more:

> Like today after school, he shows up with this new friend, Aaron Schmink—I can't believe that name—and completely ignores me while he trots Aaron around the house and grounds. Aaron is kind of small and gawks at everything like he just popped out of a burrow. But he smiled when he saw me stupidly tagging after them, and he did seem nice in a shy way . . . .

"I didn't *gawk* at everything," I protested. "Popped out of a burrow? What's *that* supposed to mean?"

"Just jealousy," Byron said. "Notice that she thinks I'm 'monstrous' and that I put her down in front of my friends."

"Well you do sort of. In front of me, anyway."

"True. But only because it's amusing."

"But it's kind of sad. Look at all this stuff she says about the barfing: *The awful, acid taste and throat pain. I dashed into my bathroom, locked the door and ran the sink faucets to hide the sound. Not just of barfing, but crying, too. The foulness. The stink.* That's not so amusing."

For the first time since I'd met him, Byron looked sheepish. "Yeah, I know. It's not that I don't feel bad her. I mean, sometimes I sort of do."

"Really?"

"Well, sure. She *is* part alien after all, with my blood—although we don't have actual blood, more like mercury. But anyway, she has to suffer Pop's badgering even more than I do. And her shrink, Dr. Nut-Bin, isn't doing her much good. I should do her analysis instead."

"Yeah, and really get her barfing."

"Ha. Talking about that, here's the part where she barfed after the James Dean movie."

"Does it mention me?" I asked, mainly interested in those parts. "Yep," he said, and I grabbed the diary.

> . . . I messed up Miki's and Aaron's days. Poor Aaron—he was trying so hard to make it a nice "date." And he fought for me, like David taking on Goliath. So as a reward he got beaten and kicked and he'll probably be sore for weeks. I think I hurt his feelings, too, the way I acted when he tried to get romantic.

Yes she did! I thought.

> But I couldn't help it. I like him a lot, but not in a boyfriend way. It's pretty obvious he likes me that way—I mean like a girlfriend, so I shouldn't encourage him if I don't feel the same way, right? I just wish that Byron and I could both be close friends with him, but even that's hard because Byron is so weird about sharing anyone. He's the one who should be seeing Dr. Nut-Bin.

"Ignore that last part, Byron said. reading over my shoulder. "I'm not weird about sharing friends. Except when I invite friends over and she butts in. Did you think I was weird?"

"Nah, just extra-tesstrial."

"You mean *extraterrestrial*? I can't help being what I am." He tapped the open diary. "So should we read more—like about her latest crush?"

"Who's that?"

"Paul Lefevre. She love-barfed twice over him."

Love-barfed. The term made it seem cute instead of awful. "I don't know," I sighed, closing the diary then opening it again. "I think I get the point. I should forget all about Keatsie."

"That wasn't my precisely my point. Actually, she'd be better off with you than her Cro-Magnons. But why bother if she's not interested? You should, you know, get romantic with Miki."

Get romantic. I blushed at Keatsie's term for my failed moves.

"Really," Byron said. "Miki *digs* you, man."

" I don't know. But, then, if I'm not Keatsie's type . . ."

"You mean big, dumb, and too old for her?"

"I guess." I flipped through more of the diary, hurrying past anything that seemed too personal for prying eyes, and handed it back to Byron. "She's a good writer, anyway."

"Because she's my twin."

Byron must have noticed that I looked more downcast than amused. "I don't know," he said, "maybe I shouldn't have brought it."

Now he looked hurt, which wasn't my intention. "No, no," I said. "It's probably best to know how she feels, as long as she doesn't find out."

"If she does, I'll say it helped us understand her better." He almost seemed to mean it, as if he truly sympathized with her pain now. But whether he did or not, I thought we had probed Keatsie's life enough now; it felt like betraying her out of spite. Besides, I wanted to hear about something else:

"Hey, man—tell me about you and Betty Lee!"

35

High risks

☺ ☺ ☹

"WHAT WOULD YOU LIKE TO know?" Byron said in a way that sounded like a*sk me anything.*"

"Everything."

"Well, let's see. It's pretty fantastic. *She's* pretty fantastic."

"I bet. When do you, you know, get together?"

"We talk at school—unless some moron or another starts glaring at us."

"Which morons? White guys?"

"Mostly, but not always. I glare back at them, but Betty doesn't want to make a big deal out of it."

"Is it a big deal?"

"It is for me. It's riskier for Betty, though. She could actually get beat up."

"Really? By who?"

"Well, certain girls who think she's trying to show them up. Or some prejudiced idiots. Or maybe her father or two brothers."

"Wow."

Before he could say more, my own father walked in on his way to the kitchen. "How's it goin'? he said. "I'm gonna grab another cup a' coffee. You want any?" He was asking Byron, not me. Byron said no thanks.

"You guys should be outside, a beautiful day like this."

"I thought I was supposed to stay in," I said. "Mom's rule."

"Yeah, well you did good for two days. I'll tell her I kicked you bums outside. Unless you wanna just sit around."

"No—I want to show Byron the neighborhood." I was already on my feet. I couldn't wait to shoot out the door after my confinement. Byron stood up with me. "This bum concurs," he said.

We went out the back door. As we turned to go down the porch stairs, we heard a commotion inside Rocco's apartment. It sounded like Rocco Sr. was howling at Adele and she was shrieking back, and that things or people were being shoved around. I thought I heard Rocco's sobs in the mix.

"What's all *that*?" Byron asked.

I sighed. "Another Sunday at the Cabruzzis. My friend Rocco lives there. Cool guy, champion make-out artist. But his parents fight all the time and he's kind of a delinquent."

"I'm all for delinquents," Byron said.

Again, I was tempted to spill the beans about wrecking the mansion with Rocco. But we'd been talking about Betty and I wanted to hear more. As we walked to the front of the house and turned downhill, I asked if he'd seen Betty outside of school other than that day at RKO Keith's.

"Twice. First we sneaked in some time at Macy's, in the Sports Department, like we were looking for presents. She knows tons about sports, but we talked about everything and then walked over to the park on South Broadway."

"And? Anything happen?"

"We held hands."

"Did you kiss her?"

"Not then."

Byron paused, milking the suspense.

"Come on, man!"

"Where are we headed?" he asked, looking around at the row of apartment buildings on our side and the modest houses across the street. I saw Chubby and Dickie sitting on one of the stoops and ignored them.

"I don't know," I said, " just walking around. So what happened?"

"The second time, we went to a movie at the Pix."

"Really?" I knew the Pix only by reputation. It was a small theater in its own neighborhood and showed a lot of foreign movies and movies nobody understood. "When was that?"

"Friday afternoon—on the holiday. Mater had already left for Connecticut and Pater was busy, so I just left him a note and took off. Betty invented some story for her mother. We went to the Pix separately and met inside, like secret agents."

"Far out! Did you watch any of the movie?"

"We had to, it was so good! You ever see *La Strada*? It means "The Road" in Italian and it's about this traveling-circus strongman who buys a poor woman to work for him and he treats her like crap but she hangs in until he kills a tightrope-walker called 'the Fool.'"

"Then what happened?"

"A long time later the strongman finds out that the woman died, and he gets hysterical and falls down crying."

"That's really sad, man. But I *meant* what happened with *you* guys?"

"Oh. Well, Betty cried at the end of the movie. I told her, 'I thought your nickname was Happy.'"

"Byron?' I said. "Did. You. *Make. Out*?"

Grinning, Byron nodded yes.

"Man! So cool! Did anyone see you?"

"Nah. There were only a few people there, in front of us. And it's not like we were breaking a law. Just kissing, but not too long because we didn't want to miss the subtitles." He saw my blank expression. "You know, the translations at the bottom of the screen?"

"Oh, okay. So did you ever make out before?"

Byron shrugged. "Not like this. She's an incredible kisser."

I didn't know what to say other than another *wow*. I found myself reimagining my afternoon at the movies with Keatsie and how stupendous it would have been if we had made out or just kissed, whether she'd have barfed "for me" as a result or not. It would have been worth everything that happened afterward.

We'd reached the overpass bridge at the bottom of the hill. I stopped to lean on the stone ledge and point out some neighborhood stuff: the last farm in White Plains, starting about five blocks farther. The shortcut leading to Todd's Pond, where I'd gone skating last winter. The corner house where Nancy Gano, Eastview's beautiful tap-dancing ninth-grader, lived.

"Where does that go?" Byron asked, leaning over the ledge and pointing to an asphalt path running along one side of the parkway. I explained that it led to the Eastview Junior High neighborhood in one direction and my former school in the other.

"You see the grass bank on the other side?" I said. "That's where a guy named Ozzie Assim fell from here and ended up paralyzed. He hit part of the road, too."

"Hmm. How did he fall?"

I told him how some neighborhood teens had gotten Ozzie drunk and dared him to walk across the ledge; how he'd almost made it. And how such a dare was still being thrown around.

"Just to walk across?" Byron said. "That's nothing." He vaulted himself up to a sitting position on the ledge, then brought his legs up, put his palms down behind him, and got to a standing position.

I was horrified, as if I'd just caused my friend's death. "Come on, man, get *down*! What the—what are you doing? Don't be insane!

"You kidding? In gymnastics we did flips on four-inch balance beams. This is like walking a highway."

He extended his arms sideways and started walking slowly to where Ozzie had fallen at the far end of the ledge. "I am-a da tighta-ropa walker," he said in an Italian accent. "They call-a me da "Fool."

"You're *being* a fool," I moaned, walking along with him. "Nobody even dared you."

"I dared me."

Traffic whizzed by below, families taking a Sunday drive or hurrying to get home.

"Please, *please*, get down, Byron. You're scaring the crap out of me!"

"Whoops!" he said, faking a little stumble.

"*Jeez*. Stop it!" I held my hand out near a leg, as if I could do anything to stop a fall. I could picture it happening, his brains all over the highway, and felt sick to my stomach. "Please come down, for God's sake."

"*Whose* sake? Ain't no God."

I knew right then that Byron was headed over the edge to splatter on the roadway, whether by God's hand or from tempting fate. My nerves short-circuited, my head buzzed, I felt dizzy, woozy, fear igniting a fire in my gut and welling up, hot and horrible. I gagged, bent over, and released a serving of my big Sunday breakfast into to the gutter.

36

Surprise caller #1

☺ ☺ 😐

"HEY, YOU OKAY, Aaron?"

I spat in the gutter and turned, groaning, to see Byron tilting his head down to me.

"Yeah, sort of. Man—just don't ever scare me like that again."

"Sorry. I didn't think it was that scary."

"Well it was. But I don't know why it made me puke."

"That *is* weird. Maybe you caught the barfs from Keatsie."

"Yeah, great. Now you'll catch it."

"Impossible."

"All I know is, it's the worst. My throat's burning and my mouth stinks. I gotta get back and wash up "

I stepped away from my embarrassing mess and started toward home. Byron hung his head and said nothing as we walked up the hill.

"You okay," I asked.

"Me? Sure. Are *you* okay?"

I seemed over it now, and I needed to do something to change the mood. "Yo mama walks a tightrope over the toilet bowl," I said, breaking my vow against yo-mama gags.

"Yo mama walks a tightrope made of pubic hair," he countered, laughing through his nose.

Byron left about an hour later, and now I worried that Keatsie would beat him home and find her diary missing. I sat in my room and read some of the new Heinlein book until Joannie got back from a day with Barbara Katz and some other friends. I decided to tell her what had happened at the ledge, hoping she'd assure me it was perfectly normal for someone to upchuck in that situation.

"You should get help," she told me. "You should see somebody."

"You mean like a shrink?"

"Maybe a counselor or a therapist. I did , and it helped."

"Come on, this is the first time it ever happened."

"Yeah, but you're a big worrier. I don't want you go through what I have. Now you know what's it's like."

"Well . . . I'll try not worrying. And please don't say anything to Mom or Dad."

"Why would I? And by the way, you're friend must be nuts."

We were all watching TV after dinner when the phone rang. I was nearest to the hallway and got up to answer it.

"If it's Doris, I'm not home," Mom called out. Her friend Doris liked to talk for hours about her troubles. But when I picked up and said hello, it was Keatsie's voice saying "Aaron?"

"Keatsie?"

I put my hand over the phone and announced that the call was for me. Again I felt a wave of panic. I braced for the worst. Keatsie would be *livid* knowing I'd read her diary, and I was sure she'd found out. Why else would she call, and what could I possibly say—that Byron had made me do it? Instead of my dreamed-of kiss I was about to get the big kiss-off.

"Hi, Barf-Boy!" Keatsie said, giggling.

"*What*?" I slumped down and sat on the floor, back against the wall.

"I heard all about it," she chirped. "I always have to know everything, right? So I pumped it out of Byron. And I think it's wonderful."

"Wonderful?" I was still calming down.

"Maybe that's not the exact word, but you showed Byron how *brainless* he was being. And—"

"You mean puking? Funny way to show anything."

"No it *isn't*. My shrink says it's the most honest reaction you can have to how you really feel."

"Well it's not the most fun reaction." Even thinking back on it made my stomach churn.

"Believe me, I know! But now you're someone I can—heh, heh— suffer with. I mean you *understand*."

"We're barf twins?"

"Yes!" she laughed.

I wondered if she was just playing with me before chopping my head off about the diary. "So what else did your real twin say?" I asked. I held my breath.

"Just that he went to your house to bring one of his sci-fi books. And your mother gave him a mayo sandwich. And he heard your neighbors fighting. And you took him to this overpass that somebody fell off once."

"Fell on the road and was paralyzed."

"He told me. And that he—my alien brother who thinks he can fly— got up on the ledge and walked all the way across. And that you worried so much you barfed."

"Something like that, I guess. Anything else??"

"That's a lot. *And* he admitted he shouldn't have done it. *Byron* telling me all this? Can you imagine?"

"No, not really. Did you tell him something first?"

"Only some boring stuff about the weekend at Mrs. Benders. I mean, boring to tell, but we had fun there. The Benders are so nice. Oh, by the way, Mrs. Bender wants your telephone number and address. Okay if I give it to her?"

"How come?"

"I don't know. She's always doing things for people, She knows everybody. You can trust her."

I couldn't see a problem and gave Keatsie permission. "So we're friends?" I said.

"Of course!"

"But not boyfriend-girlfriend."

"Aaron. It's not that I don't like you."

"I know. I'm not your type. You like the Paul Lefevre type more."

"Who told you that?"

I stopped. Could I have know that without her diary? Yes—but now I had to confess that I'd seen her and Paul from Byron's window. "I wasn't spying. I was just looking outside."

"Well we didn't *do* anything. He just gave us a ride. I don't even . . . ." She went silent.

"Okay," I said. "Never mind. It's none of my business, even if we're the famous barf-twins."

She laughed her tinkling laugh, to my relief. "Are you coming over soon?" she said. "Maybe we could all have fun together."

I wasn't so sure about that, but I told her I'd try to get there.

37

Back at school and shul

I HAD A HORRIBLE DREAM that night. Byron did fall off the ledge, screaming on his way to the concrete. When I looked down at the highway I saw car after car running him over, knocking him around like a stuffed animal. I turned to see Betty Lee standing next to me. "Well, that's that," she said. I wanted to ask her why she wasn't sad, but now Keatsie stood in her place. "Wanna barf together?" she suggested. I woke up sweating and tangled in the sheets.

At school, however, things settled back to abnormal. Byron and I had a giggle-fit when our English teacher, tiny Miss Finch, read from a poem by Henry Longfellow and came to the words "wattled gules":

Still bore the family arms, and had for his crest
a cock argent,
Combed and wattled gules, and all the rest of
the blazon.

We didn't even know what the words meant—something about the red fleshy stuff that hangs from a rooster's throat?—but they sounded so funny coming out of little Miss Finch. She gave us a scolding look, which made our veins pop from trying not to laugh.

"I thought you were going to spew," Byron said after class.

"Shut up, Tightrope Fool."

My reentry into shul that evening also went better than expected. Before class no one looked at me differently, and Moshe appreciated it when I asked how his mother was doing.

"Not so good," he told me, but thanks for asking."

"Sorry I . . . you know, the other night."

"It's okay. I'm sorry I jumped bad with you. I was upset."

"No, no. You called me some great Yiddish drags. I mean, I wish I knew them."

"Hang around my father," he said, "you'll learn them fast."

"Nice you could drop by again, A-ha-ron," Mr. Rubin said when it was time to work on my Haftarah. "Last week I was going to teach you *tefillin*, in case you wanted to learn how to wear it. You remember when I talked about tefillin, right?

"The little leather boxes you strap to your arm and head?"

"And what's inside the boxes?"

"Parts of the Torah written on parchment."

"Torah verses, good. So tefillin is worn—or 'laid,' we say—by observant Jewish men during their weekday morning prayers."

"What for?"

"It helps keep their thoughts on righteousness."

"Oh. You wear it?"

"I do. But since your bar mitzvah is on a Saturday, and you're not the most observant member of the tribes—you're probably happy to skip it, am I right?"

I thought about it a moment. I'd seen religious men wrapping the straps around arm and head and it seemed strange to me. "Yeah," I said. "It's okay."

"All right then. Besides, you're going upstairs tonight to practice with the cantor. We should have been doing it already a week ago."

"Upstairs" from the basement meant the Hebrew Institute's synagogue, the place of worship and the nicest part of the building with its two seating sections—the main one for men and a balcony for women. Up on a platform was the Holy Ark, a handsome, carved cabinet housing the Torah. Special seats on the platform were reserved for certain congregation leaders. Near the middle of the room stood a solid, elevated table where the Torah was unscrolled and read during services.

Cantor Hillel was up there working with another boy from class. Cantors, who were trained in religious singing and ritual, led Jewish congregations in prayer. Our cantor, short and roundish with shiny cheeks, had a voice like an opera tenor. When he sang a certain passage to coach the boy, it sounded magical; then the boy would try it and the magic shrank into little squeaks and squawks. As I waited my turn I thought maybe I could just do one of my imitations and sound something like the cantor. But when I got up there and went through my readings, the voice I heard was more like a wounded crow.

The cantor was generous. "Very nice, Aaron," he told me. "Looks like Mr. Rubin's doing a good job as usual. Maybe just a few places we could make some improvements."

Those few places turned out to be most of the reading. We worked for about an hour and I got home late. But Mom was so excited about a phone call she got earlier, she hardly noticed.

"You'll never guess in a million years who's coming here tomorrow night," she said, glowing.

38

Surprise caller #2

NONE OF US KNEW what to expect when Rabbi Lipschutz rang our bell the next night, arriving about a quarter past eight, just a little later than he'd estimated. From his name—as awful-sounding to me as Schmink—I'd pictured a paler, crustier, gray-bearded version of Rabbi Klein, the head of the Hebrew Institute. Even though Mrs. Bender had described Lipschutz as the most modern of modern Reform rabbis, I couldn't imagine anybody but a sour-pussed guy in a baggy black coat.

Not that my mother cared what he might look like. Yesterday Mrs. Bender had phoned to tell her a *rabbi* wanted to come to our house. As far as Mom was concerned, he could show up with two heads and a tail; she'd never had the honor of a rabbi crossing her threshold. Even my father had made sure to be home for the event, so that our supper table was fully occupied before the visit, with plenty of excitement.

"You're positive it's not because you got in trouble?" Mom asked at dinner for what seemed the tenth time.

She was clearing the dishes and preparing some snacks to put out in the living room. I was surprised she had the energy; she'd been cleaning the house since the call yesterday. Joannie and I also had to make our own rooms shine.

"He probably just wants me to switch to his temple," I said.

"So he comes all the way here for that? Anyway, for your bar mitzvah it's too late even if we could afford his place. According to Mrs. Bender, he just wants to give you a little pep talk—which wouldn't hurt with your attitude."

"Oh, I just can't wait," I groused with that same attitude.

Joannie opened the door and we all assembled to greet Rabbi Lipschutz. Before my unbelieving gaze stood a tall young man with an athletic frame. He wore a dark suit and white shirt, but he'd thrown a brown-leather bomber's jacket over his shoulders like a cape against the night's chill! And—could it be?—black loafers on his feet! His skullcap seemed to float on waves of black hair, hair thick enough to keep his head warm all winter. And instead of a bearded sour-puss greeting us, here was a handsome, glowing face with blue eyes, smooth cheeks, and a big healthy smile. We all hung there a moment with our mouths open, but Rabbi Lipschutz must have been used to the reaction. "Hi. I'm Beau Lipschutz," he said, extending his hand. "Sorry I'm a little late. I came straight from working out at the Y."

"At the YMCA, no kiddin'?" my father said, pumping his hand. "I used to go to the one in the Bronx, the only one with boxing."

"Ah, a boxer," Lipschutz said. "I could have guessed." His voice, rich and clear, sounded like someone on radio.

My mother snapped out of her trance and led him inside to the living room. He shook hands with her, then with me and Joannie as Mom introduced us. The pale-looking one was now Joannie as he clasped her hand.

Mom sat him on one of the chairs she'd set up with a tray table and began offering him a whole menu of delicatessen treats.

"No, I'm fine, thanks," he said. "I ate early. Maybe a little something to drink."

That set Mom off again with a list of every beverage in the house. He finally settled for some cream soda, which she and Joannie went off to fetch. Only Mom returned, bringing the soda and a plate heaped with fruit, nuts, and chocolates.

The four of us made small talk in the living room, Joannie mysteriously staying away. Mom went on about how honored we were by his visit and how hard her son had been working on his bar mitzvah. The rabbi asked my father what kind of work he did, and Dad told him about the all-night bakery deliveries, adding, "That's my easy job. The hard one is pickin' the horses."

Before my mother could faint from embarrassment, the rabbi laughed and said, "Sounds like my father. He spent so much time at Belmont racetrack I thought he was a jockey."

Mom told him she was surprised to see a rabbi so young, and he gave her a brief background: Raised in Long Island, graduated early from City College and did four years of rabbinical training in Cincinnati and New York. Practiced for two years in Queens, served as a chaplain in the Korean War, then got the job at the JCC.

"And so," Mom said, "this Mrs. Bender asked you to visit my son? She seems like a very nice lady."

"Nice isn't the word," Lipschutz said. "I'd do anything for her. Without her there would be no JCC." He paused to finish his soda and move the tray table aside. "But believe me, I'm happy to have a talk with Aaron. I would do it on my own, because I know the conflicts certain boys have about their bar mitzvah. I had plenty at his age."

With that he stood and asked if he and I might be excused to have the conversation. "Please," he insisted to Mom and Dad, "don't miss your TV shows. Aaron and I can talk in another room, yes?"

And so Beau Lipschutz and I ended up in my room, passing Joannie on the way. She smiled, but had a frightened look in her eyes that I guessed to be fear of getting sick. It wasn't hard to figure out the cause.

"Now, Aaron," Lipschutz said, taking his seat at my desk while I settled on the sofa-bed. "If you like, let's start with any questions you want to ask me, anything at all, including why the heck am I having a bar mitzvah?"

I thought a moment. "How'd you get a cool name like Bo?"

39

One cool rabbi

☺ ☺ 😐

"WELL, FIRST OF ALL it's B-E-A-U," the rabbi said, spelling out his name. He reached into his jacket, pulled out a card, and gave it to me. "When my mother was pregnant with me she saw an adventure movie called *Beau Geste,* and that was that, I got stuck with the name. My father liked it because it reminded him of a horse. But at least you don't spell it B-O like the underarm smell—bad enough I had to live with the name Lipschutz as a kid, just like you have to live with Schmink."

At last there was someone who understood! "*Aaron* Schmink," I noted, "*two* names I hate. They call me Aaron Stink."

"Of course they do. And what do you think they called me?"

"You mean 'Lip-sh—'" I dared to venture the dirty word.

"Wash your mouth out!" he said, laughing. "But look, 'Aaron' is a noble name. It means things like 'warrior' and it's been given to cool people all over the world. Look it up some time. As for Lipschutz and Schmink—they only sound funny to schmucky Americans, but so what? We live with our names, we honor them, and the teasing makes us stronger, just like every challenge we get through. Like the challenge you're facing now, a bar mitzvah that I understand you didn't want."

"Okay, Rabbi, so why—"

"Call me Beau, if that's all right with you."

"That's allowed? Wow. Beau. So, anyway—why the heck *am* I having a bar mitzvah, except for my parents making me have it. I don't like Hebrew school, I don't like my teacher or the rabbi there, I don't even feel very Jewish."

Beau nodded. "You have Lenny Rubin as your teacher, right?"

"Mr. Rubin? Yes."

"I know him. He's a serious teacher but a good man. A hero. Did you know he fought in Korea, two years in the freezing mud? Got pneumonia, a throat wound, the whole thing. Sometimes we misjudge people because they're part of whatever we're resisting. But they're part of the challenge, too."

"I didn't know he was in the war," I said, not quite understanding the rest of Beau's comment. "That's pretty cool. But he's . . . ."

"He's what?"

"Kind of square?"

Beau smiled. "Aaron, my man—do you sound like the twelve-year-old me or what? My parents were Orthodox, even if my old man liked to gamble. They had a thousand rules I had to follow and I got dragged to synagogue services three or four times a week. I had to eat kosher all the time. Wear a yarmulka in public school! And all I wanted to do was play baseball and go see cartoons—be a normal American kid. And then, practicing for a super-Orthodox bar mitzvah? It was like a death sentence to me."

"Right! So what happened?"

"Well, for one thing, Adolph Hitler and the Nazis happened. It was the start of a death sentence for the Jews in Europe, not just my own little dilemma. We had relatives over there—it was very real. See, unfortunately it took something horrible to wake me up, but I began to see a world outside myself. That's not an easy thing. When you're a kid, nature wants you mainly to grow your body, form an idea of 'self,' and survive as an individual."

Maybe because Beau just seemed so cool, he was getting my attention. Rabbi Klein had tried to shame me by talking about the Holocaust, but this felt different.

"So now, because of Hitler, you wanted the bar mitzvah?" I asked.

"I was confused. I was trying to understand God and why He was letting all this lousy stuff happen. I wanted to help make things better in the world, and not just my world. I wanted to become a man, and if all that ritual would speed it up, I'd give it a shot."

"And after—did you understand God?"

Beau grinned again. "You ask good questions, man, like a reporter. I hear you want to be a writer."

"I don't know. Maybe."

"Well, here's the answer. I don't think we ever understand God."

"Really? But you believe in God, don't you?"

"Mostly, yes, and sometimes I wonder about it, to tell the truth. To me and to a lot of Jews and others as well, that's not the most important thing. What's important is to live a good life and help others do the same according to what your inner spirit—call it your soul—tells you. But in the Jewish faith there's a lot of wisdom to guide that spirit."

It was so much to take in. I sat speechless.

The rabbi grinned a bright reassuring grin. "These things take time to figure out. Right now, what *your* spirit is telling you is to be cool, right?"

I shrugged.

"Or maybe it's your mother telling you?"

I laughed. "No."

"Or Rabbi Klein? If you're cool, you get one of those statues in his cabinet?"

Another laugh. "How did you know about those?"

"We all know each other and we talk. He's okay, though. I like him."

"But not as cool as you."

"I'm sure he is, in his own way. I love cool, don't get me wrong. But it's easy to dress cool and talk cool. But real cool—the hard one—is how you deal with people different than you, how you handle things you don't understand, or things that bug you, anger you. Scare you."

"What if you handle it by vomiting?" I blurted, surprised to hear it come out.

"What?"

"Well . . . I got really scared by something last Sunday, and I puked. And I have a girlfriend—I mean, she's not actually my girlfriend—and she barfs when she gets a crush on someone. And my sister . . . ." I stopped there. Joannie would kill me for my big mouth.

Beau nodded, looking serious. "Interesting—to me, anyway. I majored in psychology as an undergraduate, which comes in pretty handy in my work. I can tell you that stress-related vomiting is quite common. It can be a nightmare for some. Does this happen a lot to you?"

"No, just the one time. But my friend's headshrinker—"

He laughed at the word.

"Her head doctor says vomiting maybe is the most honest reaction to what's bothering you."

"Could be. And what's bothering you is the upcoming bar mitzvah. Are you afraid you'll—what's that funny word you used?—*barf* during the ceremony?"

"Oh, God, what if I do?"

"You won't. You know, in Korea, the Jewish soldiers I counseled had the same fear. On nights before they went into action they would puke their guts out thinking about it. They feared not only dying, but maybe—even more—being sick and useless on the battle field. But when they fought, they fought as something bigger than themselves. They fought to support their buddies and their officers and their country. And they were heroes, every one of them. Any of this making sense?"

"Sort of. I'm not sure. But what if you're not a soldier?"

"Okay, here's another example. Did you know that many actors say they feel like vomiting before each performance? I mean every time, even when they've been doing a show for years. But have you ever heard of anyone puking on stage? Doesn't happen, because first, they're now part of something bigger than themselves, a cast, a whole production. And second, it's no longer the dreaded future—it's the present, and one way or another, the worry is finished."

"So even if you mess up, at least it'll be over."

"Right. And believe me, a smart guy like you won't mess up. I've seen schlemiels who couldn't find their bellybutton do a beautiful bar mitzvah and eventually become a *mensch*—a real, honorable man. Now does something magic happen during the ritual? Do you suddenly get a hairy chest because you're called a man? Grow a foot taller?"

"I wish," I said.

He laughed. "I know. But spiritually, you *will* grow instantly taller. Because you'll be marching with the millions of men and women who took that same first step into Jewish adulthood. For boys, they call it entering manhood, a new feeling about yourself and the world. Just going through it you'll have accomplished something very difficult, a *man's* job you can be proud of, not some kid's game. And you'll be taking on a man's job for life, because all the *good* that God stands for—or even the idea of God—that's what you'll stand for now. You'll be walking tall, man! You'll be supercool!"

40

Aaron the writer

FROM the *Eastview Junior High School Dispatch:*

Thanksgiving
by Aaron Schmink

American Thanksgiving is a holiday that started in Massachusetts in order to, guess what? (Answer: Give thanks!) Before then people had thanksgiving days, but these were mainly religious events with loads of thanks to God, but (sob!) no heaps of food.

But when the Pilgrims had a jumbo harvest in 1621 they threw a party for three days. They invited the most mellow

Indians, gave some more thanks, and finally got down to the eating business. They chowed on "waterfowl (that's ducks and geese to you), venison (that's deer to you), fish, lobster, clams, berries, fruit, pumpkin, and squash," plus some wild turkey. (Excuse me, I need a Bromo-Seltzer.)

Some people call Thanksgiving "Turkey Day." Can you guess why? (Wrong: Because some dumb turkey said to.) (Right: Because we roast and stuff the poor dude and eat it as the main course!) But turkey didn't always make the varsity menu squad until about 1850. After that, it was a regular starter.

At first Thanksgivings weren't celebrated every year. In 1789, President George Washington, who couldn't tell a lie, made it a national holiday. But it was celebrated different times in different places. Then in 1941 the U.S. Congress said enough with the crazy times, from now on it's going to be the fourth Thursday in November, you dig? So that's when we now stuff our chops, gather with our families, and all that noise.

We give thanks, too, not just for the cool stuff that happened to ourselves during the year. We give thanks as part of something bigger, like our families, our community, and the human race. So happy Turkey Day, everyone, except you poor turkeys!

At first I liked the way the article came out. Then I didn't like it—too much lame joking. Then, when I got compliments in Newspaper Club, I liked it again. Mr. Salisbury said it was a little weird but had all the necessary whos, whats, whens, and wheres, so he let it go. Byron thought it was pretty good, except for the "God stuff." Later at the lockers he asked me, "What was all that horse-puckey at the end about giving thanks? To whom are we giving it?"

"Anyone who deserves it, man," I said. "Maybe even you. Uh, thanks for having me over your house? Thanks for lending me the book? Thanks for scaring the poop out of me?"

"Ah," he said, "those all makes sense."

I might have told him that Rabbi Lipschutz had inspired the final thoughts, but I was still trying to figure out exactly what those thoughts were. I'd only told Byron that the rabbi had visited and how cool he was.

"How about you?" I asked him. "What'll you give thanks for?"

He raised his chin high. "I disdain all such ceremonial gratitude."

"What about Betty Lee? You're not thankful for her?"

"Hmm. I would be—if she were mine all mine. But she's been avoiding me. Didn't you notice it in Newspaper Club?"

"Yeah, maybe, now that you mention it. Did you ask her why?"

"Not really. I think somebody said something to her. Maybe one of her brothers."

"Oh-oh. What are you going to do?"

He shrugged. "Enjoy my own fantastic company."

I laughed. "Sounds like fun."

He fussed in his locker a moment, then asked, "Want to come over this weekend? You can watch me tell myself jokes?"

"Yeah, I'd like to," I said. "But would you mind if I also visited Keatsie? You know, while you're making yourself hysterical? She kind of asked me."

"Sure, that's cool. If it keeps her away from me for a while."

"Okay," I said. "That's *if* I can come over at all. I have to do some bar-mitzvah stuff first."

"Echh."

"What do you mean, 'echh,' you antisemite!"

"I'm anti-everything."

I shook my head as if to say he was hopeless. But I gave silent thanks that I'd be getting to the Fairchild house again.

41

Who Presley?

WHEN I GOT HOME Thursday after a boring evening at shul practicing the same readings over and over, I walked in on Joannie as she hopped and twirled around her room to music I'd never heard before. Music with a beat that made me want to hop, too. From Joannie's record player came a sort of hillbilly voice singing the words "That's all right, mama." Drum and guitars behind him pounded out a rhythm like a train clacking along the tracks.

"Who's that?" I shouted over the music.

Joannie paused to catch her breath. "It's Elvis Presley!"

"*Who* Presley?"

"Elvis! Maureen says he's the biggest thing down south."

"Our cousin Maureen?"

"Yeah. She sent me the record so I'd know about him before I went down there. Isn't it great? It's so exciting! Maureen actually saw him sing in Memphis and bought a bunch of his records. She says he's super-cute and sexy and dances all crazy-legs and sticks out his groin out when he sings."

As I listened, Mom called from the hallway. "Is that you, Aaron? Joannie—Haven't you played that thing enough? Turn it down or off! Supper's almost ready."

Joannie turned it down a notch and held her arms out. "Come on," she said, "you remember how to lindy, right?"

Joannie herself had taught me the steps to this rock and roll dance. I'd also tried to imitate whatever I saw of it in movies and on TV. We joined hands and rocked back and forth, then she tried to twirl me out.

"No, I'm leading!" I insisted, and spun her out under my arm, then back for some more stylish rocking.

"That's good," she said. "You've been practicing."

"I'm a natural."

I picked up on the lyrics and began to sing along. It was about somebody's mama telling him that a girl "ain't no good" for him, and him saying to his mama that it was all right, "anyway you do," which I guessed was how they talked down south, whatever it meant. It just sounded so cool, an even better use of "mama" than "yo mama" jokes.

Dad had stayed home this afternoon, sleeping, and he joined us at supper. Mom asked him how he could snooze through all that racket. "What racket?" he said. He could sleep through anything.

Mom was in pretty good spirits—luckily, because whatever she said to me, I answered "mama, anyway you do." Joannie laughed so hard she almost choked.

Later Joannie and I played the record some more, including the other side, "Blue Moon of Kentucky," about someone who was untrue and "left me blue." At the center of the spinning disk was a yellow label that said SUN in big letters. When she finally turned off the player, I asked if I could borrow the record to take to Byron's on the weekend.

"I don't know," she said. "What if you break it? Why do you want it—to play for your girlfriend?"

"What girlfriend?"

"The one who vomits."

"Keatsie? She's my girlfriend like Rabbi Lipschutz is your boyfriend."

"Oh, God, I wish," she said, sitting down on her bed. "Why do you say that?"

"Because I saw how you looked when he was here. Speaking of barfing."

"You noticed? Oh God, you don't think *he* did, do you? Did you say something?"

"Of course not."

"Oy, he is so handsome," she sighed. "My friend Barbara knows someone who goes to the JCC, and she says every girl there almost faints when he walks in. So I don't feel so bad. Barbara was so jealous that he was *right here*, but unfortunately, he's engaged to someone."

"He's a little old for you anyway."

"So I can't dream?"

I continued to beg her to let me borrow the record, promising to protect it with my life, promising this, promising that. And though she didn't give in yet, I could see she was weakening.

42

Shabbat is kinda sharp, man

I'D ALREADY gone to seven "Shabbats," or Sabbath observances at the Hebrew Institute during the year, including one with my parents and Joannie during the Jewish high holy days back in September. But now I had to go to one more according to the shul's requirements for bar mitzvah preparation.

The others had each been on Saturday mornings and seemed endless. During all those blessings, praises, chants, readings, prayers, and a sermon, my mind had just wandered while my body imitated the motions of other people there—bowing the head, standing, sitting, swaying with a song. Sometimes I sat with one of the other boys from shul and we'd giggle at something and get horrible looks from bearded men whose prayer shawls looked like giant wings.

But for my last required Shabbat, I went to the Friday-night service instead so I'd be free on Saturday. Of course I started out by breaking one of Shabbat's ton of laws, taking a bus there and later home. You weren't supposed to ride or use the phone or turn on a light or do a bunch of other normal things on "the day of rest." So if I'd been worried about God's approval, I'd have been in big trouble.

But once the service got underway it felt different from my other Shabbats—maybe because it was so much shorter than Saturday's, or because after my talk with Rabbi Lipschutz I didn't fret so much about not being a big believer. Also, I took a seat closer than usual to the table where the Torah was read and I could see the "sent" expressions on some of the men, like they'd just eaten the best ice cream in the world. I could hear others murmur things like "I don't know this one," and "So don't worry, just read the English." They had a book up there with the Torah's Hebrew words written out in English letters.

It was a small crowd, with only three women and a couple of dozen men. I didn't turn around to look at everyone, but most of the people I saw were dressed nicely, as if going out to dinner. For the occasion I'd put on my gabardine slacks and a sweater over a dress shirt.

During the prayers, blessings, and praises of God that were sung, some of the men not only sprang up, but did little solo dances, closing their eyes and spinning around as they sang in loud voices. A couple of men looked at them disapprovingly, but the rabbi and cantor paid no special attention. Most of us sang with more spirit than I'd noticed on Saturdays, maybe to speed things up and get home to supper.

The rabbi gave a brief sermon about why we pray—something about backing up our choices and actions; I didn't really listen—I was thinking about Saturday and Byron and Keatsie and how much they'd like the Elvis record. Before I knew it the final singing rang out with gusto and then the service was over. Everybody went around shaking hands and wishing each other "*Gut Shabbos*" (good Sabbath). Some of them patted me on my yarmulke and shook my hand, too. It felt good.

As I headed toward the exit, removing the skullcap and putting it in my coat pocket, I was surprised to see Moshe Litvin standing there with a stout man who looked like an older version of himself. The man was shaking hands and chatting with some of the others.

"Hey, look who's here," Moshe said, spotting me. "I thought I saw you up front but couldn't believe it."

"I didn't see you. Were you in the back?"

"Yeah. We got here a little late."

I explained that I'd come for the bar mitzvah requirement. "Actually," I added, "the Friday Shabbat ain't bad. It's kinda sharp."

"It's okay," he said. "Unless you have to go *all* the time." He tugged on the man's arm. "Papa, this is my friend Aaron from shul."

I didn't expect the word "friend" from Moshe, but I liked it. The father interrupted his conversation with the others and looked me over.

Where's your yarmulke?" he snapped. "You're still in the synagogue."

He sounded like a policeman. I fished out the skullcap and put it back on.

"Do I know your parents?" he asked.

"I don't think so."

"They don't come to synagogue?"

"Not much."

"You speak Yiddish?"

"Not really."

"How much?"

"None."

He turned to his son and said something gruffly in Yiddish, nodding toward me. Moshe shrugged, as if apologetically. I felt that I must have made a bad impression and wanted to say something manly, something to deserve being Moshe's friend.

"I'm sorry about Moshe's mom," I said. "I hope she's feeling better."

Mr. Litvin froze a moment, then glared at his son. "How does this *fremder* know our business?"

"He's *not* a stranger," Moshe shot back. "I told you, we go to shul together."

"So what? You opened your big fat *pisk*? You're a *yente* now?"

"I was just—"

"*Zol zein shah!*" Mr. Litvin shouted, ordering Moshe to be quiet. Then he turned to me. "For your information, *pisher*, my wife is not better. She's never going to be better. And it's not your concern. So gut Shabbos and good night." He grabbed Moshe's arm and led him away.

I tore my yarmulke off and headed for the bus.

43

Bad boy Byron

THE GOOD NEWS Saturday morning: My sister decided to let me take the Elvis record to Byron's. The bad news: It was chilly and slippery outside, with light snow blowing around. A bad day to run for buses. But soon after I'd finished breakfast, Dad popped in with his bakery truck parked outside, coming to the rescue. He had to deliver a special order of cakes for an Elks Club event and was stopping at the house first. He grabbed a quick coffee with Mom in the kitchen, and when he learned that I was headed for Byron's, offered me a ride in the truck.

It was a rare treat. The mid-size truck, painted black with a gold "Duvernoy's Bakery" on the side, carried cartons of breads and pastries on wide shelves with an aisle between them. The magical aroma of baked goods filled every space, including the cab, and clung to your clothes. I tucked the Elvis record into an empty carton and joined Dad up front.

Still in his brown work uniform, Dad perched on the cab's only seat, a small, high one for the driver, and I stood on the metal floor, looking out the big front windshield as we raced up the hill to the Elks Club. Dad drove like the gardener Philippe Lefevre, like he was bronco-busting. I had to hold on to the doorframe leading to the back. After we'd dropped off the cakes, I thanked him for offering the ride. "It's way out of your way," I said.

"So what? You're my favorite son. And I hear you went to Shabbat last night. Good boy."

"How come you only go once a year?" I asked.

"Me? Because I work six nights a week. When am I gonna go?"

"You ever pray?"

"All the time—for my horses to win."

"Ha, ha. You believe in God?"

He looked at me, swerved a little on the wet pavement, looked back at the road. "What are you, my rabbi now? Sure I do. That's how I was brought up."

"Jewish God?"

"What's the difference? God's God. Why, what do they tell you in shul?"

"Oh, stuff about what God did for the Jews and all. But Rabbi Lipschutz—"

"I liked that guy."

"Me, too. He says the important thing is to live a good life, whether you believe in God or not. I'm confused."

"Well you're just a kid, so don't worry about it. After your bar mitzvah you'll be a man and you can figure it out."

"Okay."

"Don't be a worrier."

"Okay."

"It ain't worth it."

"Okay."

Dad let me off in the Fairchild driveway, giving me a box of Duvernoy's powdered jelly doughnuts to bring inside along with the Elvis record. Leena answered the back door and admitted me to the kitchen with raised eyebrows and a grunted *hmm.* I presented the doughnuts. "Would you like some?"

"Uh, uh, thank you. I'm just headed out to go home. Shoulda' been gone an hour ago." She paused and narrowed her eyes at me. "Do Mr. and Mrs. Fairchild know you comin' here today?"

"I don't know, I guess so. Why?"

She shook her head. "Ain't my business. But since you're already here, maybe you can put some sense in those children's heads."

Byron came down the back stairs to the kitchen as she was leaving. "Bye, Leena!" he called.

She looked at him and left without saying anything.

"Hey, Ace," I greeted Byron.

"Hey, man. I saw the bakery truck." He sniffed the air. "I smell cake."

I showed him the doughnuts and he swiped one to his mouth like a pet monkey. White powder and jelly spurts got all over his lips. We cracked up.

"What's with Leena?" I asked..

"Oh, man. Did she say something?"

"She said I should put some sense in you and Keatsie's heads. You 'children'."

He snickered. "She means take some sense *out.* She's still miffed about me going after Betty. The big secret is out, as if everything wasn't messed up already."

"What happened?"

Byron shook his head sadly and went to the giant refrigerator, taking out a bottle of milk. He filled two glasses and we sat at the table washing down the soft doughnuts with big gulps.

"Someone saw us together at the Pix," he said, "one of my father's regular patients. The next time the guy had an appointment with Pater, he ratted me out." Byron pinched up his face and imitated, "'*I saw your son at the movies with a Negro girl.*' Like I was burning the place down or something."

"What did your dad say?"

"Well of course he said, 'I'm not prejudiced.' And then, 'but this kind of thing isn't good for anybody.' I called him a racist and he got mad and said I'd been lying to him and I'd been spoiled and he couldn't trust me, blah, blah, blah, and that I was grounded."

"Grounded?"

"Except for school, I have to stay home until Thanksgiving, and I can't have anyone over."

"Starting when?"

"Today—but don't worry. He's working and then he has some meetings with dental suppliers or something."

"You sure?"

"That's what he said."

"Where's your mom?"

"She's at her literary-discussion group. We call it the 'Literally Disgusting Group' to bug her. She was mad about my sneakiness but she didn't think I should be punished—she's cool about interracial dating. Actually, she and Pop had a fight about it, but nobody ever changes Pater's mind."

"So I shouldn't be here?"

"Mwaa-ha-ha-ha! Zere iss no escape from ze castle, mwaa-ha-ha-ha!" He reached for another doughnut, changed his mind, and spotted the Elvis record in its envelope. "What's that?" he said reaching for it.

I slid it away. "Man, if we get jelly on it my sister will kill me! It's just some new singer for you guys to check out."

I didn't want to explain or play it until Keatsie showed up, but I didn't have to wait long. A few minutes later she bounced in from the dining room, heart-achingly pretty as ever in a cardigan sweater over a green turtleneck and the usual jeans.

"Hey—Aaron! How come nobody told me you were here?"

"He isn't here," Byron said. "I'm not allowed to have friends over."

"You're going to get us all in trouble," she said.

"Why you?" I asked her. "Byron's the troublemaker."

"Because who got into a big fight with Pop sticking up for her ungrateful sibling?"

"But," Byron said, "Pop didn't punish *your* bad self."

"Yeah, thanks to Mom."

"Doughnut?" I offered.

She gazed at the big round puffs. "No, I'd better not. They'll end up in my braces." She drew her lips back so I could get a good look at the silver cage over her upper teeth. "Pop's back on his campaign to make me wear them. I hate the stupid things. They're hideous."

"No, they're cute," I said. "Like a little tooth bracelet."

She laughed. "You mean barbed-wire fence. Hey—what's that record?"

Keatsie decided we should listen to Elvis on the big radio-phonograph console in the penthouse party room. There, as we sat down and listened, Elvis's voice rang out much bigger than on Joannie's little machine, with more twang and louder bass notes from the band. After the first playing of "That's All Right, Mama," I told them what I knew about the Presley craze down south. Keatsie thought she'd heard something about him. By the time we played side two, "Blue Moon of Kentucky," she was crazed herself, out of her lounge chair, doing backward-sliding-crossing steps over the wooden floor, swaying her head, snapping her fingers.

"I told you," I said, enchanted by her movements. "Elvis is the most! He's gone, man!"

"Sort of demented, in an amusing way," Byron said, but even he couldn't resist. He bobbed his head and flapped his sneakers to the beat.

By the fourth or fifth time we'd played both sides, we knew the lyrics and shouted them out along with Elvis, getting hysterical over our attempts to sing southern-country style. Keatsie danced her way to the piano and banged out some of the chords. I hopped to the center of the room to demonstrate Elvis's pelvis-thrusting moves as Joannie had described them. In the midst of our racket we didn't hear Mr. Fairchild arrive at the top of the stairs until he shouted, "*Byron*!"

44

Cheek-to-cheek with Keatsie

😐 ☺ ☺

MR. FAIRCHILD GLARED at his son. "What were you *told*?" Then, aiming a menacing look at me and Keatsie: "Turn off that moronic sound, whatever it is!"

Keatsie shut off the record player and retreated to the piano bench.

Byron stood firm as his father advanced his giant frame into the room. "I asked you," said Mr. Fairchild, "what were you *told*?"

"That I had to stay home."

"And what else?"

"That I couldn't have friends over."

"Then what is this *Schmink* doing here?" Mr. Fairchild said without looking at me.

As Byron's cheeks reddened, Keatsie piped up, "He's visiting *me*. *I* invited him."

"And why would *you* do that?" Mr. Fairchild demanded. His eyes darted between Keatsie and me as if his daughter had brought home a toad.

"Because he's my friend, too. Plus he has a new record I wanted to hear."

"If you're lying for your brother's sake, it's a pretty pathetic attempt," said Mr. Fairchild. He turned back to Byron. "You come downstairs with me. You don't get to have any friends here, whomever invited them."

"*Who*ever," Byron grumbled, getting up and giving me an apologetic look on his way out.

"I'll talk with *you* later," Mr. Fairchild told Keatsie. "Finish playing with your Schmink and then he's going home."

"We're not—"

Mr. Fairchild cut her off with a warning finger. "And no more of that racket from Hell, you understand?

"I better go," I said to Keatsie. We could still hear Byron and his father arguing at the bottom of the stairwell.

"No, no. Stay," she urged. "I don't know why he came home early, but Mom should be back soon."

"Yeah, but I don't want to make problems."

"They're already made, and Byron made them."

I felt pulled in two directions—get out of there before things got worse, or stay in Keatsie's company while I had the precious chance. It was no contest. "Okay," I said, "so what do you want to do?"

Keatsie said we could listen to some of the pop records she had up here if we played them quietly. And a small refrigerator behind the bar held bottles of Pepsi—everything we needed for a small party. We dug through the stack of albums and singles—both 78s and 45 rpms—and pulled out records including Bill Haley's "Rock Around the Clock," "Love Is a Many Splendored Thing," by the Four Aces, "Sincerely" by the McGuire Sisters, and Al Hibbler's "Unchained Melody."

Keatsie placed the records on the automatic changer, Haley's rock-and-roll first. After half a minute of sitting and listening, before I could down two swallows of soda, she was up doing her crouched-over, crazy-legged, finger-popping dance, mouthing the lyrics, shaking her head as if a wasp had nested in her hair.

"C'mon," she said as she slid by, hands extended.

I'd have been happy just to watch her, but now I fell into a nervous ecstasy as we locked fingers and pinwheeled to the center of the room.

"Wait," she said. "Phew—hot!" She stopped to take off the cardigan and throw it toward the piano. She grabbed one hand again and I placed the other around her waist to start a lindy, nudging her out and turning her under my arm. Each time we returned to the side-by-side position and my hand recorded the feel of her waist through the jersey, I wanted to hold the sensation forever. But the rock and roll music wouldn't allow it; the lindy soon turned into a free-for-all form of shaking and shimmying that left us flushed and breathless.

"You're a good dancer," she huffed.

"Not as good as you," I puffed.

When the ballad "Sincerely" came on, we stood facing each other awkwardly for a moment before she shrugged and put a hand on my shoulder. "You can slow-dance, right?"

"I don't know. We did it in gym. And sometimes my sister practiced with me."

"I wish I could get Byron to dance. Come on then."

With that, I held her in a foxtrot position, a respectful distance apart, and swayed in approximately the box-step pattern I'd learned in gym class and later study of Arthur Murray dance diagrams: *one-two, feet together; three-four, feet together.* I felt clumsy. My palms were oozing sweat. Even with the sides of our faces about three inches apart I thrilled at the nearness of our cheeks, the pocket of warmth they formed.

The McGuire Sisters songs ended. We stood still until Al Hibbler's began.

"Don't sway so much," she said. "Relax more."

How else could I take that but as a call to bring her closer, slow down, dance like lovers in a movie? But I dared do so only in stages: lowering the hands held in the air; bringing her waist an inch closer. Shortening my steps. Now another inch closer. Her chest bumped against mine for a second and she jumped back, then returned half way. But she allowed our faces to touch lightly—more than just allowed: she had to bend down for our cheeks to match up. The contact felt as intimate as a kiss to me. A whole network of sensations lit up and rang bells like a pinball machine.

Al Hibbler crooned how much he needed a certain someone's love, exactly my situation at the moment. I felt I had to say something as we shuffled slowly in place; it seemed lame and immature not to make conversation.

"How's your barfing?" I asked, immediately thinking, *You idiot, you just blew it*!

But to my relief she laughed. "Pretty good. How's yours?"

"No more barfing. I hope I never have to again. You, too."

"Yeah. Well I'll have to stay away from everyone who upsets me."

"Like Rizzo?"

"Yeah, that type."

"Like Paul LeFevere?"

She seemed to stiffen a little. "Paul? He doesn't upset me."

"But—"

"I don't want to talk about it. But if you think I barf every time I see him, I don't."

"Okay," I said, ears burning. "What about me?"

"What about you?"

"Didn't I upset you that time at the movies."

"Are you still thinking about that? I guess I got weird. It was just . . . you know. But you're too nice to be upsetting."

"You think I'm nice?"

"Such a nice boy," she said, mockingly it seemed.

"Well I wrecked the inside of a mansion last month." I blurted, as surprised as anyone to hear the confession come out. "That's not so nice."

Keatsie stopped moving and let go of my hand. Al Hibbler was moaning his final plea for love. "What are you *talking* about?" she said.

"My delinquent friend Rocco and me? We broke into a mansion and smashed everything we could. Railing, mirrors, chandeliers."

"What mansion?"

"Never mind. Near my house. It looked something like yours."

The Four Aces hit the turntable with their romantic ballad, but the dancing was over.

"Why are you telling me this?" she asked.

"I don't know. Because you think I'm so *nice*. I can be a delinquent, too."

"So what does that prove?"

"You know, maybe I'm your type? I could be more than just a friend?" Even as I spoke I realized I was yakking out of insane desperation and coming dangerously close to confessing I'd read her diary. *I should be nice to Aaron, even if he's not exactly my type, whatever that is. . . . I like him a lot, but not in a boyfriend way.*

"Are you crazy"? Keatsie said. "You think delinquents are my type? What's wrong with you?"

The words that welled up inside me and almost reached my lips were *I love you! That's what's wrong with me!* Even if I could mouth those words to anyone, I couldn't dare say them to Keatsie, knowing how they'd be received. But she must have seen something pathetic in my expression as I stood there limp and longing.

"I"m sorry, Aaron. I don't know why you say some things."

"I don't either. I'm a jerk when I get nervous."

"Why are you nervous?"

"You know."

She wrinkled her brow, tilted her head, as if she wasn't sure who I was. "Well, we should go downstairs before my father comes up. It was fun dancing anyway. Thanks for bringing the record."

I didn't see Byron or Mr. Fairchild on our way downstairs, but Mrs. Fairchild awaited us in the parlor. "I was just coming up," she said. "Aaron, I thought I would give you a ride home, if that's all right."

I made noises that I could take the bus, but given the wet weather outside I welcomed the offer. Keatsie asked if she could come along, a sign at least that she didn't despise me. But Mrs. Fairchild said no. "Your father wants you to stay put."

"Why? I didn't *do* anything?"

"I think both you and Byron hurt his feelings. And were dishonest."

"Mom—"

"We can talk about it later."

"Where are they now? Can Aaron at least say good-bye to Byron?"

"Byron's in his room, where he should have been. And Pop is in the library—best not to bother him now."

It felt uncomfortable leaving, but Mrs. Fairchild put me at ease as we cruised along in her Cadillac. In that drawling manner of hers that I liked so much, she asked me how it had gone with Rabbi Lipschutz. ". . . he's such a del-i-i-i-ghtful man," I said I thought he was great.

"We-l-l-l, that's good to hear. If either I or Mrs. Bender can be of any more help, just let me know."

"Thanks," I said. "Can you get me out of the whole bar mitzvah?"

She laughed. "You're joking, right?"

"Sort of. But I guess it's okay. I think I'm finally ready."

"It'll be lovely, I'm sure."

45

Turkey time

☺ ☺ ☺

DURING the short week before Thanksgiving I got two apologies, one of them from Moshe after class at shul. Before I headed upstairs to practice with the cantor, Moshe stopped me to say he was sorry for the way his father had bullied me Friday evening at Shabbat.

"I know Papa's upset about my mother, but believe me, he can be a real *farbissener* any time."

"*Farbissiner*? What's that?"

"Eh, bitter about everything. A sourpuss and a pain."

"Oh. Sorry about that. But it's another cool word."

"Oh I got plenty of those, man. When's your bar mitzvah?"

"December third."

"So bring your parents some *nahkes* for a change. It means make 'em proud."

"*Nahkes*, I like that. I'll give 'em mucho nahkes. Thanks, man."

He nodded and held out his hand. "Have a nice Thanksgiving."

I endured his powerful grip, trying not to wince. "Thanks. You, too."

The other apology was from Byron during school, for letting me come to the house after he'd been forbidden to have visitors. "I had no idea Pop's meeting would be cancelled," he said. "But you and Keatsie amused yourselves okay, right?"

I wasn't sure how I should reply. "Yeah, it was fine. Did she say anything?"

"Not to me."

To bury the topic, I asked what he'd be doing for Thanksgiving.

"Just the usual stuff. Thursday we serve turkey to po' folk at the Unitarian Church—even Pop comes to show off his carving talent. Then Friday through Saturday we go to my Aunt's fancy estate in Long Island." (He pronounced *Aunt* like *Ahhnt* instead of *Ant*, like me.) "That's Pop's sister and her family. They're surprisingly cool, actually. What about you?"

"We always go to my *Ahhnt* Sarah's in Brooklyn. She and my mother laugh so hard they pee when they get together. It'll be fun. After that, I'm not sure. I have to work on my bar mitzvah speeches. And then Saturday is my birthday."

"Oh yeah? Happy birthday in advance, young man."

"Thanks, old fart."

Aunt Sarah's house was just a small stucco one off a big boulevard, but Joannie and I had always lived in apartments and were enchanted by the idea of your own little castle, with two toilets and a basement, a garage, and patch of grass. My mother's sister lived there with her husband Bernie and my cousins Richie and Bobby, now ages fourteen and eleven.

When we arrived I inhaled the aromas of roast turkey and oniony stuffing, then headed right for the basement with the boys to play with their Lionel model-train village. Uncle Bernie had set it up over the years, a huge platform with trees and hills and tunnels and rail crossings, stores and businesses and houses with lights, barns and animals, and all kinds of people, some of them moving when the trains came by. Richie took the controls, elbowing his younger brother away, but he let us have brief turns after he'd run the trains through every possible route.

At dinner, after Uncle Bernie said a few words about being thankful, I sat at the kids' table with the boys and three young female cousins who mostly giggled at everything we said. With his mouth full of mashed potato, Richie asked me if I had a girlfriend.

"Do *you*?" I asked.

"I ahhft you furf."

"Yeah, sort of," I lied.

He swallowed his food. "So, do you make out a lot with her?"

I shrugged. "Sometimes."

"Me and my babe Rachel? We make out *all* the time."

The girls giggled so hard they almost choked.

"It's too bad you missed Richie's bar mitzvah," Aunt Sarah said to me as I brought my dishes to the kitchen. She and some of the other women were cleaning up as the men and children made their way to the living room and the chairs that were set up next to it. "You'd be dying to get to your own big day. Richie was like a movie star."

I'd had the flu at that time, staying home with Joannie while my parents had gone. Now I was glad I hadn't been there. I didn't want to have to outshine a "star." But today it seemed that every grownup relative here wanted to put pressure on me. My mother's parents could barely walk anymore; her father looked pale and coughed a lot, yet they were still promising to come to my bar mitzvah. "If we have to die doing it," said my grandmother, calling me over and pinching my cheeks, "we want to see this beautiful little face when you become a man."

My Aunt Gail, a widow who lived upstate, told me with a cigarette dangling from her lips, "You better do a good one, Buster. I'm schlepping myself all the way in from the Catskills just to be there."

After a while, the day went the way it always did: Jokes were told; family gossip and memories were shared; parents bragged about their children; some of the kids performed songs; cigarettes and cigars were smoked; plates of nuts and candies were eaten; my father fell asleep; and my mother and Aunt Sarah made each other laugh and said they were going to pee their pants if they laughed any harder.

46

Trouble next door

☹ ☹ 😐

IT WAS LATE when we got home from Brooklyn, and I stumbled into the house half-asleep, barely noticing some scraps of broken furniture scattered in the back parking area. But by lunchtime the next day, after I'd worked a while on my bar mitzvah speeches, we'd gotten the news: The Cabruzzis were gone, kicked out of their apartment by the landlord after a wild and violent scene on Thanksgiving Day.

Mom got the dirt from Marta, the Hungarian-American woman living upstairs, and passed it on to me and Joannie. (Dad was out making some special morning deliveries.)

It all began when Rocco Sr. had come by—from wherever he'd been—to take Rocco Jr. and his mother Adele to a relative for Thanksgiving. For some reason he and Adele got into one of their screaming fights. Rocco Jr. ran out into the hallway crying, and that brought Mario, the landlord's son, charging down from upstairs. Mario, the one who was crazily in love with Adele, pushed into the apartment and went at Rocco Sr. Marta heard so much breakage, so many wild howls and curses, that she called the police. By the time two policemen showed up they had to order an ambulance for Mario, who'd been knocked cold. Rocco Sr. and Adele looked pretty bruised themselves.

Mario's elderly father, the landlord, came up from his basement apartment in a such a rage that the policemen had to hold him back. The cops offered to arrest Rocco Sr., but when Mario gained consciousness and refused the ambulance, the landlord decided not to press charges. He just wanted the Cabruzzis out of the apartment by the end of the day. The family already owed a month's back rent.

"So that's what we missed while we were gone," Mom said. "My heart goes out to poor Adele and Rocco."

"What happened to their stuff?" Joannie asked.

"Marta says that Rocco Sr. grabbed a few things and took off with them. Then later Adele got some people she knows to stuff whatever would fit into their small truck. And then they were gone."

"That poor woman," Joannie said."

"And poor Rocco!" I added. "Do you know where they went?"

Mom shook her head. "I think Adele has a sister and brother-in-law somewhere over on Ferris Avenue, but who knows where they ended up?"

Ferris Avenue was an old, partly Italian neighborhood near downtown, famous for tough street kids. I imagined slight Rocco getting punched out his first day there. I felt I needed to do something, at least talk to him, but I couldn't see how.

When Dad got home and heard the story, he confided that Rocco Sr. was known to gamblers around town as a small-time gangster, a woman-chasing louse who was always in debt. "Better they're outta here," he said.

"No it's not," I argued. "I *liked* Rocco."

"Sure, I feel sorry for the kid. But you got bigger things to think about."

It took a while to get my mind back to those "bigger things," such as what I should say in my speeches—one tiny week away! But when I did return to them I wondered if there was something I could work in about Rocco's life. First, of course, I had to write all the usual stuff: Thanking my parents and other people; lessons to be learned from the holy passages I'd be reading; good deeds or "mitzvahs" that I'd done and would be doing. So far I had one: Every week, when they took up collections at shul, I'd given money from my allowance for trees to be planted in Israel, but so had almost every other student.

I felt pretty confident about the reading and chanting of my Hebrew Torah parts, but their meaning wasn't so easy. Mr. Rubin had helped a little, explaining that they told the story of the twin brothers Esau and Jacob. They'd fought over different things since they were kids, then separated for years, and finally made up. God named Jacob "Israel" and Israel got to be father of the

Jewish land. In another part, God cursed the heck out of Esau's bad nation.

There was a lot more story in my section of the Torah, some really confusing stuff about all these men's wives and daughters and other men "laying" with them and then all the children and children's children who came from Jacob and his wives.

"Those parts you don't have to worry about," Mr. Rubin advised. "The story of Jacob and Esau is plenty."

I was still confused. Jacob was supposed to be the good one in the story compared to Esau. But even in English the biblical language was a lot of mumbo jumbo to me, and I couldn't decide who the bad guys and good guys really were or what all that cursing of Esau's land was about.

On top of that I wanted my speeches to be different, the one at shul not so phony and goody-goody like the models they gave every kid. I wanted it more like it had been written by the real me. And the little speech at the reception, kind of cool and maybe funny. It would be hard putting all these things together. Then, too, I was supposed to show the synagogue speech or at least an outline of it to the rabbi, and I knew he'd hate it.

47

Happy birthday to me

SATURDAY: I was a teenager!

Every November 26 that I could remember, I heard the same thing from my mother: Thanksgiving and my birthday were too much for one week. "It's exhausting," she said. Yet every year she and Dad and even Joannie managed to make a big deal out of my day, with presents, cards, a little money, and some kind of food treat.

Sometimes it was exhausting for me, too, pretending to love some of the square clothes they bought me, like striped socks and winter hats with ear flaps. But this time they hit the target, even though Mom complained about birthday, Thanksgiving, *and* bar mitzvah all at once.

"We could skip the bar mitzvah," I said.

"Don't be a smart-aleck teenager already. Just open your presents."

From Joannie I got a nice pair of black leather gloves, very cool. From my parents, a new five-dollar bill in a card that said they loved me, plus the coolest two-tone windbreaker I could ever imagine them choosing: gray with blue collar and front panels, like the sharpest rockers were wearing. "How'd you pick this out?" I asked Mom, delighted as I tried it on.

"You think I don't know what's in style?"

I'd also gotten cards with money from Aunt Sarah and three other aunts and uncles, including my father's sister Ada in Biloxi. Altogether, with my remaining racetrack winnings and other savings, I now had more than ninety dollars tucked away in my underwear-and-socks drawer—a fortune considering I could buy three new bicycles or go to the movies a hundred and eighty times for that much. Or save it for college.

"Dad has another present for you when he comes home," Mom said.

"What is it?"

"You'll see when he gets here. If he gets here."

I worried that he'd forget and go play poker, but he got home at lunch and made me wait until after he washed up and ate. Then he called me into the bedroom, dug a card out of his wallet, and handed it to me.

"What is it?" I asked, hardly glancing at it. I'd hoped for some surprise in a big box.

"Read it, dummy."

"*One Year Membership, YMCA*. Uh, thanks, Dad. How come?"

"You said you wanted boxing lessons, right? I know the guy there. He's a better teacher than me."

"Really? You'll let me fight?"

"I didn't say fight. Just learn to defend yourself."

"Wow! It's okay with Mom?"

"Yeah, just don't come home with a bloody nose."

"When can I start?"

"After the bar mitzvah," Dad said, "You'll be all through with shul—unless you wanna keep goin."

"Yeah, I'm dying to be a rabbi."

"You could do a lot worse, wise guy."

"I know. Rabbi Lipschutz is the coolest. Anyway, thanks for the present. I love it."

"You're welcome."

"Hey, Dad? How come you were named Israel—the same as Jacob after he wrestled an angel?"

"I was named after my grandfather. Plenty of Jews are named Israel."

"Did you ever wrestle an angel?"

"Yeah—your mother, to get her to marry me."

It was a good birthday, and it got even better later in the day when Byron called to wish me a "pleasurable" one. I thanked him for remembering.

"We remember all things," said the alien.

Before the call ended I was hoping Keatsie might come on the line to say something, anything, but it didn't happen. Still, it was a great day, and at night I drifted off imagining myself in the ring with Sonny Rizzo, landing two stiff jabs, a body blow that bent him over, and then a roundhouse right that sent him flying to the canvas. Keatsie was there cheering.

48

Teenager at home

SUNDAY, my second day as a teen, started out kind of dull, but ended with a weird surprise.

After breakfast Mom and Dad took off for the Bronx, headed for our former neighborhood to go out with their best old friends. Joannie left a while later for a babysitting job. So I had the apartment to myself for part of the morning and all afternoon.

It seemed so quiet without any yelling from the Cabruzzis, and sad, too, as I thought about Rocco. If he'd been home, I probably would have gone over for a while, maybe to hear some more advice about girls. Not that his first advice had worked out so well with Keatsie, but Keatsie wasn't exactly normal, either.

I heard some voices outside and saw Googie and another kid throwing a football around. I could have joined them—it wasn't too cold out. But I was getting really panicky about my speeches. I didn't like most of what I'd written so far.

I made two decisions: I would turn my reception talk into a funny rhymed poem. Nobody expected anything very serious at those lunches. For the shul speech, though, I'd try to tie things in my life to the Torah reading. But just thinking about all that talk in front of a big audience made me sweat and feel a bunch of worms crawling around my stomach.

Could I really say something about Rocco? Or maybe the awful thing I did with Rocco, wrecking that mansion? Did I learn any lessons? Did they have anything to do with the twin brothers Jacob and Esau?

Both of those Bible characters did some pretty bad things themselves. Jacob got most of his older twin's inheritance by trading him a hot meal for it. Then later, Jacob disguised himself as Esau to get his father's blessing, which was meant for Esau. Esau turned bad by marrying women of a forbidden religion. Jacob went off and got conned into working as a slave for his uncle for twenty years. When he decided to come home, he heard that Esau was threatening to attack with his army and kill him. Jacob got scared and prayed a lot, but didn't just rely on God: he also prepared to save his family and land with some sneaky plans and gift offerings.

In the end the twin brothers made up. Jacob became the father of the Jewish tribes, but Esau ruled a non-Jewish land that got cursed by God along with all of Esau's descendants.

Of course, Byron and Keatsie were twins, too. Was one bad and the other less bad? Did Jacob or Esau ever barf when they got scared?

I ransacked my brain, put some rough ideas together, and finally sat at my desk with a pencil and pad. Amazingly, words started coming.

At about two-thirty in the afternoon my mother called from the Bronx to make sure I was all right. "I'm almost a man now," I told her. "You don't have to worry." Then, a half hour or so later, I got a call I'd never have expected in a zillion years.

49

Is it cool to come over?

"HEY, AARON, it's Miki," the caller sang. "How's it going?"

"Miki?" I squeaked. "Uh . . . hi!"

"Hi. Did I surprise you?"

"Sort of. How'd you know my number?"

"From Keatsie, natch. Was it cool for me to call?"

I had to think a second. For me, being called by any girl was pretty cool. Plus, I didn't feel helpless and nervous as I did with Keatsie.

"Sure, it's fine," I said. "Is something wrong?"

"No, no. Here's the deal, man. My sister Yoshi and me, we just visited one of her friends not too far from you? So I asked Yoshi if we could stop and say hello to one of *my* amigos—that's you, hombre. Would that be okay, you know, with you and your parents?"

"Keatsie told you where I live?"

"She tells me everything, man."

"Oh-oh. Well, okay—I mean, *si*! Come over. It's just me here anyway. Where are you?"

"At a pay phone in—where are we, Yoshi?" I heard her sister name the next town over. "Valhalla," Miki repeated. "Catch you in ten."

Now I did feel a little bit nervous as I peeked through the front windows and saw Miki get out of the car. She wore sunglasses, a beret cap, and a big scarf, looking small but cute as ever. I'd combed my hair and put on a plaid shirt, my good jeans, and the foot-killing penny loafers. But what was I supposed to do after she came in? I'd never had a female visitor of my own. What would Rocco do?

But Miki seemed nervous herself when I let her in, which made me feel better. Replacing the sunshades with her regular glasses, she peered around the front room and into the livingroom.

"My sister's waiting in the car, so I can only visit a little while," she said. "But how about coming for a ride with us?"

"A ride? Where to?"

"Just around your neighborhood. I want to see it."

"Really? How come?"

She shrugged. "You know. Just to see it. Where do you sleep, in this room?"

"No, it's my sister's. Mine's by the kitchen."

"Can I see?"

I said okay, thinking I'd left the room neat enough, and led her down the hall. Again, she took it all in with her dark eyes—the sofa-bed, my desk, the entrance to the kitchen.

"I was writing my bar mitzvah speech," I said. "It scares me to think about it."

"But you're a good writer."

"Did Keatsie say that?"

"Keatsie, Keatsie, Keatsie," Miki said, wagging her head. "I can figure some things out myself, you know. And I bet it'll be one hip bar mitzvah, right? I'd like to go."

"To the synagogue? You kidding?"

"Nope."

"You're being funny."

"No I'm not. And anyway you're the funny one. Hey, could you do that James Dean thing for me again?"

"You mean—" I bent over, put my hands in my pockets, and scrunched up my face in pain. "*You're tearing me apart! Miki—you're tearing me apart!*"

She laughed hard, staggering backward. "Oh, man—you should do your whole bar mitzvah in that voice."

I kept the Dean pose: "*And Jacob said unto the Lord, 'Esau didn't kill nobody, man—I got the bullets, look!*" I kept going as Miki was collapsing. "*And the Lord said, 'Solid, man, I dig you cats the most' And what do we learn from this?*"

"Stop," she begged. "Stop. Oh, man, I *got* to go to that cuh-ray-zy bar mitzvah."

"I think anyone who likes to be bored can come," I said. "I'll check. Just don't make me laugh there or anything."

She wanted to see the rest of the apartment. I showed her the tiny kitchen and the back porch leading to Rocco's. I told her a little about the Cabruzzis before she had to get back to the car. She pleaded with me to come just for a short ride. I said okay, enjoying the attention now. I scrawled a note to let my parents know.

Miki's sister put away the book she was reading as we got in the car. The three of us fit comfortably in the wide front seat, Miki in the middle. She introduced me to Yoshi and I reached over to shake the extended hand. Yoshi looked about nineteen or twenty, hair longer and face thinner than Miki's, voice a little deeper.

"So," Yoshi said, "you're a friend of my crazy-cat sister?"

"Uh, yeah. But I dig crazy cats."

"True, they're the best. Are you also a jazz nut?"

Miki interrupted. "It doesn't matter, Yoshi." She turned to me. "My sister goes to music school in New York. We're all music-crazy in this family."

"No," Yoshi teased, "we just like music. Miki's the crazy one."

Miki urged her to start driving. "I want to see the ledge that Byron walked across," she said.

"How—" I stopped myself. "Oh, I know—Keatsie told you. I hate to even remember it. The parkway is just down the hill if you really want to see."

"I don't get the point of this tour," Yoshi said to me, starting the car, "but Miki never takes no for an answer." She laughed as Miki bumped her with an elbow.

We stopped across from the ledge. Chubby and Brent from the neighborhood were there, leaning over it and smoking.

"You know these guys?" Miki asked. "Okay if I go over and look down?"

"Yeah, I guess. They're just jerks."

Since I had to get out to let her go, I went over with her, nodding to the other two but leading Miki several yards away from them. She looked down at the parkway. "Man," she said, "that *is* scary. No wonder you barfed."

"God, is there anything Keatsie didn't tell you?"

"Well, I was interested."

"How come?"

She hesitated, as if deciding whether to blurt something out. "Just interested," she said.

As we started back to the car, Chubby threw a cigarette butt over the ledge and turned my way. "Hey, that your little girlfriend?"

Dickie snickered. "Where'd you get *her*?" he said, then mumbled something like *Jap and Jew* under his breath that made Chubby laugh. I stopped and looked at them wondering what I had the courage to do.

But Miki tugged me away and back to the car. "Come on," she said, "I don't want any more heroics."

As we drove off I gave the high sign to the two jerks and they gave it back, shaking their fists.

"I'm taking boxing lessons after the bar mitzvah," I said. "No more jive from these clowns."

Yoshi laughed. "You'll have to fight a whole lot of clowns. They insult Asian people every day."

"I'll fight next to you," Miki said. She threw two karate punches toward the windshield. Yoshi laughed again.

I thought I would show the two of them my former school and the old farm at the end of the street, and then head home. But Miki had another idea. "I want to see the mansion you wrecked."

Yoshi said, "*What*?" and I was shocked, too. Of all the things Keatsie should have kept secret it was that. Before I could stammer something Miki said, "It's okay—everybody gets mad sometimes. I once smashed a mirror in the girl's room at school. Bad luck."

"I don't know . . . ," I said. "I mean, it was already kind of wrecked. We just wrecked it some more inside."

"We?" Miki said.

"Me and Rocco next door. We pretended the mansion was everything we were mad at. But Rocco had real reasons to be mad. I feel stupid about mine now."

"What did you wreck?"

"Chandeliers. Lots of mirrors. That's tons of bad luck now that I think of it."

Yoshi slowed the car down. "Well, where is this bad-luck place?"

Miki looked at me, then her sister. "That's okay," she said. "We don't have to go there." She gave my hand a little pat as if I were the disappointed one. I liked the touch.

50

Byron's secret

😐 ☺ 😐

I ALREADY had a load of stuff on my mind when Byron added his new secret to the pile. As we left math class, he stopped, looked around, and said, "Guess who I was with yesterday?"

"I don't know. Alien beings?"

"No, that was Saturday. I was out with Betty yesterday."

"No lie!"

"No lie. And it was her idea, too. She had to go to White Plains Hospital to visit an aunt and said we could meet after. It was perfect, because the same day I was playing touch football with some kids at my old school—you know, it's near the hospital? I didn't even have to make something up."

"Man! What did you guys do?"

"Mostly walked around holding hands. It got kind of cold but we didn't care. Oh yeah, we went into a drugstore for a hot chocolate and the guy said he couldn't serve us."

"Really? That's stinks. Did you say anything?"

"Of course. First I gave him the world-famous Fairchild sneer"—Byron made a snooty face, looking down his long snoot—"then I said, 'Well *we* don't wish to be served by a prejudiced ignoramus."

"Ignoramus! Cool. What happened?"

"He chased us out, and naturally I couldn't help knocking over a candy rack before we took off running. We were laughing so hard we almost forgot how mad we were."

I was excited for them, proud of Byron, but also worried that they'd get in trouble. I didn't have a secret to share, but I told him all about Miki's visit, including how Keatsie had blabbed to her about me.

"Keatsie is the blab queen," Byron said. "But what do you care? Miki obviously craves you in spite of your many imperfections. Do you like her?"

"I do," I said. It felt like I was just learning the news. "I like her a lot."

"So there you go. Keatsie's all flustered over some ape of the week anyway."

"Really? Who now?"

He shrugged. "I don't really keep up."

Before we parted, I made sure he knew he could come to the bar mitzvah if he wanted. I had already invited him to the reception after my parents said it was okay to have one friend there. But as for the synagogue, he said, "I? Enter a house of *worship*?"

"They told me everyone is welcome, even Martians."

"Yeah? Can I bring Betty?"

"Sure," I said, imagining how the two of them would be received. "If you want to cause a riot."

"I can't go where she's not welcome."

"I don't blame you," I said. "I wish *I* didn't have to go."

51

The holy shawl

THAT EVENING at schul, Mr. Rubin gave us a lesson in the "tallit," the big shawl worn by prayer leaders and other Jewish "adults"—usually males over thirteen. They put it on, he said, during morning prayers, certain holy days, and other occasions. My parents had already bought a version of the shawl for me to wear on Saturday.

As he spoke, Mr. Rubin held up a long rectangle of cloth that seemed half the size of my bedsheet. White in the middle with black stripes toward the ends, it had short fringes at the bottoms and long knotted strings called *tzitzit* at each of the four corners.

"Sometimes it's worn like this," he said, draping it over his head and shoulders, "but mostly like this." He lowered the shawl to drape it only around his shoulders with the fringes in front, at belt level. I noticed it had a collar pattern where it wrapped around his neck. "Some men wear a sort of tallit vest under their outer garments all morning and night," he said, "but I don't expect any of you to do so unless you're very religious."

Or really uncool, I wanted to say, but I saw Mr. Rubin looking at me as if expecting a wisecrack. He smiled slightly and said, "Mr. Schmink, since you'll have the honor of wearing your first tallit this Saturday, you should take it seriously."

"I am," I said. My urge for mischief dissolved into a wave of nerves as I thought about the upcoming performance.

"The tallit," he continued, "reminds us to obey the laws God gave the Israelis, and thus avoid the temptations of the flesh."

I heard a titter from the back. Mr. Rubin shot a look there, and I turned around to see Frankie Solomon's pale cheeks turn pink. "I believe your bar mitzvah is in March?" Mr. Rubin said to Frankie. "So maybe then you'll grow up."

Mr. Rubin picked up a Bible from his desk and continued the lesson. "The Old Testament tells us how God introduced the tallit ritual to Moses." He opened the Bible and read: "'*Speak unto the children of Israel, and bid them that they make them fringes in the borders of their garment throughout their generations, and that they put upon the fringe of the garment a ribband of blue.*'

"'Ribband' is a fancy word for ribbon," Mr. Rubin explained. "God next instructed that the Israelis should look at this fringe to remember all His commandments and to do them. '*And that ye not seek after your own heart and your own eyes* ' In other words, don't go looking for trouble and getting into it.

"So," Mr. Rubin continued, putting the Bible back and picking up the shawl, "the tallit is one such garment with fringes, which we call tzitzit. In the modern day we have four tzitzit, woven with a bunch of little knots. Each knot stands for one of the many commandments that guide the Jewish faith. The tallit is a holy garment to be treated with respect. The full-size one for adults can be worn at home for prayers, but never in the bathroom."

He looked at both me and Frankie to stop any wisecrack in its tracks. "Questions?"

"What do the stripes stand for?" one of the students asked.

"Blue sometimes stands for Israel. The black may symbolize certain tribes, or for some Jews the destruction of the Temple in Jerusalem and the exile of the Jews—" He glanced at his watch. "But this is a longer story. If you'll excuse me, I have to go see Rabbi Klein for about five, ten minutes, before he leaves. Can you behave yourselves that long? Don't touch the tallit."

As soon as he was gone I had to stifle an urge to grab the shawl, put it over my head, and amuse Frankie by imitating a woman wearing a big kerchief. *How about a hot date, Frankie boy?* Frankie looked like he could use a good laugh. But I thought, with all the bad luck I'd earned from breaking those mirrors, I wasn't going to insult anything supposed to be holy. Besides, I saw Moshe waving at me from his corner and I didn't want to kill our new friendship. So I gave Frankie a laugh with an imitation of Mr. Rubin—"Grow up already, Mr.

Solomon, or I'll put you in diapers!"—and went over to Moshe to ask about his mother.

"She's about the same," he said, "but my father is driving me *meshuge*. Did you know I was supposed to be bar mitzvahed two months ago? He's breaking all the rules, but he still keeps putting it off because he says he can't deal with it now. I'm supposed to wait till she's dead and can't see it?"

"Man, I hope not. You did all the study already? For the bar mitzvah?"

"Yeah, everything."

"So how come you're still hanging around here?"

"To get away from him."

"Hey," I said, "you want to come to my bar mitzvah on Saturday?"

Moshe looked pleasantly surprised. "Sure, I'd like to if I can get away. Thanks! Sometimes I go to Saturday services anyway."

"You can watch me screw up."

"Don't worry. Even a schmuck becomes a man afterwards."

52

Ringing off the hook

WEDNESDAY. Less than three days remained before I would take the stage before a synagogue full of people expecting big things of me: Perfect performance of the ritual. Correct Torah reading. Nice chanting. Beautiful speech, including descriptions of the *mitzvahs*—good deeds that I'd been doing or planning.

My immediate family would be there rooting for me in their hearts, gazing at me like I was the Messiah. Around them more family and some friends, waiting to be impressed. And then the regular Saturday congregation, eager for the service to be done with, or angry that some kid was interrupting their serious rituals. I felt nervous enough when I had to stand and read something aloud in school; now I was wrestling with panic.

But at least I had my synagogue and reception speeches written, and pretty much the way I wanted them except for the mitzvahs—my weekly contributions for trees in Israel didn't seem like enough. Still, I practiced reading the words aloud every minute I could, closing myself off when anyone else was home, refusing to let anyone in the family read them.

After dinner, the phone in the hallway started jangling about every fifteen minutes, calls for Joannie, calls for Mom, and some for me. Out-of-town relatives and family friends asking for details about the events and wishing me luck.

Joannie picked up the next ring and called me over. "Some girl named Miki?" she said. "You're very popular tonight." I grabbed the phone and shooed her away.

"Hi," Miki greeted. "Sorry to bother you. I just called to say I had a nice time Sunday."

"Oh—Thanks. I did, too."

"Did what?"

"Had a nice time," I said.

"Really? I bet you think I'm crazy."

"No. I mean, maybe a little, in a good way."

"What else?" she said.

"What else what?"

"What else do you think about me?"

"Umm, I don't know. Nice things."

"Like?"

"Uh, you're smart. Pretty. Very cool."

"Thanks! Hey, by the way I hear you like Elvis Presley."

"Gee, I wonder who told you."

"Yeah. But I like him, too! They've been playing him on the radio. And guess what his middle name is."

"I didn't know he had one."

"It's Aaron! Elvis Aaron Presley, Jr.!"

"You kidding?"

"I kid you not, man. Yoshi found it out somewhere. It's Aaron, just like you. What do you think of that?"

I thought a moment. I loved it, of course. And for telling me, Miki deserved an Elvis imitation. *Well that's all right mama*, I sang to her.

She laughed. "You're so funny. But I gotta go. See you. Bye!"

Joannie asked about Miki and I brought her up to date, glad to have something else to think about besides the bar mitzvah. Things quieted down for about an hour after that, and then the phone rang again.

"Who's that calling so late?" Mom asked from the living room.

I hurried and picked it up, thinking it might be Miki again, but it was a struggling, wisp of a voice I didn't recognize until it said, "It's me, man, Rocco."

"Hey, man!" I didn't know what to say, after all that had happened to him. "Uh, you okay?"

Mom wanted to know who it was and I yelled, "Just a friend." I asked Rocco again if he was okay, and the answer was a whimper I couldn't quite understand.

"I can hardly hear you," I said. "Where are you?"

"I *ain't* okay," he said with a little more volume. "I ain't even supposed to be using the phone, so I gotta talk quiet. I'm at my Aunt Marie's and Uncle Don's apartment, but they don't want us here and we got no place to go."

"Jeez. How come they don't want you?"

There was a pause. Then, meekly, "'Cause I took some money outta a drawer and got caught."

"You stole from them?"

"No, man! I just wanted to help my mother. We ain't got nothin'! We didn't have no chance to take our stuff, we don't got no money, we don't even got our clothes. I'm gonna kill my old man if I ever see him. He beat on me and my mother. I'll stab him with a butcher knife, man."

"Did you give back the money?"

"'Course. After they found out. They didn't want us here anyway. They're afraid of my old man. And we had to sleep in the cold living room, with me on the floor. Maybe you can help us out, you know?"

"Me?

"I don't know nobody else to call, man. You're my best friend."

I hadn't realized I was, but he sounded so miserable I felt as sorry for him as for anyone.

"All's we need is a little money for a month's rent somewheres," he said, starting to talk fast. "Like fifty bucks. My old lady's got some money comin' from welfare and she's gettin' a job in a supermarket. Then later we can take my old man to court. You still got that money from the horse races? I'll pay you back."

"She know you're asking?"

"Ma? She don't know nothin'. She just keeps cryin'."

I was silent, trying to figure out what to do.

"You know where the bus terminal is at?" Rocco said. "The one by the train station? I can walk there and meet you. Maybe you could bring the money tomorrow, after school?"

I had shul tomorrow after school, an important meeting with Mr. Rubin and maybe Rabbi Klein, the last before the bar mitzvah.

"I gotta go in a minute," Rocco said. "We really need the help, man." His voice was breaking into sobs. "They're gonna throw us out on the street."

I took a breath. "Okay. I'll see you there at three-thirty, okay? But then I have to hurry somewhere else."

"You'll bring the money?"

"Yeah. Some."

I heard a man's shrill voice yelling in the background, getting louder. Rocco hung up quickly without a goodbye.

53

Mitzvah

😐 😐 ☺

JUST ABOUT any bus in town ended its route at the central terminal, near the train station. Right after school I jumped on one headed in that direction and got there about ten minutes before Rocco was supposed to show up. A zippered pocket of my coat held an envelope with two twenty-dollar bills and two tens. I patted the area every few minutes to make sure nothing had disappeared.

I didn't see Rocco outside the terminal and it was cold, so I went inside to the long, heated waiting room. It lived up to its bad reputation. Through a cloud of cigarette and cigar smoke I saw men who looked like they'd been sitting or sleeping there for years, in the same rumpled clothes. Besides smoke, the place smelled of bodies, liquor-breath, bathroom stench, and greasy hot dogs and fries being cooked behind a snack counter. Some older guys gathered in a small group, joking and swearing, and a few tough-looking kids sprawled on benches or leaned against the grimy walls. Regular-looking people came through, too, but they didn't stay long after warming up. I touched the zippered pocket again.

When Rocco hadn't shown by a quarter-to-four, I went outside again to look for him. It stank out there, too, with long lines of busses coughing exhaust fumes. Trains ran their engines nearby, waiting to pull into the main station.

I was getting nervous; I was supposed to be at shul by four o'clock and it was already that time. Just as I was ready to leave, Rocco appeared at the end of the boarding area, walking as if in pain and hugging himself against the cold. He wore only a light windbreaker and jeans, no gloves.

"Sorry, man," he panted when he reached me. "I can't walk too fast in these shoes." I looked down to see the remains of what had once been black gym sneakers, worn almost to shreds. "I couldn't find my loafers," he said, shivering. "Me and my ma we didn't have time to take nothin'. Okay if we go inside?"

We found space on one of the benches, but some scary guys glared at us and I was afraid to take out the money. Rocco looked a little scary himself, still bruised, hair a mess, face pale and thin. He suggested we go into the men's room.

"In here," he said, leading the way into an empty stall and closing the door, which didn't lock, behind us.

"Man, it stinks here," I said, feeling sickened. I unzipped the pocket and took out the envelope. "Sixty bucks," I said, holding on to it.

"Sixty! Oh man, thank you! You're really *savin'* us, no lie."

"Promise to give it to your mother?"

"I swear to God."

"To use for rent?"

"We have to. We ain't got no place."

"And you'll pay it back?"

"I promise. Not—not for a little while, maybe."

"That's okay. It's for college." Right away I felt stupid for saying that. Sure, college for fancy Aaron, compared to a place to sleep and something to eat for Rocco and his mother. If this was going to be a mitzvah, it didn't matter if I ever got it back or not. "Yeah, whenever you can," I added, knowing that could mean never

Someone banged on the stall door and opened it part way. A big guy in a worker's uniform. Through a dangling cigarette he barked, "What're you two doin' in there?"

We scooted out past him. Rocco took the envelope, put it deep in a front pocket. "I gotta go. She needs it fast, you know?"

"Don't get robbed."

"I won't, I'm goin' right back." He stuck his hand out. "Friends, right?"

"Friends," I said, taking the freezing paw.

54

Final prep

I DIDN'T KNOW which bus or busses to take to the Hebrew Institute, so I walked there in a hurry, arriving out of breath and more than a half-hour late. Mr. Rubin acted as if I were invisible and continued his lesson about Chanukah, the holiday coming up about a week after my bar mitzvah. It seemed interesting, but my mind wandered all over the place, from Rocco to Miki to Keatsie to Byron and Betty to my talk in front of all the people who might show up at the synagogue. By the time I relaxed enough to focus, the class had ended.

Mr. Rubin came over to my seat. "What happened? Everything all right?"

"Yeah. I had to do something. A mitzvah."

"Oh, a mitzvah? Well that's good. You and I have a meeting, remember, so maybe you can tell me about it. I'll be back in five minutes."

I had time to chat briefly with Moshe and Frankie before they left the room. I reminded them to come Saturday if they wanted to. Neither was sure they could make it. When Mr. Rubin returned, he sat next to me on one of the classroom chairs. He crossed his long legs and folded his hands over a knee.

"I'm afraid Rabbi Klein had an emergency call," he said, "so he won't be joining us. He said he wishes you good luck and that he'll see you there. He asked me to answer any questions and to go over your speech with you if you need."

I felt a shudder of relief. The Rabbi might have insisted on seeing the speech, which I hadn't even brought. "I have a question," I said. "Can anyone at all come to the bar mitzvah?"

"I suppose, as long as there's room. You expecting thousands?"

"I hope not! I'm pretty nervous already."

"It's normal. Everyone's afraid of an audience. I was afraid, too. Don't worry, the courage comes when you need it. You'll do very good, I know it."

"Will you be there?"

"No, regretfully I won't be able to make it. I have a family obligation. I'm sorry."

"It's all right. You were in the Korean war, right?"

He shrugged. "What's that got to do with anything?"

"I don't know. About being afraid?"

"Who told you about me?"

"Rabbi Lipschutz from the JCC? He said you were wounded and everything."

"'Everything' is the word. How do you know Lipschutz?"

I explained how he'd been asked to advise me.

"He's a smart cookie," Mr. Rubin said. "He's not Orthodox, but I'm sure whatever he told you is good advice. A non-religious kid like you should probably be in the Reform temple anyway."

It seemed a good moment to get something off my mind. "My speech isn't very religious," I said. "It's about the stuff you're supposed to say, but in my own words."

"Hmm. Maybe you should show it to me? You know, you should have been practicing the *d'var Torah* with me or the rabbi for weeks already. But you, you like to have your own way of doing things, and then I got busy coaching other students, plus my own work, and time slipped by. Someone should hear it, at least let me see."

"I didn't bring it."

"Oy. You're afraid we wouldn't like it?"

"I guess. I mean, I just wanted it to be my own words."

"That's fine, as long as you're respectful of the religion and the meaning of your Torah reading, which we discussed together. I hope you're not trying to shock anyone."

"No."

"You'll honor your parents?"

"Yes."

"Explain the reading, what it means to you?

"Yes. You helped me a lot."

"I hope. You'll talk about your mitzvah?"

"Yeah. I think I did a good one today."

"Okay. Just remember, I'm the one who coached you. Don't make me look bad."

"I won't."

"I'm still a little concerned. You haven't shown it to anyone? Someone with experience in the ceremony?"

"No."

"You might be saying something very offensive and you wouldn't know until it was too late." Mr. Rubin rubbed his chin, made a clucking sound. "How about this? If you want to read it to me tomorrow morning, you can reach me here. Or at least read it to your pal Rabbi Lipschutz. The bar mitzvah is a sacred, once-in-a-lifetime occasion, Aaron. You don't want to ruin it."

"Okay. I'll be really careful."

"Oh, and one more thing—keep it under seven, eight minutes. Nobody needs to pee in their pants while they're waiting for you to change the world."

I laughed. "Okay. Thanks for all your help and everything, Mr. Rubin."

To my surprise he reached over and gave me a quick hug. "You're a smart-aleck, Aaron, a real *lets*, but you're a good student and you read the Hebrew very nicely. If I don't see you back in shul, good luck. Do me proud."

"I'll try," I said. This time—knowing him to be a soldier—I felt a current of strength and courage as I shook his hand.

55

Barf boy

MY MOTHER fried an egg for my breakfast Friday, and I told her I couldn't stand the smell of it.

"Since when?" she said. "You always love a nice egg. Besides, you need the nourishment."

I waved the offering away like it was a plate of worms. I tried eating some Cheerios instead but felt queasy after a few spoons. "My stomach doesn't feel good," I moaned.

She looked horrified, as if the world was about to collapse. "Oy, one day before his bar mitzvah?"

"Don't worry, Mom," Joannie said from across the table. "It's just nerves. I get the same thing."

Mom studied me. Touched her fingers to my forehead. "No fever. Do you feel like throwing up? Do you have—"

"*No*, Mom, I just think I should stay home today. I need to practice some more. It doesn't matter if I miss a school day."

"I don't know. . . I have to go to work and I don't like you staying home by yourself."

"I'll be okay. I'll just be practicing in my room."

"Well . . . Dad will be home by the afternoon. I could make you a sandwich . . . If you really need to practice . . . ."

She persuaded herself to give in, saying she'd call later. After she and Joannie cleared out, I paced around in pajamas, fighting my butterflies until I felt a touch of hunger and nibbled at a piece of bread and jelly. There was nothing to do then but take out my synagogue speech—which I'd copied on to note cards—and read it again and still again, hunting for things sure to ruin the ceremony, offend the Jews, shame my parents, and disgrace myself forever. As I did so, trying to put myself in everyone else's shoes, I could no longer tell what I wanted to say from what I didn't. I needed help.

I thought of calling Mr. Rubin, since he'd offered. But what if he wanted me to make a change I didn't like? It would be hard to say no to my bar mitzvah teacher and a pretty cool guy as it turned out. But Rabbi Lipschutz felt more like a friend, more understanding. I decided to try him first.

I got nervous and a little dizzy as I dialed the number he'd given me. A woman answered and said in a raspy impatient voice that the rabbi wasn't there. I asked when he'd be available. She said she didn't know.

"Could he call me back later?" I asked.

"Who is this?"

"Aaron Schmink."

"What do you want him for?"

"I need his advice for my bar mitzvah speech."

"Is you bar mitzvah with us?"

"No."

"Look, the rabbi is very busy on Friday."

"Please just tell him I called?"

She sighed. "Give me your number. I'll leave it, but like I told you . . . ."

It sounded pretty much like I wouldn't hear from him. A touch of panic crept in. I looked at the note cards and the words seemed like some kind of foreign code, making no sense. The more I looked the more a cold sweat chilled my arms and forehead. I started thinking about the bad luck I might have brought on myself. Something stepped on my stomach and triggered a dry heave. I hurried to the bathroom, leaned over the toilet, and returned the Cheerios and the bread and jelly to the universe.

Strangely, that helped a little. I washed the foul taste out of my mouth and drank some water. The words and their meaning came into focus again, but still left me wondering how they'd be taken by my family, the religious people, and others. I read it aloud once more and made a few small changes.

Parts of the speech were supposed to be humorous. What if nobody laughed? What if people booed or walked out? Maybe the rabbi would pull me away from the reading table and throw me at my screaming, crying family like a scrap of forbidden pork.

I walked back and forth down the hall past the phone, as if that would make it ring. When it finally did, I grabbed my note cards and picked up the receiver. It was my mother.

"Is everything okay, honey?"

"Yeah, fine, Mom."

"What are you doing?"

"I'm practicing."

"Your stomach feeling better? I'm worried."

"It's okay, Mom, but I gotta go. I'm expecting Rabbi Lipschutz to call."

"Rabbi Lipschutz? Why would he call?"

"Just for some advice. Ma—I gotta go."

"Okay, okay. Dad should be there soon."

My father got home at about one o'clock. The baked-goods aroma that he carried with him, which usually stirred my appetite, only tightened my stomach. "How's the Bar Mitzvah Kid doin'? he asked. I told him "fine," and buried my nose in the note cards like a religious scholar.

He washed up and rustled around in the kitchen, banging pans and dishes in his rough style of cooking. He yelled out, "J'u have somethin' to eat?"

"No thanks," I called from my room.

"I think your mother made a sandwich for you. Baloney. You want it?"

"No. You eat it."

"You want an egg?"

"No, Dad! I have to practice."

"You gotta eat somethin.'"

"I will, later."

"You ready for tomorrow?"

I took a breath to calm the flutters. "I think so."

"That's my kid—I mean man."

After lunch he closed himself in his bedroom and tuned the radio to the racing results. Soon I heard him snoring when I passed near the door.

It turned gray outside and started to drizzle. Then, as the afternoon darkened, I heard little ice pellets hitting the windows. The same kind of weather was predicted for tomorrow. Maybe nobody would come.

56

Final advice

TWO O'CLOCK and I still had no appetite. I killed some time looking at tomorrow's clothing outfit: a blue-gray double-breasted suit still smelling of the drycleaners, starched white shirt, and cool tie with a crisscross pattern. My best shoes were shined up and ready to go—ugly Buster Browns, but at least no one would see them from the audience.

At about three o'clock, as I seriously considered letting Mr. Rubin tear the speech apart, the phone rang. Notecards in hand I picked up the receiver and said hello. To my joy, the hoped-for radio voice answered.

"Beau Lipschutz here. What's hap'nin', Cap'n?"

I sighed in relief. ""Hi, Rabbi! Thanks for calling back. Sorry to bother you. The woman who answered said you were busy."

"She always says that. But I have a little time before Shabbat. What's up?"

I poured it out: How nervous and confused I was again about the talk. To be more convincing I confessed that I'd barfed earlier.

"You threw up? That's good. You'll be brave in battle tomorrow."

"But I haven't shown my talk to anyone," I said. "I wanted to do it my own way, but now I can't even tell how it'll sound."

"Hm. I'm surprised you got away without rehearsals. But it happens—we get busy and can't keep track. So Rubin hasn't heard it? Your parents?"

"No. You're the only one I can trust."

"Trust for what?"

"I don't know. I think . . . to understand what I'm trying to say, and maybe know a better way to say it."

"Well, I'm not sure about that, but I'm flattered. You want to read it to me? How long is it?"

"Seven minutes. I timed it."

"Okay, maestro. You're on the air."

I heard him chuckle a few times, but when I finished reading he was silent. Had he left? Fallen asleep? "Hello?" I said.

He spoke. "Sorry. I was just making notes. You wrote all that yourself?"

"Yeah."

"Aaron, I think you *are* going to be a writer one day. That's one of the boldest, most honest bar mitzvah talks

I've heard. And I'm proud you used some of the things we talked about before."

"Really? You like it?"

"Yep. Has some funny parts, too. I like the Yiddish and the big words. And you did a pretty good job with the Torah story. Just a couple of things, though, where I think you might want some small changes."

I thought *uh-oh*; but as we talked I could see how much better Beau understood the bar mitzvah audience than I did. He could see what they'd misunderstand, what I was saying in the wrong way or too many times, what was missing, what would have the opposite effect of what I wanted. For example:

BEAU: "You forgot to thank Rabbi Klein."

ME: "He didn't do anything."

BEAU: "No, he just holds the synagogue together, ran your shul, led prayer services, and tomorrow ushers you into manhood. That's not nothing."

BEAU: "This is not the place to say you don't believe in God. Besides, you're not sure you don't believe, right? Maybe just say you're confused or working it out, if that's the truth."

BEAU: "I wouldn't scold the synagogue for not allowing a Negro to attend. You don't know if that's true. Rabbi Klein happens to be very active in interracial causes."

BEAU: "Did you really wreck that mansion, as you're about to tell everyone?"

ME: "Well, it was already pretty wrecked. We just broke some more stuff inside. It was stupid, just because we were mad at something."

BEAU: "Why mention it in the speech?"

ME: You know, to show I did bad things, like Jacob and Esau."

BEAU: "I'm not going to judge you, but a bar mitzvah is not a confessional for crimes. Have you told your parents?"

ME: "No."

BEAU: "They'll drop dead in front of you. Just . . . I don't think you want to go into those kinds of details and incriminate yourself in a holy ceremony. Not cool, man."

We kept talking—almost a half hour by the time Joannie came home and asked who was on the phone. I waved her off so I could listen. Beau didn't insist on any changes. He said he just wanted to offer me the benefit of his experience, but the speech was up to me."

As I already mentioned," he said, "I think it can be a great speech. But I have to caution you—I may not be the typical audience. Even with changes, if you make them, you'll still be saying things some people won't like. Maybe even the tone itself. Being unconventional is always risky, so just make sure you're willing to take that risk."

"Okay."

"Good luck, then. I wish I could be there, but tomorrow I have to make another bar mitzvah boy into a *mensch*. Let me know how it went when you get a chance."

"So who was it that was so important?" Joannie asked as she passed me in the hall.

"Oh, just Rabbi Beau Lipschutz."

"Oh God, really?" She put a hand over her heart.

"Yeah, he was calling to ask you out on a date, but I told him you were busy."

She made a fist at me. "Keep it up. You won't live till your bar mitzvah.

During dinner Dad was in good spirits but Mom looked as nervous as I was, worrying about how all the arrangements would go tomorrow. Tonight she'd made lamb chops served with mint jelly, usually one of my favorites, but she kept watching me as I picked at my plate, barely interested. She'd get up to feel my forehead. She'd push more water at me. She'd tell me I needed to build up my strength.

Everyone was impressed that Rabbi Lipschutz had called. "Whatever he told you I'm sure was wonderful advice," Mom said.

"Any advice on pickin' horses?" Dad asked.

"Yeah," I said. "Don't sit around waiting for God to help you."

"Just what your old man always says."

Again the phone jangled late into the evening: more calls from relatives and friends just arriving in town or asking for details or simply to wish me luck. Even our most Orthodox relative checked in, defying the religious ban on Friday night phone calls.

I picked up on one of the calls and there was Miki with that cheery voice, boosting my mood.

"You still coming tomorrow?" I asked her.

"Of course! Are you ready to be a star of stage and screen?"

"You mean did I barf yet?"

She giggled. "Why would you barf?"

"I heard that's what stars do before they perform."

"They do? I didn't know that."

"It's true. Soldiers in the war, too. So yeah, I spewed a little."

"Oo—I'm sorry."

"No, it's good. Get it out now instead of tomorrow. Oh, and speaking of barf, do you know if Keatsie's coming?"

She was quiet a second. "Why?"

"Just wondering. I mean, I'm hoping Byron'll be there."

"Yeah, I think he will be."

"Oh, did you talk to them?"

"Just to Keatsie."

"And?"

"I don't think she's coming."

"She said that?"

"I . . . hey, I only called to wish you luck. Keatsie's Keatsie."

"Okay, sorry. I'm glad you called. I'm glad you'll be there."

"Super cool, daddyo. See ya then."

57

The big day arrives

SOMEHOW I managed to get to sleep by ten o'clock, but of course I had a nightmare about giving my speech. Blank note cards. Missing cards. Everything written in strange symbols. My throat unable to utter a sound. The rabbi and cantor and other readers crowded over me like they were peering into my grave.

I woke up in a sweat and heard my parents still talking in their room. It must have been about midnight. The next thing I knew Mom was shaking me awake. It wasn't even light yet. "Time to get up, honey. Lots to do before we leave."

It was chaos. Dad trying to get a few more winks. Then everyone wanting to use the bathroom at once. Lots of fussing about clothes. A piece of toast on the run. (Mom: "There'll be plenty to eat later!" Dad: I'm hungry now.") I paced around in my suit and tie, wishing I could wear the black penny loafers without suffering their bad-luck curse. I checked every few minutes to make sure I had the speech cards in a jacket pocket so my nightmare wouldn't come true. Another pocket held my little entertainment script for the lunch reception afterward. Finally we made it outside to a cold, foggy day with drizzle and ice pellets, but then Mom and I had to run back inside to get my prayer shawl, which we'd forgotten.

When we came out again Dad had the hood of the car up and was gazing at the engine. Joannie stood by a rear door under an umbrella. I smelled gasoline.

"What's *wrong*?" Mom cried.

"It won't start," Joannie said.

Mom panicked. "Oh *no*! Oh *no*! We won't get there! I told you to check the car before—"

"Calm down," Dad told her. "It's just flooded. Smell the gas? Just gotta wait a minute."

While we all did a dance of death, Dad shut the hood, got in the driver's seat and waited a torturous minute or two. The engine cranked . . . coughed . . . and started.

The regular congregation hadn't arrived yet at the synagogue, but a gang of our relatives awaited us in the lobby. I received a flurry of hugs, handshakes, and lipstick-heavy kisses before Rabbi Klein appeared with his wife—whom I'd never seen before. It surprised me how beautiful she was, with big dark eyes and high cheekbones. No wonder the rabbi didn't have more time for me.

After he and his wife greeted the family, the rabbi led me away for some last-minute instructions. Mr. Rubin had already run me through the ritual, but now it took on a weighty reality as I looked out on all the seats soon to be occupied. The synagogue had never looked so big, with all its rows and balcony. Against one wall was the wooden Holy Ark from which the Torah would be withdrawn and carried to a central table for the reading.

"So, Aaron," the rabbi said, putting a hand on my shoulder. "I sometimes wondered if you'd make it to this day. But here you are, and I understand you're very good at the Hebrew, according to Mr. Rubin and Cantor Hillel. So I'm looking forward. And the speech? I'm sorry I didn't get a chance to—but I trust Mr. Rubin liked it okay?"

I didn't know what to say at this point. I wagged my head from side to side and sang a little *mm-hmm*, meaning neither yes or no as far as I was concerned.

"Anyway," he said, "we have to get going now. You'll make us proud, right?"

He started off, but suddenly it popped in my mind to ask: "Rabbi, would a Negro girl be allowed at a bar mitzvah here?"

He cocked his head. "You're expecting someone?"

"I don't think so. Just wondering."

"Anyone who respects the Jewish faith is welcome here. Any color."

"What about atheists?"

"Oy," he said, shaking his head. "You're choosing this time for such questions? Let's worry about right now, because we're starting. All right?"

He directed me to the front row to await my family. Soon, the doors opened and in they came, my audience, each one of them giving me a new jolt of butterflies. Would I offend that religious-looking one? Would that sour-pussed man laugh at anything? Would the lady with the scowl walk out in a huff?

I felt a little better when my father settled down beside me, his prayer shawl over his shoulders and mine folded on his lap. Mom and Joannie blew a kiss my way and went out a back door and up to the balcony, where the women sat. They had a box of small candies to hand out when I was called up to speak, another of the traditions. Supposedly, I would be "showered" with these candies when officially a man.

I patted my jacket to check on the note cards and adjusted the white skullcap on my head.

"Stinkin' lousy weather," Dad said, "but it looks like everyone's gonna make it. You're a some big attraction."

"I don't feel so big. Were you scared at your bar mitzvah, Dad?"

"Me? All I thought about was the presents—all that *gelt* I'd be gettin' to spend. Why, you scared?"

"A little. But yesterday I was afraid I'd throw up. Actually I did throw up."

"You did? No kiddin'. You feel sick now?"

I had to take stock for a second. Nervous, yes; but nauseated, no! Butterflies in the guts, yes; slimy worms, no! So maybe it was true—that finally your stomach says *I did my work, man, go do yours.*

"Not now," I reassured my father.

"Attaboy. That's Izzy's kid."

Cantor Hillel now mounted a raised platform called a *bimah*, smiling at me on the way up. More people kept coming, filling the synagogue. Joannie's friend Barbara Katz. More relatives, including Aunt Sarah and Uncle Bernie and their son Bobby. It looked like Richie the older son had begged off. (I imagined him making out with his "babe" Rachel while they were alone.)

Mom's parents, each hobbling on canes, were helped along to their seats. Both of Dad's parents had died young, but his two brothers, little Sammy and tall Jack, had come in from Long Island with their wives and college-age children.

The sight of Frankie Solomon and his parents cheered me up. Frankie was already grinning—I'd get one laugh at least. Moshe Litvin arrived soon after and gave me a pumped fist. He'd managed to come without his father—who I didn't need glaring at me again as if I'd stepped in something.

I missed Miki's entrance, but when I turned to scan the audience, there she was, up in the balcony with her "chauffer"—her sister Yoshi. I caught her eye with a wave and she waved back crazily with both arms as if to fly out over the congregation. My heart warmed to her another degree.

I'd pretty much given up on Byron as the clock approached ten and an usher started to close the double doors. Then abruptly he opened them again.

"Ain't that your rich pal?" Dad said. "That his mother with him?"

It was Byron as I never thought I'd see him: in sports jacket and loose tie—and wearing the skullcap required of all men entering the synagogue. Byron in a *yarmulke*, a *kippah*! He could have passed for a bar mitzvah boy. The woman with him, however, was not Mrs. Fairchild but her friend Mrs. Bender, moving confidently and nodding at people. I suspected she helped persuade Byron to come, as well as drove him here.

Byron spotted my wave and waggled a few fingers at me from his hip. He seemed ill at ease in this unfamiliar house of God. Mrs. Bender gave me a deep head bow as if to some prince she'd secretly made king. She looked around, then proceeded to the balcony.

Everyone I'd hoped would come was here, with one exception. But then I hadn't held out much hope for Keatsie, not after Miki's alert yesterday. Still, wasn't she supposed to be my friend? Where was she today? With who? With *whom*? If even Byron could be persuaded to show up, couldn't she at least have. . . .

I pulled my thoughts away from her and back to the moment. Cantor Hillel had moved to the podium, tapping the synagogue's recently purchased microphone. It had been set up with its amplifier Friday morning, before Shabbat, and now the cantor tested it with "one, two, three," moving back when it screeched at him. Soon the congregation settled and the ceremony began with a big burst of his tenor voice, rising and falling with passion as he sang the first of many Hebrew prayers and blessings that would precede my performance.

Most of the people had picked up a prayer book distributed at the door, but not everyone turned the pages to keep up with the cantor. I did so only half-heartedly, finding it hard to concentrate. After a while, like many in the congregation, I just mumured the Hebrew words that opened familiar prayers, like *Barukh ata Adonai Elokaynu, melekh ha'olam*—"Blessed art Thou, Lord our God, King of the Universe." I stood when the congregation stood and said *aw-mane* (amen) when they did. My family did much the same, although Dad still seemed to remember some of the blessings. I was dying to turn around and see what Byron was doing during these prayers, but I feared he'd make me laugh or to feel ridiculous.

Finally, after what seemed forever to me, the prayers ended and it was time for the Torah readings. Following tradition, a synagogue official called a *gabbai* came up and summoned certain qualified men to the bimah for the first readings of the day's Torah passages. Three of these "readers" were older gray-haired men, and one younger, with a dark beard. As the cantor sang more blessings he led them to the Tabernacle, the Holy Ark, and they tenderly removed the Torah, still in its embroidered gold-and-blue cover. They carried it like a sleeping child it to the reading table. The gabbai remained at the table to help with the readings.

With the cover removed and the Torah unscrolled by its big wooden handles, the men took turns reading the correct passages, sort of half-chanting, half-singing, as I would soon be doing if my legs didn't melt under me. Like them, I would be touching the corner fringes of my prayer shawl to the beginning and end of my passage on the scroll, and then kissing those fringes. Unlike them, I would be taking my time and singing, not droning through it like they were reading baseball scores.

The readers finished and moved away from the podium. The gabbai came forth and issued my *aliyah*, the honored call to come up with my father and to read my passages: "*Ya'amod* (Let him arise), *Aharon ben Yisrael* (Aaron, son of Israel) . . . *Vayishlach* (my reading) . . ."

Showtime!

58

Like an angel

☺ ☺ ☺

DAD AND I mounted the platform together and I climbed a stepstool so I could look down on the Torah and out onto the crowd. Directed by the cantor and the gabbai, my father unfolded the prayer shawl and read a blessing, using the spelled-out Hebrew words on a sheet the gabbai put before him. Dad then draped the shawl over my shoulders and stumbled through another blessing. After that, he stepped away and left me at the podium. The cantor stood off to one side, and the gabbai arranged sheets of text and set down a fancy silver pointer for marking my passages on the Torah as I read them. The gabbai leaned close and whispered, "If you can't read the Hebrew, you'll read from here." He pointed to the blessings and readings spelled out in our alphabet.

"I think I can read the Hebrew."

"Wonderful. Just in case." He adjusted the microphone for me—"Don't put your mouth too close to it"—and stepped back.

"The Big Attraction"—yours truly—now stood at the podium with every eye on me, every ear waiting to hear what would come out of my mouth. It was like nothing in my life before. I felt huge and powerful and tiny and insignificant at once. But Rabbi Lipschutz had been so right: First, I was now part of something bigger than myself; and second, *"it's no longer the dreaded future—it's the present, and one way or another, the worry is finished. . . . even if you mess up, at least it'll be over."*

I took the fringes of the prayer shawl and touched them to where the passage began and ended, then kissed them. I cleared my throat and let fly in my sweetest Al Hibbler voice the ritual blessings to God.

Ba-r'chu et A-do-nai ha-m'vo-rach.

The congregation—mainly those who knew the words—sang the response. It was thrilling, directing a whole crowd to do something! I repeated the response as taught, then crooned a long blessing that thanked God for the Torah:

Ba-ruch a-tah A-do-nai Eh-lo-kay-nu meh-lech ha-o-lahm, a-sher ba-char ba-nu mi-kol ha-a-meem, v'na-tahn ahla-nu et Torah-toh. Ba-ruch a-tah A-do-nai, no-tayn ha-Torah.

As the congregation responded its *aw-mane,* I could make out my mother already wiping her eyes, with Joannie patting her arm. But now it was time for them to distribute the candies and for me to launch into the Torah passage about Jacob and Esau, then another reading, a *Haftarah,* about the cursing of Esau's land and descendants. The gabbai put the silver pointer in my hand and guided it to my starting place. I took a breath and, loud and clear, belted out what I'd practiced so often it felt like my own language.

When I'd finished, I took a moment to look out on the crowd. Okay, a few of the older ones seemed half asleep and little kids were focused their candies. But in almost every other face I thought I saw a glow of something—delight? admiration? *He sang like an angel.* Mom was beside herself. Still on the platform, my father beamed at me, raising a thumb. Up in the balcony Miki raised two thumbs and mimicked applause. When I dared look at Byron he made a funny, scrunched up, what's-all-this-God-stuff? face. I had to stifle the giggles because more ritual lay ahead: more blessings, the putting away of the Torah, some words from the rabbi, and then my speech—which, I began to fear, might undo all the triumph I was feeling now.

I almost wished I could quit while I was ahead; but that wasn't the Aaron I wanted to be, not Aaron the writer, not Aaron who was bigger than his own worries, not Aaron who would soon tell the congregation what he learned from the reading, not Aaron the *man*, man.

When it came time for me to recite the final blessing—another thanks for the gift of the Torah—I gave it my grand-finale voice, backing away from a screech of feedback, and then helped the readers close the scroll and cover it. The men put the Torah in my arms and helped me raise it up high to the congregation, walk around the platform with it, and finally return it to the Ark.

The rabbi took his turn at the podium as I and the others stepped back. He talked about how God revealed himself to Jacob and how He reveals himself in different ways today. But now I was thinking about my own speech and didn't pay much attention until he mentioned my name, congratulating me and my parents for the bar mitzvah.

"And now," he said, "it will be our pleasure to hear from *Aharon* himself, his thoughts and the lessons of his reading, *d'var Torah*, upon his entrance into Jewish manhood."

I came forward. *Oh God.*

59

My famous (to me) bar mitzvah speech

😐 ☺ ☺

BACK UP ON THE STEPSTOOL. Microphone readjusted to my height. Note cards pulled out of my pocket. One card falls from sweaty hands to the floor; I pick it up. Where does it—oh, good thing I numbered them. Okay. Deep breath. Everyone so quiet, waiting. Clear throat. Smile at the audience. Look up between sentences. Go!

Hi, everyone. (*Joannie puts a hand to her ear, mouths the word 'louder.'*) HI, EVERYONE. (*The microphone screams a feedback. I go softer. Joannie nods; just right.*)

I'm glad to be here finally. A bar mitzvah is a big deal for a kid to face. It's hard work and makes me proud and confused at the same time. Very scared, too, like I am right now in front of everybody. (*Some laughter. Joannie makes the "slow-down" sign with her palms.*)

I want to say some things I hope won't be too boring, but first I'd like to thank some special people:

My dear parents, Izzy and Vivian, who made a zillion sacrifices for this day and always love me like a son, even though their son is sometimes a wise guy. (*Looking at my mother:*) Try not to *kvel*, Mom, I'm trying to bring you some *nahkes*. (*Laughter at the Yiddish words for "joyful crying" and "satisfactions."*) Next, my sister Joannie, best sister ever because she listens to my troubles and shares her rock and roll records. And Mr. Rubin, my schul teacher and Torah coach, who finally knocked some learning into this smart-aleck, this *lets*. (*Laughter.*)

Also Rabbi Klein, head of the synagogue and schul—thanks for sparing my parents some bad reports. Cantor Hillel, thank you for showing me how to sing the blessings, even about a millionth as good as you. I was also lucky to meet Rabbi Lipschutz of the Jewish Community Center, who helped me understand about being cool and still being a *mensch*. And *muchas gracias, hombre,* to my genius pal Byron Fairchild and to my friend Moshe Litvin. They all taught me some fancy words I'm using today. Finally, thanks to all my family and everyone else who came especially for my bar mitzvah. (*A glance up to Miki.*)

My reading today is *Vayishlach*. It's part of a whole Torah story about Isaac's twin sons Esau and Jacob and how they forgave each other and made up after a whole bunch of troubles. Esau was the older one. He was *livid* at Jacob for tricking him out of his father's inheritance and blessing. But then later, the family was angry at Esau for marrying wives from a forbidden religion. After a while, Jacob moved away and had his own family while he worked for his Uncle Laban, but the uncle deceived him into working twenty years for *bubkas*, zilch. (*A few chuckles. I hear Frankie's phlegmy laughter.*)

So in my reading, Jacob decides to go home and he sends Esau a message: I come in peace. I want to make up. But a messenger comes back and says Esau's on his way to meet you—only with four hundred men. That sounds like an attack to Jacob and he's scared. He prays to God, but doesn't just sit back and rely on him. He does things on his own to protect his family. He gathers men and makes battle plans. But he also has a whole bunch of gifts to offer Esau in case he's willing to make up.

Before they meet, Jacob goes off again and ends up wrestling all night with somebody who turns out to be an angel of God. The angel says from now on your name is Israel. And Israel will become the father of the Jewish land and people.

So, Jacob comes back to face Esau, and when Esau shows up with his men, guess what? He hugs his brother, he kisses him, he cries. He doesn't even want the gifts because he's rich already. Everybody is forgiven. But then later on, God curses the descendants of Esau's land forever because of the sinning.

I know there's a lot more to the story in the Torah and the prophets, but that's kind of how I understand my readings so I can apply it to life.

(*Some people looking bored. Let's see how the next part goes.*)

In the last few months—before I was a man—I did the same kind of *insufferable* things as the twins. I was sneaky. I was disrespectful in shul—to a war hero no less who taught me. I hated another student without knowing what a good guy he really was—is. I was mad at a really *phenomenal* girl just for liking somebody else. I was angry at my father for trying to protect me. (*Dad puts a knuckle to his eye. Is he kvelling, too? He'll make me cry!*) I was mad at my mother because she wouldn't let me get cool shoes that would mess up my feet. In my anger I did something really stupid. (*Puzzled looks when I don't say what it was.*)

But for all this anger I was understood and forgiven. I'm learning how important it is to understand someone before you judge them, because if a jerk turns out to be a great person, then you're the jerk for the way you treated them. You can't just sit back praying to God or counting on other people to make everything right. Like Jacob, you have to take a chance and do the proper things yourself. (*Lots of head-nodding on that one.*)

I'm still trying to figure out religion, so I haven't done a lot of praying by myself. Except last night. I prayed that I wouldn't throw up during my speech, and I think my prayers were answered—so far! (*Modest chuckles. A couple of sour faces. Don't look at them.*)

Like Jacob, I will try to be thankful for the many good things I have and not jealous of everything else. Also like Jacob, I'm not going to give up when I'm troubled by something.

(*Here goes:*) Right now, though, I'm sort of confused about God. My family believes in Him. I have a best friend who doesn't. I have an Orthodox Jewish friend who bops me on the head when I joke about religion. But a respected Jewish person gave me this advice: Live a good life by doing the things God stands for. You know, don't do any harm, have respect for everyone, be honest, be understanding, and do mitzvahs to help others. Also stand up against wrongs, like prejudiced *ignoramuses* for example. Do all that, and you'll be okay. (*Some heads nodding, but others shaking in disagreement.*)

So in conclusion, or almost, I have a lot of things to figure out starting today, as I enter manhood. Who's right, who isn't, how to live a good life and still be funny. (*Titters.*) I think I would like to be some kind of reporter or writer one day, and maybe I could do some good that way, even some mitzvahs.

So far, I did a little mitzvah by giving money for trees in Israel. But I also did a bigger one this week that my parents don't even know about. I helped a poor friend and his mother who were evicted from our building. (*Mom, Dad, and Joannie jerk their heads up.*) I gave them rent money from my savings. I never did anything like that before, and I don't think anything ever felt so good. Except finishing this speech. That probably feels really good for everyone. Thank you for listening.

(*Applause. Hearty clapping from Dad, Joannie, and my friends. Mom clapping but still looking puzzled. Some meager applause from stern-looking types.*)

As I let out a deep breath, I felt Rabbi Klein's hand on my shoulder again, turning me back toward the seats. "Well," he said quietly, "that was *different*."

60

Kudos, kvetches, and Manichewitz

😐 ☺ ☺

AFTER MY TALK and the final Shabbat prayers, I endured a hail of candy tossed at me as I moved to the lobby with my father. Once there I felt like a beanbag being passed from one relative to another as the congregation joined us. A long table with sweet wine and light snacks had been prepared for everyone attending.

Rabbi Klein appeared and gave blessings over the wine and breads. He congratulated my parents, but before leaving with his wife he shot me an odd look, like, *glad to be through with you, Mr. Smartass*. Or maybe I imagined it.

Between the congratulations and gushing over my Torah reading, my mother kept trying to ask me about the money I'd given to Rocco—why and when and how much and who said you could. "And what was that 'stupid thing' you did when you were angry?" But before I could explain, someone in the crowd would push in to give me a hug or a kiss, a handshake—or even a quick lecture. An elderly relative stuck his face at mine and said, "Since when do you stand up in a synagogue to announce you don't believe in God?" A woman in a black veil stopped to scold me: "You sound like a smart boy, but smart boys don't talk about vomiting during a *d'var Torah.* That was disgusting."

As I stammered to respond to such challenges, the next person would barge in to tell me that I'd expressed exactly how they felt about belief and being a good Jew. I was quite the center of attention, anyway, second only to the paper cups of Manichewitz wine and a stack of miniature hot dogs. Some of my parents' acquaintances—those who wouldn't be attending the small family luncheon coming up next—slipped a gift envelope into my jacket pocket. These I gave to Mom to hold in her purse, the *gelt* to be tallied up later. Dad gave me permission to have some wine now that I was a man.

As I sipped a small cup of it, Byron made his way through the crowd, followed by Mrs. Bender. He had one of the little hot dogs stuck in his mouth like an extra tongue. While Mrs. Bender introduced herself to my parents and congratulated them, Byron gulped down the hot dog and gave me his mock-stern look.

"Pretty cool speech," he said, "but how can you be confused about God? Did I not make it *irrefutably* clear that there is none?"

"You better take off that skull cap," I said, laughing. "No atheist wears a yarmulke."

"I'm declaring myself the first. Hey, I liked your line—my line—about 'prejudiced ignoramuses.' Thanks for the credit."

"Thanks for the fancy words, man. I used one of Keatsie's, too. *Livid.* Is she livid at me, by the way?"

"Dunno. Why?"

"Oh, I thought she might come with you today."

He scrunched up his nose. "Can't have her in a holy place. She's possessed by demons."

Before I could pursue it any further, Mrs. Bender came over and gave me a warm handshake. "I'm so happy you spoke with Beau Lipschutz," she said. "I'll let him know you mentioned him and how well you used his advice. I assume it was his."

"Yeah, it was—and he's super-cool, like you said. Thanks for helping me and for coming here and everything."

"Always my pleasure."

After she parted and the crowd began to thin, I finally spotted Miki and Yoshi hanging back behind the stragglers. I waved for them to come over. Miki scooted up first, paused, then hugged me for just an awkward couple of seconds before stepping back. "Aaron, you were so boss! I dug your talk the most. And that singing—you wailed, man! I wanted to cop some drums and sit in."

"It was very good," Yoshi said, joining us. "*Solid*, man."

"Thanks," I said, laughing. "I'm glad you guys came. I dug seeing you cats up in the balcony while I was wailing."

"Well," Miki said, extending her hand. "I'm glad we came, too."

I held the warm hand as long as I dared. "I wish you could come to the luncheon," I told her, "but it's mostly for family—oh, and one alien of my choice." I nodded toward Byron, still in the yarmulke.

"*Svoort za znukuxa, Gwanqu!*" Byron said in Martian.

Miki laughed. "Hey, I'm thinking of having a little party soon. Would you guys come?"

Byron and I assured her we would. Yoshi shook my hand, then led her sister out. I thought of taking a few more sips of wine before leaving for the reception, but I felt lightheaded already and had one more performance yet ahead of me, the fun one.

61

Wishing you lots of lox

☺ ☺ ☺

THOSE FEW family members who were too religious to drive on a Sabbath began their ten-minute walk to Gordon's Delicatessen and banquet room, site of the reception. It was still miserable out and I felt sorry for them as we climbed in our car—Barbara Katz, Byron, and me in the back seat—and drove over.

Barbara reached across Byron to shake my hand and congratulate me. "I didn't get a chance inside. I loved the way you sang. As good as Elvis!"

I answered her Presley-style: "*Well, that's all right, mah Barbara, that's all right with me.*" She threw her head back, big laugh. I liked Joannie's devoted friend Barbara. Pleasantly chubby, she was known as "a sweet girl" with "a sweet face."

Joannie turned around to Byron, "And how did *you* like the service?"

"Hmm," he said, rubbing his chin. "Infinitely superior to the boring bar mitzvah I went to last year. Especially since the reading was about me.'

"About you?"

"Well, about twins like my sister and me. I'm the bad twin, she's the strange, sneaky one."

"Oh? Why are you bad?"

Byron glanced at me—should he tell her about his "forbidden" girlfriend? But my mother turned around and interrupted with her earlier question to me: "When are you going to explain about Rocco and the money? And whatever else you did?"

"After you give me all the *gelt* in your purse."

"Maybe I never will," she said, smirking. She turned back.

"Better watch out," Dad told her. "He's a bigshot man now."

Gordon's Deli had a street-level food store with long delicatessen case, plus a large room downstairs for catered parties. My parents already knew Abe Gordon and his wife, who did many of the receptions for the Hebrew Institute. It was one of the few dining rooms we could afford on top of the day's other costs. Besides, we loved his food, our favorites for Sunday breakfasts. Abe, with his small eyes and receding curly hair, ran around in his apron like some magic elf, doing everything at once. Mrs. Gordon and another woman stayed behind the deli counter dishing out chopped-herring salad, dill pickles, slices of lox—smoked salmon—and other salty delights to salivating customers.

Downstairs the tables were arranged in a horseshoe, with about twenty-five places set up. On the tablecloths sat flowers, bottles of wine, plates of rye and challah breads, small pails of dill pickles, and dishes of celery, radishes, and olives. As we sat—Dad, Mom, Joannie, Barbara, me, and Byron at the center table—Abe took orders for drinks. When Dad ordered a whiskey and ginger-ale highball, I did, too. "Without the booze," Dad instructed. But all I really wanted was the maraschino cherry that came with the ginger-ale "shirley temple." Byron ordered the same, stuck the cherry in his mouth like a cork.

Dad proposed a toast to the bar mitzvah "man." As we raised our glasses Uncle Bernie called to me, "Don't get drunk before your speech!"

"It's not really a speech," I said.

"Good," shouted one of Uncle Jack's sons. "I'm hungry!"

"You still feel like vomiting?" Cousin Bobby piped in, reaching for a celery. His mother Aunt Sarah grabbed his shoulder—"Bobby!" Lots of wise-guy answers to the vomiting question came to my mind, like *Yeah, when I look at your face.* But I was a man now, above those cheap shots. Today, anyway. Everyone was in such a good mood, laughing, joking, recalling their own or their childrens' bar- and bat mitzvahs, I wouldn't have dared spoil it. Besides, Abe's wife had come down to help serve the first course—chopped-liver salad—and it was time to clink a glass and deliver my thing.

"I just have a few words," I said, standing up and tapping my ginger ale glass. "It's a poem. And you can eat your liver while I recite."

"Something's already eating my liver!" Uncle Sammy cracked, getting a big laugh and encouraging more wisecracks. I opened the sheet of paper I'd prepared and began.

"'Today I am a man,' I say to all around this
table,
but what the heck was I before—a bagel?"

"With cream cheese! "Uncle Sammy yelled, extending the laugh.

"Well, yesterday I was a boy, today I *am* a man.
It could be worse—I *could* be an orang-utan."

"You look like one!" young Bobby ventured, getting only his own laugh. *Yo mama*, I thought, but his mama was right there, not looking like at all like an ape. And wasn't I already through with those *yo-mama* jokes? I continued:

"I welcome friends and family to Gordon's
delicatessen.
Before we stuff ourselves, I have a small
confession:
I used to hate what I got called because
my name is Schmink.
You know what words they rhyme it with,
like Aaron Stink."

"Believe me, we know," said Uncle Jack's son Manny. Others nodded. I went on:

"But now I've entered manhood, and I'm bigger
than my name,
I can be Stink or Tiddledewink and be
cool all the same."

"Always with the *cool*, these kids," said my mother's Aunt Essie, looking at my grandparents. "Everything has to be cool, whatever that is."

"Not everything," I said. "I'm *explaining*."

"Oh, excuse me. Go ahead, darling."

"I wanted to be *cool* when dressed for my
bar mitzvah,
but Mom said no to loafers, 'wear the shoes
that fit ya!'"

"Beautiful Buster Brown orthopedics!" Mom called out. "They cost a fortune." Laughter. I proceeded.

"A mellow rabbi told me that cool means
more than shoes,
more than being atheists or Protestants
or Jews.
It's how you deal with people who are
different than you
and how you handle scary things and
things that are untrue."

"Absolutely," Aunt Sarah affirmed. Uncle Jack's wife added, "Hear hear!"

"And that's what I'll be working on, now that
I'm a man."
So *thank you* for your gifts today to help me
with my plan."

"You're welcome!" little Uncle Sammy shouted amid cheers and applause. "Can we eat already?"

"My son, the writer," Mom beamed.

I had one more verse, with my best rhyme (*learn to box* and *mushy piece of lox*), but the chatter and the clink of silverware were at full volume. I thought of one of the lessons of the Newspaper Club: Important stuff first, so you can cut the ending. I cut it and attacked my liver.

62

Thank you, thank you

I'D THOUGHT that all the emotional stuff would be over by Wednesday, following the bar mitzvah. The last relative had gone home Monday and the phone had finally stopped ringing. Now I had a pile of bar-mitzvah cards to sort through, most of them containing money or check, and Mom insisting I write one of my famous thank-you notes to everyone who had given something. She'd pulled out a box of flowery notecards to get me started.

But when I got home Wednesday after classes and Newspaper Club, Joannie told me that Mom had been crying.

"Why, what's wrong?"

"You should ask her. She just got off the phone with Rocco's mother."

Mom greeted me in the kitchen, her eyes red-rimmed. "Come here," she said. I did so and she gave me a jumbo hug.

"What is it?" I asked, a little uneasy.

"I realize now what a beautiful thing you did," she sniffled. "Rocco's mother called a little while ago. She wanted to say how that sixty dollars you lent them saved their lives."

"Really? She said that?"

"Oh, you should have heard her. She kept breaking down in tears, that's how much it meant to her. She made me cry, too. Anyway, they were able to get into their own little place so they can hold on till her job starts and some help comes through. Meanwhile she's trying hard to get Rocco back in school."

"I only lent them some of my gambling loot," I said, beaming at the news. "I don't even care if I get it back."

"Well, you may not get it. She didn't say anything about that."

"It's okay, I got lots of money now."

She rolled her eyes. "Not that much, kiddo, considering what you'll need. But it was a real mitzvah you did. We're proud of you for the thought."

"Thanks."

She stepped back and raised a finger. "But the *next* time you decide to spend that kind of money, mister, you talk to us first. Do you understand?"

"When do I get to spend my own money without asking?"

"When you work for it and your college is paid for. Otherwise, you can use your allowance and that's it."

"I thought I was a man now," I said, already knowing what she and others would be saying to that claim.

And she said it: "A very, very young man. You still have plenty of growing up to do."

I stood on my toes and stretched my body upward. "There—I just did it."

She laughed. "And you're still my beautiful little boy."

"Ugh!"

Dad and Joannie also thought I'd done a noble act, so everything was now cool on that score. Also, Mom had stopped asking about "the stupid thing" I'd mentioned in my speech but hadn't revealed. Thus my rampage with Rocco in the old mansion remained my secret, smoldering in my gut when I thought about it. Mom must have decided that my "stupid thing" was one of many she already knew about, like the penny loafers. Or she had enough other things on her mind not to dwell on this one.

I didn't see what a confession would do now except upset everyone. What was I supposed to tell my parents, that I almost fell from a balcony and killed myself trying to smash a chandelier? Maybe it wasn't such a terrible crime to wreck a wrecked house some more. Okay, trespassing. Vandalism. But I felt plenty guilty about it already, and I didn't want to get Rocco into more trouble. Wasn't "being a man" partly knowing when to handle things by yourself? So now I was handling it. I would just learn from the experience—that such actions have bad consequences, even if only in your own head.

I thought about Rocco and all the bad things he'd been going through. He never seemed to worry much about his own actions and their consequences. Still, he'd been my best friend in the neighborhood and I knew I'd miss him. Maybe I could find out where he lived and visit.

This week and next, though, I had a million things to do. Not just the thank-you cards, but lots of schoolwork I'd been kind of neglecting because of the bar mitzvah study. Christmas vacation was just two weeks away. I felt too busy to even think about Keatsie and Miki, except that I *was* thinking about them. A lot. For example, who—*whom*—did I like more? I wasn't sure. Miki always cheered me up and I was excited about seeing her again, maybe at the party she said she'd be having. I kept replaying that hug she gave me at the synagogue—a cute, smart, funny, cool girl who wanted to hug Aaron Schmink! Definitely one of my best feelings since becoming a man.

But still, I missed Keatsie, talking with her, watching her crazy-legged moves, or just looking at her. Maybe she had a reason not to come to the bar mitzvah, but she could have called or sent me a card. She didn't even sign the card her mother sent, which just said "From the Fairchilds." What was her problem? Was she finally afraid she'd barf if she saw me?

Ha, dream on, Schmink.

I'd quit trying to sneak any Keatsie information out of Byron. He either ignored the hint or made some new crack about her. He even looked a little annoyed when I kept on, so I stopped. But in a way it was thanks to Byron that I got to see her, briefly, on Friday afternoon.

By then Miki had already called to invite me to a big party at her house next week, on the Saturday evening after this coming one. She'd explained, in her chirpy way, that her father would be throwing a *bōnenkai*, a traditional Japanese forget-the-year blast for friends and work colleagues. While they'd be carrying on upstairs, Miki and friends would be in the finished basement, a kind of party room, with music, dancing, lots of food, plus liquid refreshments. "Non-alcoholic, of course," she said. "We're not all official adults like you."

So when I saw Byron that Friday at school, a week earlier, we were already talking about the party. Miki had invited him, too, with permission to bring a "date." He was struggling over whether to ask Betty Lee and how she'd feel at a party where she hardly knew anyone—if she could even get away.

When we met at our lockers after classes, Byron said that his "mater" would be picking him up shortly. Later on, he and the family were going to a dinner party with "boring talk" at the "estate" of one of his father's friends.

"And you think our place is big?" Byron said. "Theirs makes ours look like a bird house." I tried to imagine such an estate as we walked outside to wait for Mrs. Fairchild. The best I could conjure was a great storybook castle with walls, towers, and a moat.

As Mrs. Fairchild's white Cadillac approached, I saw a second figure in the front seat, leaning against the passenger door. The car pulled up, and there was Keatsie. She glanced at us, looked down for a moment, then opened her window and managed a smile that seemed forced.

"Hi, Aaron."

I mumbled a hello. She looked different, even more beautiful—but who was she? She wore lipstick and eye makeup, which I didn't remember seeing on her before. She had already dressed for the fancy evening. Between the lapels of a coat I could see a white blouse worn under a black sweater, with a string of pearls. Her hair looked different, too; less curled, neater.

"I would prefer to sit in the front," Byron told her.

Mrs. Fairchild leaned over to greet me and told Byron to squeeze in or sit in the back.

"No," Keatsie said, "I'd actually rather be in the back." She opened the door and got out for the transfer. She wore a longish grey skirt, stockings, and short heels—making our height difference even greater. I felt like an elf as I gawked at her.

"I heard your bar mitzvah went great," she said, as Byron squeezed by her into the front. "Miki loved it."

"Yeah, I think you would have liked it, too. I sang just like Elvis."

She smiled. A slight flush appeared on her cheeks. "I know, but . . . I couldn't go. I'm sorry."

"It's okay," I said, filling an awkward pause. "Maybe next time. I'm doing one every year—for the presents."

She laughed, that lovely tinkling laugh. "Good idea. Well . . . I better go. We have this dinner thing."

"I know. Have a good time."

"Thanks. See ya."

"See ya."

As they pulled away, I thought of all the things I might have said before the "see ya's." I should have asked her *why* she couldn't have come. I should have asked if she was going to Miki's party. But these questions would be answered soon enough.

63

Meet the parents

MIKI had made it pretty clear, when inviting me, that I was her date for the party. She made it even clearer when I got to her house and she answered the door, grabbed my hand, and yanked me inside.

"Aaron—I'm so glad to see you! We're gonna have so much fun."

I had come over early, at two-thirty, so that my father could give me a ride and still get to his Saturday card game. Miki's party was officially from three until seven; the adults' party had already begun.

Miki put my coat and scarf away and tugged at me again. "Come on, meet my parents."

I imagined a stern couple looking down at me and shaking their heads. But Miki didn't seem worried. She led me through a short hallway to a room where about a dozen people crowded around a table, snacking from small plates, drinking out of tiny cups, and laughing and shouting at full volume. A phonograph in another room blasted a jazz tune. Some of the people looked Japanese, some were white, and three—two men and a woman—black. It surprised and excited me to see the mix, unusual, as far as I knew, in this neighborhood with its cozy homes near the town's public high school. I felt part of some cool thing taking place against prejudice.

"Hi, everybody!" Miki said. "This is my friend Aaron."

A few people raised their cups our way, hardly looking.

"Sorry," Miki said to me, laughing. "A *bōnenkai* is for getting drunk and forgetting the year's troubles. So everyone's drinking *saki*—rice wine—and acting insane. That's my father over there—" She pointed to a smart-looking man with horn-rimmed glasses and a goatee. "He teaches music at the high school. And that's my mother next to him—"

"She's beautiful," I said of the slim woman, her dark hair cut to frame her face.

"And she knows it," Miki said. "She teaches part-time at Good Counsel College. Music, naturally. I told you we were music-crazy. Not only that, but my parents play in music groups with half these cats. Classical and jazz."

"Man!"

"Let me try it again," she said, moving closer to the table. "*Mom*! *Dad*! Please excuse me. I'd like you to meet my friend, *Aaron*!"

"Ah!" her father said, breaking away from the table and coming over. His wife followed, slightly wobbly. They shook my hand warmly as I stood up straight in my best, pleased-to-meet-you behavior. I was glad I had dressed smartly in crisp shirt, argyle sweater, and slacks with a crease.

"I hear you did some mellow crooning at your bar mitzvah," the dad said, to my astonishment.

"Miki said you were 'real gone,'" added the mom, taking a good look at me.

"Sorry about the, uh, noise here," said the father. "Just an old tradition. Ignore us and have a good time downstairs, okay? Cool to meet you, Aaron."

"Great—solid—to meet you, too!" I said, giddily.

The parents bowed at me briefly, and by reflex I bowed back before they returned to their guests.

As we headed toward the basement stairs, I peeked into a room with piano, big phonograph speakers, and a wall of books and vinyl records.

"You have the coolest parents in the universe," I gushed.

"Yeah, they want to be super modern and fit in. It's hard for Japanese people after all that World War II stuff. But they can be strict with us, too."

"How so?"

"Like schoolwork. They push me hard. And respect for elders. Very important. Anyway, I'm sure your parents are cool, in their own way."

"What makes you so sure?"

"'Cause they made *you*, man," she said with a laugh, elbowing my arm.

Miki's sister Yoshi greeted me as we entered the "rec" room in the basement. She'd been laying out snacks on a long table. Balloons and crepe-paper streamers decorated the ceiling and woody-looking paneled walls. A large space on the hard, smooth floor had been cleared for dancing, and opposite the food table, a smaller table held a phonograph and stacks of record albums.

"Are you attending the little kids' party?" I asked Yoshi?

"You joking? I'm your chaperone. I'll be upstairs, too—I have to control my parents."

"Her boyfriend's coming over later," Miki said.

"He's not my boyfriend."

"Okay. He's a friend and a boy."

"That's all."

"A really gorgeous boy."

"Shut up. Go get *your* boyfriend a soda."

Miki didn't dispute the term "boyfriend" as referring to me. Was she my girlfriend then? It didn't quite feel like it yet, but it didn't feel like a bad idea, either.

"Ginger ale?" I requested, as Miki headed to a small refrigerator in a corner.

The doorbell rang and Yoshi went upstairs to start letting people in, now that party time had arrived. Miki handed me my drink and came close, speaking low. "Listen, Aaron, I have to tell you something. Keatsie's coming. I invited her, of course, and . . . she's bringing somebody. I kind of promised her we wouldn't make a big deal out of it, if that's okay with you."

"Why? Who's she bringing?"

"Just—"

A freckled, redheaded girl came hurrying down the stairs, arms open.

"Hey, look who's here!" Miki cried. They hugged and spun around to me. "Aaron, meet Beverly, my cr-a-a-y-zy schoolmate."

"No, *she's* the crrr-ayyyyyzy one," Beverly said in a cartoon voice.

They came downstairs one after another now: More girls from Miki's school, boys from various schools, some my age, some a little older; a cousin of Miki's with a buddy; whites, "Orientals," a black girl and boy, and even a boy Miki said was from Mexico. It was like a Human-Relations-Day dream!

But no Keatsie yet. Or Byron.

A few of the kids had come with a parent or parents attending the party upstairs, which was becoming louder by the minute. Some of them wore jackets with an embroidered school emblem.

Miki put a Frank Sinatra record on the phonograph and set the volume to compete with the upstairs racket. Sinatra belted out "Learnin' the Blues" at a swinging tempo, and people started to dance a slow lindy.

Miki and I joined them. Some of the girls from Miki's school danced with each other or alone, mixing in impressive ballet and modern-dance moves, leaping around, giggling. Miki the dance student threw in extra pirouettes or backward dips as I twirled her outward. It made me feel like a real dancer myself until we would stumble over each other and fall into a laughing fit.

We went through more records, stopping only to stuff our faces with little sandwiches, sweets, and a salty, crunchy mix that Miki said was popular in Japan. It was fiery, too, and Miki broke up as I ran around fanning my mouth.

As great a time as I was having, I couldn't stop thinking about Keatsie coming here with someone else. I was dying to learn who her date would be, but didn't dare push Miki any further about it.

Miki introduced me to the other kids, most of them smart, quick, and easy to talk with—when we could hear each other over the loud music.

I spoke close to Miki's ear: "I used to think private-school guys were lames."

"They mostly are, except for the guys I invite!"

As I chatted with the boy from Mexico, trying out my few Spanish words, the door to the basement opened and down came two late arrivals: Byron with Betty.

Betty had never looked more beautiful, as pretty as I'd always thought her to be. She wore a dark skirt and a colorful cardigan over a high-necked white blouse, and she'd done something new to her hair. She seemed nervous at first, but as she looked around and recognized me and saw kids of different colors, her normally loveable smile became even more so, magical. While Miki introduced herself and started introducing Betty to others, Byron and I moved off to talk.

"Hey, man," I said, "where's your yarmulke?"

"Oops, forgot it!"

I looked to make sure Betty was out of earshot. "So you guys worked things out?"

"Sort of, for today. Tomorrow they'll probably murder us."

"Who will?'

"Parents, if they find out."

"You both had to lie?"

"Mm, not exactly, just didn't say. I'm worried she'll get in trouble. I don't care about me." He looked over at her, dreamily. "Ain't she beautiful, though?" He put a hand over his heart. "*Bedazzling.*"

"Yep. Way too bedazzling for you."

"Yeah, probably true. How are you and Miki doing?"

"She's the most, man. She kind of called me her boyfriend. So maybe now I have a girlfriend?"

"See, I knew she was your soul mate."

Byron wanted a Pepsi and some food and to get back to Betty. As we started toward the table though, he stopped me by the shoulder. "Oh, I almost forgot. I'm supposed to deliver a message from Keatsie. She's waiting outside, actually, and wants to talk to you before she comes in. So weird, but I'm just the weirdo's messenger."

"Outside! All this time? Who's she with?"

Byron looked down, shrugged. "You should go out there."

64

It ain't over till the party ends

😐 ☹ ☺

"NO BIG SURPRISE," Miki said when I told her Keatsie was waiting for me outside. I asked if she wanted to come out with me.

"Mm, I don't think so," she said. "I have a pretty good idea of what she wants. Just make sure you come back."

"I will!"

I got my coat and went out, pulling my collar up in the chilly air and looking around for Keatsie. A parked car beeped its horn from across the street—a souped-up Chevy with three people in the front seat. As I approached, Keatsie got out of the car on the curb side.

She closed the passenger door and waved me over. Two men or boys remained in the car; I could see only the backs of their heads.

"Hi, Aaron," Keatsie said quietly when I reached the car. "Sorry to make you come out and all, but it's better if . . . well, we should talk here first."

She nodded toward the front seat and I bent slightly to look through the closed window. The big ruddy face of Sonny Rizzo greeted my hang-jawed gaze. He raised two fingers in a feeble wave and forced a smile. The driver of the car, another big guy, about twenty, glanced my way.

I looked at Keatsie, huddling in her coat. "*Rizzo* is your date?"

"It's different than it was," she said. "*He's* different."

"I can't believe it! I thought you hated him."

"I did. Especially that day after the movie. But he's really changed. He's been just the sweetest guy since then."

"*Sweet*? Yeah, I bet. What made him suddenly change?"

"Me, I guess," she said, looking uncomfortable. "If he wants to see me, he has to follow my rules."

"So he doesn't still, you know, make you, uh . . . ?"

"What? Make me barf?" She allowed herself a smile. "No, no more Barf Girl. Which is exactly what I *mean* about 'different.' It's . . . just hard to explain." She looked at me, head tilted, as if trying to read my feelings. I wasn't sure myself what they were. "But anyway," she added, "he wants to say something to you."

"To me?"

She nodded and opened the door. Sonny slid over and out of the car. He stood between me and Keatsie and held out the very hand that had once slapped me to the ground. I noticed that the thumbnail had been chewed all the way down. "Hey, man, how's it goin'? he said. "Wanna shake?"

I kept my hands in my pockets. "I don't know. Why?"

Keatsie bonked one of his shoulders from behind. "Tell him," she ordered.

Sonny bowed his big, curly-haired head. I thought of how I might throw a jab and a hook at it—after I learned how to box.

"I'm sorry," he said to me.

Keatsie bonked him again.

He looked at me. "I apologize for everything that day. Calling you names, hitting you."

"Yeah? What about insulting Keatsie and all?"

"I would never do that again. I love my girl. I would never hurt her."

Keatsie moved out from behind him. "Or any of her friends, right?"

"Right."

I had more: "What about the prejudiced things you said? You know, about Betty Lee."

He looked puzzled for a moment. "Oh—yeah, Byron's girl." He looked at Keatsie. "Sorry about that, too. It was just dumb talk."

"Why don't you guys shake, then?" Keatsie said. "I don't want to go inside with any hard feelings."

Sonny put his hand out again. Slowly, as cooly as I could, I shook it.

"That's Sonny's brother Mario," Keatsie said, pointing inside the car. I looked in and Mario nodded to me. He had a thinner face than Sonny, with a long nose, angled as if broken once.

"Nice wheels," I said, for something to say.

"Thanks, man. If you need a ride later, I'll be pickin' these guys up."

"Yeah, thanks, maybe." *Just what I need: a ride with the two love birds.*

"So," Keatsie said, "can we go inside now? I'm freezing!"

Back at the party, about half the kids were jabbering around the snack table or sitting on chairs and an old couch, devouring food and drinks. The other half—including Byron and Betty and another interracial pair—were slow-dancing to one of the hit tunes in Miki's collection. Most of the boys were shorter than the girls, as I would have been with Keatsie, by a mile. When Miki led me out to dance, I felt happy to have a partner my size, even a little shorter.

But I felt good about more than our heights. Miki followed my blocky Arthur-Murray dance steps so gracefully I didn't have to think about my feet. She pulled my left hand to her shoulder and moved in close. Her black, glossy hair smelled thrillingly floral. I held her a little tighter around the waist, and we glided off to Roger Williams' tinkling, romantic version of "Autumn Leaves."

"Are you okay about Keatsie and Sonny?" she asked as we moved around the floor.

The question prompted me to sneak a look at the two, melted into each other as they danced, both with their eyes closed. "I still don't like him" I said. "But it's not my problem."

And incredibly, it really wasn't any more! Now past the first shock of her and Sonny Rizzo, I realized that it all made sense in a Keatsie kind of way. It wasn't about me. She just liked big, strong, older guys for boyfriends, okay? And maybe when they stopped scaring her, when she actually took command—no more nervous barfing.

And maybe she *was* changing Rizzo into a half-decent or only half-horrible guy. My bar mitzvah had helped me become a *mensch*; Keatsie Fairchild might do the same for Rizzo—as long as he was so nuts about her he'd do anything.

So, good for her! I felt more relieved than anything else, mainly that I didn't have to keep mooning hopelessly or make excuses to see her when I visited Byron. Maybe I could finally relax and just enjoy her as Byron's fun twin.

Miki interrupted my thoughts, as though reading them. "You had a crush on her, though, didn't you?"

"I'm not sure."

"Come on, it was pretty obvious."

"Maybe. . . . But that's before I became a man."

She laughed. "Can't men have crushes?"

"Sure. But they're much better with girls who dig them."

Miki rested her cheek against my shoulder. "Well," she said, taking a breath. "*I* dig you."

I tittered.

She pulled her cheek away. "Why are you laughing?"

"You hair was tickling my nose."

"Oh."

"I dig you, too," I said.

She looked at me. "You do?"

"Uh-huh."

"Mmm," she sighed, moving in close again.

As the song ended and "Only You" by the Platters began, I thought about what I'd just said. Did I really "dig" Miki now? Yes—I liked everything about her, including her jazzy boldness, and she made me feel good inside. Was it a crush? Maybe. Sort of. I knew I'd think about her when we were apart and that I'd want to be with her again soon. I knew that she liked me for the things I liked best about myself, and she didn't seem to care about my four-eyes, flat feet, feathery hair, shortness, or chubbiness in embarrassing places.

Would my family like her? How could they not? I'd never heard them say anything bad about Orientals. I wouldn't let them. Plus she would show them her respect for elders, which they'd love. I imagined the two of us doing *mitzvahs* together and delighting everyone. As for her parents, I already felt accepted by them, even if they were woozy when they met me.

Would the neighborhood kids make fun of her, as Dickie already had? Probably, and I'd sock them right in the chops—as soon as I learned how to box.

Yoshi came back downstairs after a while to check on us. And as if to assure me that non-Japanese guys were okay with her parents, she brought a tall, handsome blonde guy in a white cardigan down with her. He took her hand and moved her to the dance floor. She laughed and danced half a song with him before leading him back upstairs.

"That's Tim," Miki told me. "The boyfriend she says isn't her boyfriend."

"He looks cool."

"Well, he's kind of a frat boy and jock, but he's okay."

"Yeah, it must be awful to be a big, handsome, popular jock."

"Who cares about that stuff?"

"Why, you like small and ugly?"

"Yeah," she laughed. "Like me."

"No, I'm the ugly one. You're super pretty. Bedazzling."

"Bedazzling! Wow." She tucked her head back on my shoulder and made a purring sound.

A few records later the phonograph played "Moments to Remember" by the Four Lads, about the romantic times you remember always, after the years go by. I wondered if I was having one of those times now. It looked that way for Byron and Betty as they danced—or more like swayed in a clinch. Byron caught my eye and made an OK sign behind Betty's shoulders. I made one back.

The time sped by, and soon the last hour of the party approached. Some of the kids had already left, including Byron, who had to make sure Betty got home before her family began dinner. What was going to happen with them? Byron the walker of highway ledges would take any risk, but what about Betty and the chances she was taking? They had to make their own decisions, but being My Mother-the-Worrier's son, I couldn't help worrying about them.

Keatsie was next to leave, with her new-and-improved Sonny Rizzo. I actually talked with him a little as we stood by the snack table. He told me how he had run into Keatsie downtown one day and suddenly couldn't stop thinking about her. That was how it all had gotten started.

"Cool," I said, for lack of a better response. What else was there to say? I guess it was cool that he stood there being Mr. Polite instead of his old rotten self.

"Gotta go," he said, gathering Keatsie to him. "My brother'll give you a ride if you want."

"No thanks," I said. "I'm gonna stay with my girlfriend a while."

I watched for Keatsie's expression. A double-take, then a smile and an approving nod. Or maybe just the smile and my imagination again.

Yoshi did her last check on us and went back upstairs, where the adults' party had calmed down to some weary singing and an occasional shout. With only a few of us still dancing, Miki turned off all the lights except a small one above the phonograph.

"I'm going to play some real music now," she announced, rearranging the record stack. "Some mellow jazz."

"We can't dance to it," said one of the boys..

"Oh, you can dance to these, believe me."

She put on a Sarah Vaughan album. Soon that velvety low voice was crooning out "Tenderly," "I Don't

Know Why I Love You Like I Do," and "It's Magic." Miki pressed her warm cheek against mine and we swayed like in a dream, the music sending us into its own place, the universe of romance, where nothing else mattered. The lyrics of "It's Magic"—about the "fantastic things" that begin when you're in somebody's arms—seemed to be written for all of us as we held our partners. When the song ended, with a sweep of harp and violins, there seemed to be nothing for me to do but . . .

Miki had the same feeling. She faced me and raised her chin.

Our glasses collided. Then our noses. We laughed, and tried it again.

This time our lips touched lightly and we tested the feeling, that electric feel of a kiss in the making—and for me the realization that I had never kissed anyone this way before.

I'd always wondered why people talked about a "first kiss," when ever since you were two years old you'd been kissing people back, like relatives and friends of your parents, even on the lips. But this was different, so different it didn't even seem to be your same lips. These were lips that felt every position, every movement, temperature, and pressure, and sent urgent messages right to your heart.

This was a kiss. And I felt better than ever about being Aaron Schmink.

Appendix:

Some Fun (mostly) Vocabulary Used in this Book*

1) Byron Fairchild's fancy words

insufferable: Can't be suffered another minute
putrefying: Rotting
inscrutable: Can't be figured out
ergo: Thus, therefore
pestiferous: Annoying, like a disease
mater: Latin for mother
pater: Latin for father
impeccable: Perfect, flawless
***paterfamilias*:** Head man in the household.
phenomenal: Amazing (but a less lazy word)
festooned: Hanging in a loop, like a chain of flowers
imperative: Required to be done
infamous: Famous in a bad way, having a bad rep

sanctum: A room or other place for privacy
minimally: At the very least
peeved: Annoyed, bugged
extraterrestrial: Existing outside Planet Earth.
Cro-magnon: An early human. Insulting term for one's intelligence.
concurs: Agrees
disdain: Scorn, disrespect

2) Fancy words used by Aaron, other characters, and the author

distress: Misery, suffering, grief
emphatically: Definitely!
extricate: To free (from something)
ignoramus: Offensive term for a supposedly unlearned person
irrefutably: In a way that can't be disproved
laconic: Uses few words where others use many
magnanimous: Generous
rapport: Easy connection with a person or people
sheepish: Timid or embarrassed about something
trait: Someone's certain quality, like cheerfulness or grossness
unconventional: Not what's called the usual way of behaving or thinking.

*3) Yiddish words from Moshe and others***

Note: Some of these words were brought directly to the New World by Jews coming from their old countries, while others ("Yiddish-isms") were coined after the immigrant communities settled in the new land. A number of the terms used by the characters in this novel are obviously insulting or offensive.

bubkas: zilch, nothing at all, worthless; (literally, a goat's droppings)

farbrissen[er]: stubborn; bitter sourpuss; generally unsympathetic person

gelt: money, usually cash

goyem: gentiles; non-jews

k'vell [kvelen]: to take pride in, smile beamingly, often over children or grandchildren

lets: clown, smart-aleck

mensch [mentsh]: decent person, flawless, of high integrity and humanity

meshuge [-gueh]: crazy, nutsy

nakhes [naches]: pleasure, delight, joys derived from one's children

nebbish, nebish: spineless, fearful, fainthearted person; simpleton

nudnik: pest, bore, nag

patsh: slap

pisk: mouth, specifically a fresh or smart-alecky mouth

putz: ignorant, pathetic, insensitive person (vulg.,the male sexual organ)

schmendrik: a nobody, yokel, "nincompoop"

schmuck: jerk, schmo; vile person; literally jewel, ornament (vulg., the male sex organ)

shnook, shnuk: sadsack; meek, self-dissing pushover

yold: a sap, chump

4)Hebrew words

aliyah: In *bar* or *bat mitzvah* terms, the act of being called up and proceeding to the platform for one's reading from the *Torah*

bar mitzvah; bat or bas mitzvah: The coming of age ceremony for 13-year-old Jewish boys and (*bat* or *bas*) for 12- or 13-year-old Jewish girls, requiring a period of instruction and preparation and culminating in a synagogue reading from the *Torah* and comments on its personal meaning.

bimah: An elevated platform in the synagogue from which *Torah* readings are given

D'var Torah: A synagogue talk relating to a section—ordinarily the weekly reading—of the *Torah*, usually given by the rabbi or, during a bar or bat mitzvah, by the boy or girl

gabbai: A layperson assisting in the running of synagogue services

Haftarah or haftorah: A Sabbath Synagogue reading from the Prophets, part of a bar mitzvah or bat mitzvah ceremony

kippah: A *yarmulke* or brimless cap, the head covering customarily worn by men entering the synagogue

tallit: Prayer shawl worn by men for morning prayers

Torah: In Judaism, the "law" or "teaching," consisting of a section of the Hebrew Old Testament (*Pentateuch*) and customarily contained on a scroll from which synagogue readings and commentary are done. It is also a body of related, rabbinical commentary passed down in written and oral form.

tzitzit: Knotted fringes on the *tallit* serving as reminders of responsibilities to God and man

---

*Simplified definitions for a particular use of the terms, not necessarily for their additional forms and functions.

**Selected sources:

Gross, David C., *English-Yiddish, Yiddish-English Dictionary,* romanized, expanded edition, Hippocrene Books, 1995.

Rosenbaum, Samuel. *A Yiddish word book for English-Speaking People.* Van Nostrand Reinhold, 1978.

Michael Wex. *Born to Kvetch.* Harper, 2006.

Acknowledgments

I am profoundly grateful to all those who read and gave advice on this story, including on the details of Orthodox Jewish bar mitzvah training and ritual. In particular I thank writer Bill Teitelbaum for his extensive counsel; lay rabbi Ira J. Block, who tragically died of an illness shortly after giving his wise and generous assistance; Carolee Shudnow for her informed comments; my agent Roger Williams for his general encouragement of my work; those, living and dead, who inspired my characters; and of course my beloved wife, artist Mary H. Phelan, infinitely supportive and as keen a reader as I have known in a life of writing, editing, and a passion for words.

Author Note

ARTHUR PLOTNIK is the author of nine books, including two Book-of-the-Month Club featured selections, plus award-winning fiction, poetry, and creative nonfiction. With many successful works of advice for writers, he has been called "a freaking genius-god in the writing world" (PowellsBooks.blog). A long-time editor of *American Libraries* of the American Library Association, he was honored by the profession as one of its foremost leaders. Father of two daughters who have given him bountiful *nakhes*, he grew up in White Plains, New York, and lives in Chicago with his wife, the artist Mary H. Phelan.

Made in the USA
Monee, IL
17 September 2019